SUPER
HUMAN

SUPER HUMAN

MICHAEL CARROLL

PHILOMEL BOOKS

AN IMPRINT OF PENGUIN GROUP (USA) INC.

PHILOMEL BOOKS

A Division of Penguin Young Readers Group.

Published by the Penguin Group.

Penguin Group (USA) Inc., 375 Hudson Street, New York, NY 10014, U.S.A.

Penguin Group (Canada), 90 Eglinton Avenue East, Suite 700, Toronto, Ontario M4p 2Y3, Canada (a Division of Pearson Penguin Canada Inc.).

Penguin Books Ltd, 80 Strand, London WC2R 0RL, England.

Penguin Ireland, 25 St. Stephen's Green, Dublin 2, Ireland (a Division of Penguin Books Ltd).

Penguin Group (Australia), 250 Camberwell Road, Camberwell, Victoria 3124, Australia (a Division of Pearson Australia Group Pty Ltd).

Penguin Books India Pvt Ltd, 11 Community Center, Panchsheel Park, New Delhi—110 017, India.

Penguin Group (NZ), 67 Apollo Drive, Rosedale, North Shore 0632, New Zealand (a Division of Pearson New Zealand Ltd).

Penguin Books (South Africa) (Pty) Ltd, 24 Sturdee Avenue, Rosebank, Johannesburg 2196, South Africa.

Penguin Books Ltd, Registered Offices: 80 Strand, London WC2R 0RL, England.

Published simultaneously in Canada. Printed in the United States of America.

Design by Marikka Tamura.

Text set in Palatino.

Library of Congress Cataloging-in-Publication Data
Carroll, Michael Owen, 1966–
Super human / Michael Carroll. p. cm.
Summary: A ragtag group of young superheroes takes on a powerful warrior who is transported from 4,000 years in the past to enslave the modern world.
[1. Superheroes—Fiction.] I. Title. PZ7.C23497Su 2010 [Fic]—dc22 2009029965
ISBN 978-0-399-25297-6

5 7 9 10 8 6 4

To the Mighty Tharg,
his droids,
and all the Squaxx dek Thargo

PROLOGUE

4,493 years ago . . .

The afternoon air was thick with dust and screams, blood and war cries, flashing blades and piercing arrows. So much blood had already been spilled that in places the desert sand had turned to red mud.

Krodin had long since abandoned his shield and was now swinging a sword in each hand, the weapons almost too heavy for the average man to lift, let alone wield.

He was of average height, though well-muscled. His bronzed skin was flawless, completely lacking the battle scars and tattoos of his comrades. He kept his dark beard close-cropped, and his long, sweat-drenched hair hung loose, free to whip around his head as he fought.

He was the greatest warrior the Assyrian empire had ever seen, and today's battle was only serving to strengthen his reputation.

A desperate Egyptian lunged at Krodin with his spear, but Krodin simply spun: The blade in his left hand severed the spear's shaft, the tip of his right blade passed through the Egyptian's torso.

Krodin had already sent another Egyptian to the next world before the spearman's body had collapsed to the ground.

A quartet of swordsmen surrounded him, rushed at him with their shields raised, their weapons flailing. Krodin leaped at one of the men, ducked under his swinging sword, crashed into the man's shield. Behind him, the Egyptian's colleagues slammed into each other, stumbled.

It was a moment's work to cut them down: He sliced at the knees of the first, punctured the stomachs of the second and third with a double-thrust of his swords, and slashed at the fourth with such force that the man's feet left the ground.

Krodin's hands and arms were thick with his enemies' blood. He dropped both swords and took a moment to flex his fists—the knuckles cracking loud enough to be heard over the roar of the battle—and wipe his hands on a dead man's tunic.

There was a wound on his upper right arm, a deep cut that seeped his own blood. He didn't recall receiving it and didn't care. It was already healing, and within the hour his skin would be as flawless as ever.

From the west came a low rumbling. Krodin didn't waste time looking to see what had caused the sound—it was all too familiar. He snatched up two of the dead Egyptians' shields and ducked down behind them.

Moments later the sky darkened. Like rain from Hell, ten thousand arrows fell on the battlefield, piercing friend and foe alike.

Protected behind the shields, Krodin grinned. Only a truly foolish or desperate leader would order his archers to take such action at this stage in the battle.

As the last arrows thudded into the shields, Krodin grabbed his swords and began to run.

For as far as he could see, the bodies of the dead and dying littered the sand. The air was laced with the metallic tang of blood, and filled with screams and moans and panic-filled prayers.

He leaped over bodies, skirted around shattered and burning siege vehicles, and—without slowing—slaughtered every Egyptian in his path, regardless of whether the man was fit enough to hold a weapon.

He knew that somewhere to the west the Egyptian general was watching. And he was sure that the general was praying to the war god Onuris that Krodin would be struck down before he got too close.

Another rumble, another barrage of arrows was loosed.

Krodin took shelter in the lee of a half-dead rhinoceros, tucked himself inside its bronze armor-plating. The stench of the animal was almost strong enough to block out the smell of blood, and the ground shook from its desperate, pain-filled roars.

Then the arrows fell, and the rhinoceros shuddered, bellowed one last time, and was still.

The Egyptian general would be already planning his retreat, Krodin knew. The coward would disappear across the desert and lie to his king about the success of this attack.

In terms of numbers, the Egyptians had already won. They were remarkable warriors, highly trained and well-equipped. Krodin's own men were also excellent warriors, but the Assyrian empire had been greatly outnumbered and was unprepared for this attack—though Krodin knew that it was hardly unprovoked. It was retaliation for an earlier incursion into Egypt by the Assyrians, which in turn had been sparked by a previous event.

Krodin didn't know for certain how many of his men had fallen, but he strongly suspected that by now almost all six thousand of them had been guided toward the short, agonizing path to the afterlife.

But Those Who Dwell Above—the gods of the other world, if they existed—would have to wait a long time before they greeted Krodin at their gates. He would not die this day.

And the Assyrian empire would not fall this day, not to the Egyptians.

He broke cover and raced for the enemy's encampment.

A frenzied cry rose from their ranks, and their archers began to shoot at will, no longer waiting for orders.

Again, this was a good sign. Krodin grinned, and—still running—he closed his eyes.

An arrow whipped toward his face. Krodin knocked it aside with the sword in his right hand, and with his left sword he split the shaft of a thrown spear.

Less than a minute later he was too close to the Egyptian pikemen for their archers to fire.

A dozen or more pikemen rushed at him at once. Krodin ran, tensed his muscles, leaped over their heads. He spun and twisted in the air, slashing out with his swords, taking down four of the pikemen before he touched the ground.

The Egyptians came at him with swords, and he hacked at them with a speed and fury like they had never imagined.

Now desperate and mindless of their own men, the archers unleashed a thick cloud of arrows, and Krodin dodged or shattered every one.

They launched spears and tridents and nets. His flashing swords moved so fast that nothing could touch him.

An enormous, enraged, armored rhinoceros was set loose. Krodin stood his ground, waited until the beast was almost on him, then dodged to the right. His swords pierced its armor-plated headgear and the rhinoceros crashed roaring to the ground. Krodin, still holding on to the swords' hilts, vaulted onto the beast's back and jerked the swords free.

The Egyptian slaves—promised freedom if they could stop the Assyrian—launched themselves at him with daggers and clubs. Krodin knew that they were not warriors, neither bred nor trained to fight. They were weak, terrified, and clumsy. Even a moderately experienced fighter would be able to disarm them without issuing a single fatal wound. They did not deserve death, certainly not like this.

Still Krodin killed them all.

Then a deep, powerful voice bellowed, "Enough!"

Krodin stopped. His breathing was heavy now, his body drenched in sweat and spattered with blood.

The voice boomed out once more. "We yield, Assyrian! Enough!"

Krodin finally opened his eyes, and turned in a slow circle. The scene was much as he had pictured it in his mind. So much destruction and death that the desert floor looked like a dense field of scarlet flowers.

The remaining Egyptians encircled him, their weapons at the ready. They were out of reach of his swords, four or five men deep.

But Krodin knew that they would not attack.

Then a parting appeared in the crowd, and a tall, thin man

strode through. He had coal-black hair and bronzed skin, and wore a long, spotless white tunic. There was a simple gold loop around his forehead.

"I am Imkhamun, first general of the royal guard of the palace of his sacred majesty—"

"Kneel," Krodin said, his teeth bared. "Kneel before the might of the Assyrian empire."

Without hesitation the Egyptian dropped to his knees, lowered his head. Then Krodin looked around at Imkhamun's men. "Drop your weapons."

The sound of spears and swords hitting the ground was almost deafening. Krodin pointed to one man at random, an archer. "You. Water. Now."

The archer stumbled backward into his colleagues, then pushed through them and ran.

"Raise your right hand, Egyptian," Krodin said to Imkhamun. "Spread your fingers."

Trembling, the thin man did as he was told. Krodin's sword flashed, and Imkhamun's right thumb dropped to the ground. The Egyptian screamed and doubled over, cradling his wounded hand to his chest. A crimson blossom appeared on his tunic and grew rapidly.

The archer pushed his way through his fellows, carrying a skin of water. He slowed almost to a crawl as he approached Krodin.

Krodin snatched the skin from his hands, passed it to Imkhamun. "Drink, so that I know it is not poisoned."

Fumbling, hindered by the loss of his right thumb and his shaking, blood-slicked hands, the Egyptian pulled the stopper from the skin, took a long drink, thin streams of water spilling from the corners of his mouth.

Krodin watched him for a moment, then, satisfied, took back the skin and sipped from it.

"You are mine," Krodin said. "All of you. Every man in your army now belongs to Assyria. You will move through the battlefield. Scavenge the dead for weapons and supplies. Any Assyrian you find who still lives, tend his wounds. Any Egyptian too badly wounded to march, you will kill."

Half-whimpering, Imkhamun asked, "You . . . you would take us to Assyria?"

"No. We will march on Memphis. Your king will be put to the sword, your vaults plundered." Krodin leaned closer. "And you will burn your crops, salt the land so that nothing will ever grow again. Before the week is out, Egypt's lush fields will be a desert. Your kingdom will fall. This is the price you pay for attacking Assyria."

Slowly, awkwardly, Imkhamun climbed to his feet. "This will not happen."

Krodin grinned. "Earlier I thought you a coward, for only a coward attacks without reason or warning. But . . . you are not a coward, Egyptian. You stand up to me even though you have seen me devastate your army. There are many humans I would call brave, but surely you are among the bravest." He raised his left sword, pressed its point against Imkhamun's throat. "Or the most stupid."

"Then strike me down, Assyrian. I have lived well and served King Sahure with unwavering loyalty, and I am ready to walk the fields of Aaru. But before you extinguish my light, tell me your name that I might warn Osiris and Ammit of your eventual coming."

"Oh, I have had many names, Egyptian. I have called myself Krodin these past two centuries."

Despite his fear, despite the sword at his throat, Imkhamun frowned. "Two centuries? Impossible. No man can live so long."

"I have lived that, and longer. And I will live longer still. The gods of your afterlife have no need to fear me, Egyptian, for I cannot die. I am immortal, ageless, indestructible. Already I have walked this Earth for more than five hundred years. I have seen many empires rise and fall, and I have no doubt that I will see many more. I ally myself with Assyria simply because it suits me to do so. But make no mistake: I am not Assyrian."

"You . . . you are a god?"

"No. I am not a god. Nor am I human."

CHAPTER 1

It should have been a good day. It was late spring, a warm, sunny Thursday, and school was out because almost half of the teachers had called in sick. Even better, the kids knew that there weren't many teachers who'd take a sick day on Thursday and then come back to school on Friday. That almost certainly meant a four-day weekend.

For most of the kids of Fairview, South Dakota, it *was* a good day. But not for Lance McKendrick. The day had started out well, but it had turned sour pretty quickly.

Lance was on the run again. His sneakers pounded across the huge mall's polished floor tiles as he darted left and right around the late-afternoon shoppers.

Behind him three of the mall's security guards were shouting for everyone to clear the way. He couldn't understand how this time they were so close to catching him. Usually he was able to give them the slip in a matter of seconds.

And then he glanced back and spotted his marked playing cards spilling out of his pocket, leaving a handy trail for the guards to follow.

Lance threw the rest of the cards into a trash can, vaulted over a wooden bench, ducked under the outstretched arms of the clown selling overpriced helium balloons, skidded around Uncle Harry's ice-cream stand, and raced up the down escalator.

Panicked parents dragged their children aside as Lance apologized his way up the moving stairs. "Sorry, sorry, comin' through . . ."

He emerged into the sprawling food court and couldn't resist a smile. He'd been worried that the recent flu epidemic might keep people away from the mall, but it was quite the opposite: The place was packed. He was going to get away.

He pulled his distinctive Red Sox cap from his head. He knew how the security guards' minds worked: They were chasing a teenager in a red cap. They wouldn't remember anything else about his appearance.

Behind him, the guards were bellowing orders into their walkie-talkies. That was a good thing, Lance knew: It made everyone stop and stare at them.

He spotted a large crowd of kids his own age and zipped past them, then doubled back and stood among them as they watched the panting rent-a-cops charge past.

Idiots, Lance said to himself.

The last of the security guards—a large, potbellied man whose wheezing and coughing suggested that he really should have taken a sick day—lumbered past and Lance sidled away from the other teens.

He opened his backpack and was about to stuff the cap into it when he changed his mind. If the security guards decided to search bags on the way out he'd be caught. He dropped the cap onto a table close to the Golden Path Eatery and kept moving.

Lance didn't consider himself to be one of the bad guys. Most of his scams were pretty basic and technically not illegal, like buying a dozen cans of cola from the Supersaver Drugstore for twenty-eight cents each, sticking out-of-order signs on the vending machines in the mall, then waiting around for unsuspecting thirsty people to become frustrated that they couldn't get their caffeine fix. Lance would kindly offer to sell them one of his cans for a dollar.

He'd never stolen anything. Not really. Occasionally he might take something that didn't belong to him, but in his mind that wasn't the same as stealing. Or he might sneak into a warehouse while the loading dock was open and no one was watching and look for things that probably wouldn't be missed. Big companies always allow for a certain amount of lost or damaged goods, so Lance told himself that wasn't really stealing either.

Lance was fourteen, attended Martin Van Buren High School with his older brother, and by his own choice had no close friends. He never volunteered for anything in class, made sure his grades were exactly average, never joined in with any of the social activities or did anything that would make people notice him. His goal was to make it all the way through high school—and later college—and have no one really remember much about him.

He was of average height and build for his age. He had

ordinary brown hair, blue eyes, a straight nose, and mostly even teeth. He was aware that he wasn't particularly good-looking, but he was fairly sure that he wasn't ugly either.

His brother Cody was two years older. He had jet-black hair—always perfectly groomed—and deeply tanned skin, and was considered to be quite a catch. Cody played on the school baseball team, where he was something of a minor celebrity as a good all-rounder. He was involved in a dozen different social groups, excelled in most of his classes, and could play the guitar well enough that he was constantly turning down offers from his many friends to form a band.

Everyone liked Cody, even the ultra-cynical kids who dressed only in black, hated everything, and thought that happy people were losers.

And Lance liked his brother well enough too. The only thing that bothered him about Cody was his popularity. Lance didn't want to be known as "Cody McKendrick's little brother." It wasn't that he didn't want to be compared to Cody—he didn't want anyone to notice him at all.

Lance's philosophy was simple: If he ran a scam on someone and they remembered him, he'd failed. Even if he somehow still got away with it, it was a failure. The only true success was when he deprived someone of the burden of their money and they walked away without realizing what had really happened.

He wanted to be like the superhuman who called himself Façade, except that Façade was a villain. Lance knew that if he could change his appearance at will then he'd be practically unstoppable.

He didn't see *himself* as a villain. He never took money

from anyone who couldn't afford it. Even when he was running a three-card monte con, he made a point of not taking *all* of the mark's money. He knew that if the mark still had enough money to get home, then he'd be less likely to think he'd been ripped off. And there'd be a greater chance that he'd try again next time, in the hope that he might win his money back. Sometimes, if the mark insisted on risking the last of his money, Lance would give a few dollars back to him after he lost. That way the mark would think that Lance was an OK guy—and then he'd definitely come back again.

Anyway, if they were dumb enough to believe that it was possible to win at three-card monte, they *deserved* to lose their money.

Lance believed that there was nothing wrong with persuading people they could beat a game with impossibly high odds. The government did it all the time with the state lotteries. The chance of winning the Powerball jackpot was less than one in a hundred million. Statistically it was much, much harder to win than it would be to open the phone book at random in the dark, stick a pin in a page, do it forty times in a row, and hit the same number every time.

He made his way back through the food court, down the escalator, and toward the west entrance.

There was a large crowd clustered around the doorway. *Perfect,* Lance thought. *Easy enough to get away if everyone is looking at something else.*

It was only as he was squeezing through the crowd that he began to wonder just what it was that had drawn hundreds of people to the entrance.

He stretched up onto his toes to peer over the sea of heads, and spotted something shiny and silver. For a second he thought it was a guy in a motorbike helmet, but then the man turned his head, scanning the crowd.

Oh no . . .

Lance ducked down again, sidestepped past a woman holding up her toddler, and did his best to look completely innocent as he passed through the doors and began to amble away.

He'd taken less than a dozen steps when he realized his mistake: When a big-time superhero makes an appearance at the local mall, only the guilty would leave the scene.

It was too late.

A heavy hand landed on Lance's shoulder, and a deep, almost mechanical, voice said, "Where do you think you're going?"

Lance dry-swallowed. The hand on his shoulder was encased in metal. It was holding him firmly. Not tight enough to hurt—though it certainly looked as though it could do that—but tight enough that he couldn't easily duck out of the grip and make a run for it.

"Well?"

"Just, y'know, uh . . . home?"

He turned around slowly and looked at his distorted reflection in the polished, opaque visor of the armored man.

The crowd had formed a circle around them. Lance knew now that he was not going to get away.

Paragon was a head taller than Lance and covered head to toe in polished metal armor that seemed to be bristling with weapons and pieces of equipment. Fixed to a socket on his left hip was what looked like an oversize handgun; a three-pronged hook protruded from its barrel. His famous jetpack was strapped to his back, and three pairs of handcuffs were clipped to his belt, along with half a dozen stuffed pouches. Even his steel-covered gloves had small storage areas around the cuffs.

Lance couldn't help but notice a close grouping of dents and scratches in the silver chest-plate, and was glad that he wasn't the guy who had shot at Paragon only to discover that the armor was bulletproof.

"Your heartbeat and perspiration are way up. You're the one the security guards were chasing. The junior cardsharp." It wasn't even a question. The armored man's head swiveled smoothly from side to side. "Interesting situation we have here, kid. . . . You're hardly worth the trouble of arresting. So what should I do? What would *you* do, if you were me?"

Lance tried to shrug himself out of his jacket. "Um . . . give me a stern warning and let me go?"

"And the money you've taken? How much?"

"Ten bucks."

Paragon leaned closer, his helmet almost pressing against Lance's forehead. "*How* much?"

Lance swallowed again. *Man, I am so busted. . . .* "Hundred and forty-five."

"One hundred and forty-five dollars." Without turning away from Lance, Paragon pointed through the onlookers toward a girl standing by the mall's entrance with a collection tin. "Which you are kindly going to donate to charity, right?"

"Oh, absolutely," Lance said, nodding. "That was the plan all along."

"Perhaps you'd be even kinder and round it up to, say, two hundred?"

"I don't have that much on me," Lance stammered.

"Just give as much as you can. That's what good citizens do. Name?"

"Jason Myers." Lance was comfortable with that. It was the name he always used when doing business. He'd used it so often that when anyone called out the name Jason he automatically turned to look.

"ID?"

Lance reached into the back pocket of his jeans and withdrew the fake student ID card, held it up for Paragon to see.

After a moment, the armored hero nodded. "All right." He plucked the card out of Lance's hand. "You won't mind if I keep this, will you? I'm going to add it to my collection. . . . Gotta tell you, though, this is one of the best I've seen. It's almost perfect."

Lance sighed. "OK. You caught me. But you can't do anything. I'm fourteen. You can't arrest me. You're not a cop."

With a trace of amusement in his voice, Paragon said, "I could hand you over to the security guards here."

"We're outside the mall," Lance said. "They're only allowed to make arrests inside."

"So you know the law. Good for you. How about I hold on to you long enough for your parents to come looking? How's that sound?"

"Sounds like kidnapping." Inwardly, Lance relaxed. There was no way that was going to happen. "And my folks won't miss me for *hours*, 'cos they're sick at home with the flu. You really think that this is a good use of your time? Surely

16

there's some real crooks out there that you could be bothering instead."

"Leave. Don't come back."

Lance allowed his shoulders to sag, tried to look defeated. "OK, OK. I'm going." He sighed and turned away. He muttered "jerk" under his breath, deliberately loud enough for Paragon to hear—he didn't want the superhero to know how relieved he felt. The situation could have turned out a lot worse.

Red-faced, he pushed through the cheering crowd. Everyone would remember him now: He'd never be able to work this mall again. But there were other malls, and there was also the tourist district downtown. Tourists were easier to scam anyway.

From behind, Lance heard the whine of Paragon's jetpack kick into action, and glanced back to see the armored hero slowly rise into the air.

The crowd clapped and hollered. It wasn't every day that a superhero showed up in a small town like Fairview.

What's he doing here anyway? Lance asked himself. *Have the supervillains all got the flu too or something?*

Then the jetpack's whining grew closer, and Lance was buffeted by the blast as Paragon passed close overhead.

The armored hero touched down in front of him, and stood with his arms folded. "Forgotten something?"

"Um . . ."

"The money." Paragon extended his gloved hand.

Reluctantly, Lance reached into his pocket and handed over a roll of bills. "There. Happy now?"

"I wasn't born yesterday, kid," Paragon said. He flipped through the bills. "This is your decoy roll, a bunch of ones wrapped up in a twenty. Where's the rest of it?"

Someone in the crowd went "Oooh!" and sparked a ripple of light laughter.

"Go on," Paragon said. "Be a good citizen and make a charitable donation."

Another member of the crowd shouted, "Get a receipt, kid! It might be tax-deductible!" which triggered an even bigger laugh.

Yeah, that's hilarious. Lance could feel his cheeks burning as he passed back through the crowd with Paragon following close behind. A few snide comments were thrown his way, but he knew this wasn't the right time to respond.

The girl with the collecting tin smiled at him as he approached. If she'd been a crotchety old woman, it would have been bad enough, but she was young and pretty and cheerful.

Lance dug deep into his other pocket and took out his real roll of bills, handed it all over to the girl. "Happy now?" he said to Paragon. "Can I go, or do you have to humiliate me even more?"

"You think *this* is humiliation? Consider yourself lucky you're not being arrested. Go on, get lost. But you just remember this next time you get the urge to rip people off."

Lance turned away, but the girl reached out and took hold of his arm. "Wait, wait!"

Oh, what now?

She pinned a tiny paper flag to the lapel of Lance's jacket.

CHAPTER 2.

Almost three hundred miles to the north, fifteen-year-old Roz Dalton felt her stomach clench in protest as the customized Bell 222B helicopter dipped and swerved and swooped over the landscape.

She did her best to pay attention to her older brother and not think about how embarrassing it would be to throw up all over the floor. She'd never had a fear of flying until about a year earlier, when her brother insisted that it was time she learned. Then she started to have nightmares about the copter's engine suddenly cutting out while she was at the controls.

Her aviophobia had eased a little in the past couple of months, but she still knew she'd never be comfortable with sitting inside a wingless metal box that weighed over two tons and flew at one hundred and fifty miles per hour.

Roz was slim with lightly tanned skin and black hair that

until recently had reached most of the way down her back. Now it was so short it was almost a crew cut. She liked it better this way: It was easier to manage and took only a few minutes to wash and dry.

Her brother Max was five years older. He was of average height and had a slim waist with a disproportionately large upper body, the result of far too many gymnasium hours on the pull-up bars and not enough on the rest of the equipment. Max had the same dark hair and piercing brown eyes as Roz, a family trait they'd inherited from their late mother.

They both wore matte-black two-piece uniforms made from a lightweight bulletproof material that Max was in the process of patenting.

"We'll be going in fast," Max was saying to Roz. "We don't know who these people are or what they can do. And after last month's debacle I don't want you taking any risks. Got that?"

Roz nodded. The knot in her stomach tightened as she recalled the battle, and she unconsciously rubbed her left arm just above the elbow: A violent but low-powered supervillain called Gladius had slashed at her with his sword, coming within an inch of removing her forearm. The wound had left a deep scar that Roz just knew was going to be permanent.

Accompanying Roz and Max in the copter were three members of Max's support team: Oliver French, Antonio Lashley, and Stephen Oxford. Unlike the Daltons, Ollie, Lash, and Ox were ordinary humans, but they were former U.S. Army Rangers, highly trained in hand-to-hand combat, weapons use, strategies, and survival.

Sitting next to Roz was the white-clad superhero Quantum.

He was about Max's age, but tall and lean. Most of his face was hidden under his mask, and Roz sometimes envied his anonymity: Superheroes like Quantum and Titan didn't have to worry about everyone recognizing them when they were off duty.

Max, however, had never hidden the fact that he was superhuman—and because everyone knew who he was, there had seemed little point in Roz hiding her own identity.

Quantum nudged Roz with his elbow. "You all right, Rosalyn?" He was one of the very few people who called her by her full name, but despite that she still liked him.

She shrugged. "I'm fine."

This was only Roz's fourth official mission. Her superhuman abilities had begun to develop four years earlier, but Max had always kept her at home with their younger brother Josh. Much as Roz had hated being left behind, she had never complained.

"Whatever happened to that boyfriend of yours?" Quantum asked. "Someone with his abilities could be pretty useful on a mission like this."

"I think you're confusing me with someone else," Roz said. She tried to keep her expression neutral. It hurt that she'd had only one relationship and it hadn't lasted very long.

"No, I'm certain it was you. You were seeing that guy who could—"

Max loudly cleared his throat, interrupting them. "If you two are done? Thank you. The Midway power plant is due to go online next month," Max said, unrolling a map of the target area. "That's almost three months ahead of schedule, but I'm told that the safety checks were all in the green as of this morning. They've only got a minimum complement of security and staff."

"How many are we up against?" Quantum asked, peering at the map.

"Unknown." Max tapped the map with a gloved forefinger. "They crashed through the perimeter here in a stolen Securicor truck. Took out the guards and shot their way into the plant. We believe there are at least four of them still outside, using the truck as cover. We don't know whether they're trying to sabotage the plant or steal from it. Fact is, the reactor doesn't have a core yet—there's no plutonium for anyone to steal. We'll be landing zero-point-five miles to the north. Quantum, you'll scout ahead, let us know what we're up against. Just keep to the perimeter—check out their defenses."

Quantum nodded, then said, "I can phase myself through the walls and—"

"No," Max interrupted. "We can't take the risk. Remember Cádiz?"

Roz noted the exchange of looks between the two men, and she knew what it meant: On a recent mission to the Spanish city, the supervillain Termite had rigged a warning device that could detect when Quantum was using his ability to phase through solid objects—it had almost cost three hostages their lives.

"Until we can find a way to block that sort of detector, phasing yourself is off the table." Max turned to his sister. "Roz, you hang back with the chopper until we have a better idea of what's going on, understood?"

The pilot called, "Ninety seconds to target. Hold tight, I'm taking her down."

22

The copter banked to the left and dropped sharply. Roz clutched the edges of her seat and tried not to lose her breakfast.

The swooping and lurching didn't seem to bother the men at all. The Rangers were running a last-minute check on their weapons and body armor, and Max was pulling on his uniform's matching helmet.

Ollie jumped up and slid open the door, and a blast of hot, dusty wind howled through the copter.

"Suit up, Roz," Max shouted.

As Roz was picking up her helmet the copter lurched, dropped even more sharply. The helmet slipped from her grasp and rolled toward the door.

She reached for it with her mind, stopped its roll, lifted it up, and plucked it out of the air.

She looked up to see Quantum smiling at her. "Man, I wish I could do that!"

Roz's telekinesis was almost second nature to her now. Just by concentrating, she could move almost any object, as long as it was in her line of sight. The size of the object didn't seem to present any problem, but its mass did. So far, she hadn't been able to lift anything heavier than her own weight.

Her helmet wavered in the air as the copter touched down with a bump. Max yelled, "Quantum—Go!"

The speedster vanished.

Half a mile there and back, Roz thought. *How long is that going to—*

Roz jumped: Quantum was suddenly standing in front of her. He picked up the map, snatched a pencil from Ox's hand, and began marking Xs and circles on the map. "Eight on the outside. Four here, two here, two over this side. At least three more on the way out through the doors, heading this way." He drew an arrow on the map. "The gate and wall provide them with cover here and here, but the terrain shelters us from their view up to about here. . . ." He drew a larger circle, then wiped the sweat from his upper lip on the back of his glove. "The men are armed with HK11Es, looked like. Standard lightweight body armor, all gray. No insignia that I could see. Max, there's not one of them under thirty and they look like they know what they're doing."

"Good work," Max said. "You . . . Quantum, you're sweating."

"Yeah, it's pretty hot in here." He swayed a little.

Max grabbed his arm to steady him. "Ollie?"

The Ranger stepped up to Quantum, put one hand on each side of the speedster's face, and tilted his head back. "Can't see too much without taking off his mask, but he looks sick, Max." He pressed his thumbs under Quantum's jaw. "Yeah, glands feel a little swollen. You're sitting this one out, kid."

Quantum brushed Ollie's hands away. "Forget it. I feel a little woozy, but I'll be fine."

Ollie steered him back to the seat next to Roz. "No way. I'm the medic; you do what I say."

Max pulled on a camouflage jacket over his uniform. "If it passes, come and find us."

Quantum nodded.

"All right, let's do this." Max leaped out first, followed by the Rangers.

Roz watched as the team split into two pairs, each pair

skirting around opposite sides of a low fern-covered hill. The men dropped to the ground and began to crawl forward. Beyond the hill she could see the tops of the power plant's enormous cooling towers.

She was more concerned now that Quantum wasn't with them. He wasn't officially a part of Max's team, but they had worked together on a few missions and he was a great asset.

He doesn't look good, Roz thought.

Her concern must have shown on her face: Quantum smiled weakly and said, "That's one problem with being superfast—I get sick a lot quicker than normal people." He leaned back and closed his eyes. "But I heal quicker too. I hope."

Roz could do nothing but sit and wait. She'd been expecting that anyway, but with Quantum out of action, the success of the mission was now less certain than when Max had planned it.

Quantum moaned softly, and Roz saw that his eyes and nose were streaming.

Roz jumped from her seat and leaned next to Ernie Wieberg, the pilot. "We have to get him to a doctor."

Wieberg shook his head. "Mission comes first."

Roz glanced back at Quantum. "Yeah, but he looks *really* sick. I'll see what Max says."

She reached for the radio handset on the dashboard, but Wieberg grabbed it before she could. "No, we have to maintain radio silence. They—aw hell! I think they're jamming us!"

"That could mean they know we're here. I should get out there. . . ." She looked back toward Quantum. He was sitting forward, elbows on his knees and head in his hands.

Wieberg turned to her. "And do what? Sit down, Roz. You're not ready for something like this."

Roz jumped at a sudden voice inside her head: Max was communicating telepathically. "You hear me?"

I hear you, she thought.

"Don't recognize these guys, but I don't think they're superhuman. There's at least a dozen outside now, maybe more. We're pinned down—can't get to the wall."

Can't you get inside their minds and control them?

That was Max's greatest power. He could read most people's minds, and communicate directly with some, but the ability to control someone else's thoughts made him one of the most formidable of the superheroes.

"I'm not getting much," Max's voice said. "I've got one for sure—he's currently running for the hills convinced that a swarm of spiders is after him. But I'm not getting through to the others. Think something's blocking me. Hold on. . . ."

After a moment, Max said, "Roz, we're going to have to call in backup. Our radios are down here—get Wieberg to contact the air force. He knows the codes."

Max, he says the copter's radio isn't working either.

There was a thump behind her: Roz turned to see that Quantum was lying facedown on the floor. She rushed back to him. *Quantum's down—he's fainted. Max, he looks* really *sick!*

"Gotta be some kind of weapon—they're hitting us with it too. French just got a bad dose of the shakes; Lashley's doubled over coughing his lungs up."

Roz bit her lip. *Do you need me?*

"I don't think we have any other option, Roz. Get out here and stay low. And keep your eyes open. Tell Wieberg to take the Bell back to the nearest safe house and get medical attention for Quantum."

Roz did as she was instructed, and the helicopter was already starting to rise as she leaped through the doorway.

She hit the ground, rolled to her feet, and ran in a half-crouch toward the small fern-covered hill.

CHAPTER 3

Lance was more than halfway home before he finally calmed down. It was bad enough that Paragon had taken his money—the man didn't have to humiliate him as well.

He was sure that some of the people in the crowd had recognized him as Cody McKendrick's little brother.

Mostly, he was concerned with how his parents were going to react. Maybe, if he was lucky, it would all blow over before they recovered from their bout of flu.

The McKendrick house was like a hospital ward at the moment. His father had it the worst. He'd woken up Sunday morning in a cold sweat, shivering and coughing up great big lumps of green phlegm. Then Lance's mother had caught it. In between her bouts of coughing and sneezing, she'd ordered Lance and Cody to take over the housework.

So every afternoon since, when Lance returned from school, he diligently dragged the vacuum cleaner out to the hall and switched it on. After twenty minutes, he switched it off again and shouted "All done!" up the stairs.

He promised himself he would actually use the machine sometime before they recovered. He'd also throw out the pizza boxes and the half-empty cartons of Chinese takeout on which he and Cody had been living for the past few days.

As he turned left on Jade Avenue he heard the familiar whine of Paragon's jetpack. *Oh, not again! What does he want this time?*

He looked up to see where the sound was coming from, cupping his hands around his eyes to shade them from the sun. Paragon was a dot high against the sky, but dropping quickly, growing larger as he approached. Lance debated whether to run or hide, but before he could do either a battered Ford Pinto screeched around the corner so fast it almost went up on two wheels.

He had a brief glimpse of the driver—an official-looking man wearing a dark suit and sunglasses—before the Pinto careered across the road, coming within inches of clipping the front of a bus. The Pinto's driver spun the wheel, zoomed around the bus, but oversteered. The car hit the median with an ear-shattering bang as one of its tires blew.

Seconds later it slammed into a thick concrete lamppost.

Lance dropped his backpack and ran toward the car. The driver was slumped over the wheel, blood pumping from a deep gash in his forehead where it had collided with the now-shattered windshield.

The driver's door was buckled. Lance ran around to the passenger side, pulled open the door, and leaned in. "Can you hear me? Are you conscious?"

The only response was a weak moan.

His mind racing, Lance tried to remember what he was supposed to do in a situation like this. He'd attended first-aid classes in school but hadn't really paid much attention. *Get him out or leave him? If I move him, I could make his injuries worse, but if I leave him—*

A dull *whump* from the engine made up Lance's mind: Already he could smell the smoke. He grabbed hold of the man's right arm, pulled him back from the steering wheel. *There's no way I can lift this guy.* He tried to pull the driver over onto his side so that he could slide him out. "C'mon, mister! Can't do this on my own!" *Please don't let his legs be trapped!*

The man suddenly jerked upright. His head whipped around and for a second he stared at Lance. "Get me out of here!"

"I'm trying!"

The man wrenched his arm away from Lance, started grabbing for the door handle.

"That one won't open!" Lance said. "You need to—"

The driver's-side door was ripped off its hinges. Lance stared. *How did he . . . ?*

Then a metal-gloved hand reached into the car, grabbed the man by the collar, and dragged him free.

"Get out, kid!" Paragon's amplified voice bellowed. *"Move!"*

Lance jumped back out of the Pinto and tripped over his own feet. He landed on his backside and started scrambling backward.

There was another *whump* from the engine. Lance got up and had just reached the far side of the street when the car erupted into a ball of fire. The shock wave knocked Lance back to the ground, rocked the entire street, and shattered the bus's windows.

Lance opened his eyes and saw a large chunk of red-hot metal that had landed only two feet away from his head. *Oh man . . .* He tried to push himself up, but his arms were quivering and weak and he had to roll onto his back first. He quickly checked himself for injuries. *I'm OK, I'm OK.*

The same couldn't be said for the Pinto's driver. Through the thick cloud of oily smoke that billowed from the car, Lance could see that the wound in the driver's forehead was still seeping blood, but Paragon didn't seem to be too concerned with the man's well-being: He lifted him into the air by his shoulders and roared, "*Where is it?*"

The driver's head lolled back and forth.

Lance couldn't help himself: He shouted, "Hey! You can't do that! He's injured!" He got up, wavered a little.

"Shut up, kid," Paragon said. "A couple of minutes ago this maniac was doing over a hundred down on Canal Street. He went up on the pavement and hit a guy and didn't stop." He shook the driver again. "One more time: Where is it?"

Lance ran over, skidded to a stop next to Paragon. "You're supposed to be one of the good guys! You can't . . . You have to wait for the paramedics!"

"He's faking," Paragon said. He lowered the man to the ground. "Now get lost, kid." The hero's opaque visor momentarily turned in Lance's direction, then did a double take. "You again."

The driver took the opportunity to roll to his feet and begin to run.

"Told you he was faking," Paragon said.

Lance and Paragon stood side by side for a moment, watching the driver race along the street, then Paragon said, "Stay here. Tell the cops everything." He patted Lance on the shoulder. "You did the right thing back there, kid. You might wanna consider giving up the life of crime before you end up where this guy is going to be."

Then Paragon broke into a run. After a few steps he activated his jetpack and soared along the street after the running man.

Lance did as Paragon instructed. He waited for the police and paramedics, explained what had happened.

The white-haired, red-faced police sergeant told Lance he was a hero and shook his hand. "Yer gonna get yer pitcher in the papers fer this."

Oh fantastic. There goes my low profile.

"I seen you somewhere before. What's yer name?"

He almost responded with "Jason Myers" but then realized that he was too close to home: A lot of the onlooking neighbors knew who he was. "Lance McKendrick."

"What? Not Cody's kid brother. . . ." The sergeant grinned. "Seems bein' a hero runs in the family, huh?" Lance wanted to say that being able to hit a baseball out of the park didn't make someone a hero, but he kept his mouth shut.

Paragon returned a few minutes later, dropping out of the sky with the driver—unconscious for real this time—in his arms. He handed the man over to the police, talked with them for a few moments, then was engulfed by reporters and autograph-hunters.

The sergeant had told Lance to stick around until they were sure they were done with him, so now all he could do was watch as Paragon awkwardly tried to sign autographs with his metal-gloved hands. Eventually Lance remembered his backpack and wandered over to where he'd dropped it.

The accident felt like it had happened hours or even days ago, but in reality less than a quarter-hour had passed. The burning car had now been extinguished, and already a tow truck was approaching, slowly trying to get through the crowds.

The massive concrete lamppost had survived the crash intact. *God, if that thing had fallen back on the car . . .*

Lance walked up to the car, peered along its path. If the lamppost hadn't been there, the Pinto would have crashed through the Sternhams' hedge and probably plowed into the front of the house. Two-year-old Ricky Sternham was nuts about cars and frequently spent hours on the porch watching the traffic.

As Lance was turning away, something beyond the Sternhams' hedge caught his eye. A glint of polished metal. He checked to make sure that no one was watching, then he ducked past the hedge.

On the lawn was a small leather briefcase with brass clasps.

Is that what Paragon was looking for? He kept asking the guy, "Where is it?"

Lance picked up the briefcase and stuffed it deep into his backpack. *Today might not be a total loss after all.*

CHAPTER 4

Roz Dalton kept as low as she could as she crawled over the fern-covered hill.

She hadn't heard from her brother in several minutes.

Max? Are you there? Max?

A moment later Max's voice appeared inside her head. "Yeah, I'm . . . Roz, they've got me too. I'm shaking like Jell-O here! Has to be some kind of subsonic weapon. I've got aches in my back, my legs. . . . Even my jaw feels like I've been trying to chew marbles. Keep your distance until we know for sure."

The gunfire died down, and Roz could hear shouting from the far side of the copse. She crept forward on her hands and knees, and wished that Max would allow her to carry some sort of weapon.

Then Max's voice—much weaker than before—said, "Roz, get away. . . . They've caught us. Can't move, too weak . . ."

For a second Roz froze, unsure of what to do. With the radio signals blocked, she couldn't contact Wieberg in the copter.

I've got to do something. *They won't be expecting me—they'll have seen the copter leave, so they'll probably think that they're facing only Max and the others.*

She couldn't help wishing that she had Max's powers instead of her own.

A woman's voice: "Cuff them and drag them inside. The more hostages the better. Have you . . ." A pause. "Tell me that's not the famous Maxwell Dalton!" The woman laughed. "Oh, this is better than Christmas and the Fourth of July all rolled into one!"

"There'll be others," a man said. "Quantum or Energy or one of that lot."

"Them I don't care about. It's Paragon that worries me—his armor could be environmentally sealed. Now move. The Helotry don't like to be kept waiting."

There were scuffling and grunting sounds, which quickly died away. Roz dropped flat onto her stomach and squirmed forward. Making as little noise as possible, she crawled through the bushes, but stopped before she reached the clearing.

Halfway to the power plant's wrecked gateway, eight men were dragging Max and the Rangers along the ground, one leg each.

The eight men were dressed in full-face ski masks and light body armor over gray combat fatigues, but she couldn't see any sort of insignia that might give her a clue as to who they were or where they had come from. The men were carrying machine guns and were accompanied by two others—one leading, the other taking up the rear.

It was clear to Roz that these men knew what they were doing: The man at the rear of the pack was walking backward, his head swiveling back and forth as he kept watch.

If I wait until they get inside the building I won't have a chance, Roz thought. Whatever she was going to do, it had to happen within the next couple of minutes.

But even if she could somehow disable all ten of the gray-clad men, Max and the Rangers were still handcuffed, and almost certainly still weak from whatever it was they'd been hit with.

Then she saw her chance: Stephen Oxford suddenly doubled over, his body racked in a violent coughing fit. Roz hoped Ox was faking it—if he wasn't, he was definitely in a bad way—but didn't waste time wondering: The gray men had dropped him, instinctively stepped back.

She leaped to her feet and ran straight toward the distracted men. The rear guard saw her first, raised his weapon to his shoulder.

Roz concentrated on the machine gun, telekinetically ripped it out of his grip, then spun it in the air. The butt of the gun viciously clipped him across the forehead, sent him staggering backward into one of his colleagues.

Before the others realized what was happening, she focused on one of the two men dragging Max and twisted his ski mask around his head so that it covered his eyes. He didn't react as she'd hoped, by dropping Max's leg or lowering his weapon: Instead he shouted, "Incoming!"

The other gray men immediately crouched, automatically forming a defensive circle with their backs to each other.

Roz changed course, darted away from them toward a shallow depression in the ground. Before she reached it a bullet whizzed past her head, and another clipped the right shoulder of her uniform.

Roz dove headfirst to the ground, rolled onto her back, and began to squirm backward. From this angle she couldn't see the gray men—which meant that they couldn't see her.

Then her hand brushed against something: a discarded fist-sized half brick. She grabbed it, threw it into the air, and before it could fall back to the ground she took hold of it telekinetically, launched it toward the gray men. She climbed into a crouch, just high enough to watch as the gray men saw the brick coming and dodged aside—but they clearly weren't aware that they were facing a telekinetic: Roz steered the brick straight into the chest of one of the men. The impact knocked him over.

The one with the twisted ski mask ripped it off his head and ran for the compound. Roz didn't care whether he was running away or going for help—either way it was one less for her to worry about right now.

She picked up the brick again, set it on a course for another man's head. This one was clearly not as panicked as the others: He waited until the last second before ducking aside.

Need something bigger than just a brick. . . . A large sheet of cement-spackled plywood was resting against the compound's wall. She lifted the plywood sheet into the air, whirled it about, placed it between herself and the men. She pushed it forward—the closer it was to them, the more it restricted their view.

Then one of the men opened fire.

Roz threw herself back to the ground as a ragged line of bullet-holes appeared in the plywood sheet.

There was a shout of, *"You idiot! No!"* followed by a long, sharp scream.

The gunfire abruptly stopped.

Someone had been hit.

Roz stared. The perforated sheet of plywood wavered in the air.

For a moment, there was nothing but silence.

Then the guns erupted once more, a torrent of bullets that tore the plywood sheet into sawdust.

CHAPTER 5

Twelve miles away from the Midway nuclear power plant, Abigail de Luyando glared at the six kids in the corner booth and wished they would either order something else or get out. She'd been working since eight-thirty that morning and it was now coming up on seven in the evening. Almost eleven hours on her feet and so far today she'd made only eight dollars and twenty-five cents in tips.

Every seat and booth in the 1950s-style diner was occupied, and outside the door the long line of potential customers was growing, even though those at the end of the line probably wouldn't get a table for over an hour. The kids in the corner booth were taking up space that could otherwise have been occupied by people a little more generous with their money. She had given them the check twenty minutes ago and so far all they'd done with it was make a paper plane.

But Abby knew that she couldn't push them too hard. Some of them knew who she was and if she got on their bad side they might tell her manager that she was only fourteen. Worse, they might tell her mother that she hadn't been to school in weeks and was now working full-time at Leftover's Finer Diner.

She walked over to the booth, pulling her notepad and pencil out of her apron pocket. "Can I get you guys anything else before you go?"

The nearest boy leered at her, a big cheesy grin on his face. He grabbed hold of her bare arm, holding on tight enough to leave a white mark on her dark skin. "How about your phone number?" Abby thought that he would have been good-looking if not for his impressive collection of acne scars and his tarnished silver nose ring.

Abby pulled her arm free. "No can do. I don't have a phone. But I'm saving up my tips for one."

Four of the boy's friends went "Oooh!" and laughed, but the one closest to the wall—a white girl Abby vaguely remembered from middle school—made a face and said, "*Here's* a tip: Be nicer to the customers and they might keep coming back."

Abby faked a laugh while she mentally pictured herself beating up the girl with a chair. "You got me there. Look, guys, if you're not going to order anything else I'll have to ask you to leave." She tilted her head toward the door. "There's a whole line of people waiting."

"Sure, yeah," the nose-ring boy said as he turned back to his friends. "Coupla minutes, OK?"

Abby nodded and returned to the counter. The manager—a

pale twenty-year-old with limp hair and a shirt that was three sizes too big—tapped a cheerful, rapid beat on the counter with his hands and said, "Come on, kiddo, pull it together. Only three more hours to go!"

"Easy for you to say, Dave. You've only been here since five."

Dave's grin slipped a little. "Table four are waiting for their check and the guy on seven dropped his cheeseburger. New one's coming up now." The cook passed three plates through the little window from the kitchen, and Dave slid them toward Abby. "Table two. Bacon fries, club with no lettuce, tortilla platter. And they want a strawberry malt and a Diet-Pepsi float."

Abby spent the next fifteen minutes bustling back and forth between the tables, the register, the counter, and the kitchen window. The only other waitress on duty that evening was Mandy, a forty-three-year-old mother of four who had spent almost the whole shift sitting in the kitchen and complaining to the cook about how busy the diner was.

There should have been four people covering the floor, but Keith and Jasmine had called in sick at the last minute, so Abby was practically working the whole place on her own.

Mentally she was exhausted, but physically she still felt as fresh as she had that morning. It took something a great deal more strenuous than a double-shift in the diner to wear Abby out. *There's got to be a better way to earn some money,* she said to herself. *I hardly need superhuman strength to carry plates around.*

Almost exactly eight months earlier, Abigail de Luyando discovered that she was not an ordinary person. It had

41

been a Friday night—early Saturday morning, really—and she'd been locking up the diner when two men pushed open the door and demanded that she hand over the contents of the register.

Without thinking, she'd picked up a steel tray and thrown it at the nearest man. It slammed into his forehead and knocked him backward over a table. The second man lunged at her: Abby grabbed his arm, picked up a fork, and stabbed it down through the sleeve of his leather biker's jacket and into the counter. As he struggled to get free she punched him in the face, knocking him out cold.

When the cops arrived to arrest the would-be robbers they had to leave the jacket behind: No matter how hard they pulled, they weren't able to remove the fork from the countertop.

The following morning, Abby arrived at the diner to find Dave the manager's normally pale face red with effort as he struggled to wrench the fork free. "How did you *do* that?" he'd asked her.

"Just lucky, I guess." When she was sure he wasn't watching, Abby grabbed hold of the fork. It came free of the counter as easily as if it had been stuck into a stack of pancakes, and the jacket slid to the floor.

After the morning rush was over, Abby had gone out to the large, cluttered yard at the back of Leftover's Finer Diner. Piled up in one corner was a collection of weather-tarnished aluminum tubes and panels, discarded after the diner's refit the previous year.

Abby picked up one of the longer tubes and twisted it into

42

a knot like it was Play-Doh. Shaking her head with disbelief, she threw the tube to one side and—just to see what would happen—she aimed a punch at one of the aluminum panels.

It was like pushing her fist through rice paper.

Over the following weeks, Abby had experimented and practiced every free moment. She was stronger and faster than a normal fourteen-year-old girl should be, but she quickly discovered a strange quirk of her abilities: She could just barely pick up four cinder blocks in one go, but had little trouble tipping over a much heavier Dumpster. She was able to flick pennies across the counter with such force that they buried themselves so deep in the wall that she couldn't dig them out, but couldn't throw a ceramic cup much farther than an ordinary person.

Her powers really worked only on metal objects.

By seven-thirty the line outside the diner had thinned a little: Mandy hadn't taken a break in half an hour. The pressure eased enough for Abby to tackle the corner booth once more.

"Sorry to interrupt your fun, guys, but we're running a business here. Time you moved on."

The boy with the nose ring smirked. "And what if we don't?"

"See the sign by the door? The management reserves the right to refuse admission. You do want to be allowed in next time, don't you?"

"All right, all right. We get the message."

Five of them slid out of the booth, but the last—the girl Abby remembered from school—lingered. She began poking through the pile of dollar bills and loose change on the table. "Let's see. . . . Check comes to thirteen seventy-five. . . ." The girl counted out fourteen dollars and scooped up the rest. In an overly cheerful voice she said, "Keep the change!"

"Wow, a whole *quarter*? Thanks!"

Nose-ring boy laughed. "Cheer up, babe! Better than nothing!" He slapped Abby on the backside.

She rounded on him. "Get out!"

His grin spread. "Y'know, my friends are still a little hungry. Maybe they'll stay a while and you and me can—"

A soft but clear voice from behind him said, "Maybe you'd better do as she says."

Nose-ring turned to see a tall African-American teenage boy staring at him from the counter. "What's it got to do with you, beanpole? You can just—" Nose-ring boy's mouth kept moving, but no sound came out. He paused, frowned. Tried to say something else. His eyes grew wide and he looked like he was on the edge of a panic attack.

His puzzled friends clustered around him. "Marlon, what's wrong? Are you choking?"

He shook his head, pointed at his throat, and mouthed the words, "I can't speak!"

Abby glanced around the diner. Everyone was staring, but as she looked toward the counter the tall, slim teenager was hastily turning away—Abby was sure he was trying to hide a grin.

What was that? Did he *do something?*

Nose-ring—who looked like he was on the verge of tears— was quickly led out of the diner by his friends.

The slim boy was sitting at the counter with a half-eaten

burger in his hands and a copy of *Record Collector* open in front of him.

Abby kept watch on him as she cleaned up the vacated booth and wiped down the table. The boy seemed to be completely immersed in the magazine: Even after she had seated the next customers and taken their orders he was still on the same page. Either he was a very slow reader or he wasn't actually reading at all.

She moved around to the far side of the counter, and stopped in front of him on the pretext of washing some glasses. "Interesting article?"

He looked up. "Hmm?"

Abby guessed he was a little older than her. He had a thin build, but large hands and wide shoulders that suggested he wasn't done growing yet. His hair was close-cropped, and his skin was almost as dark as hers. He had the beginnings of a mustache on his upper lip. Abby realized now that she had seen him at the diner before, many times, and he'd always been alone, always sitting in the same spot and ordering the same food.

"What you're reading," Abby said. "Interesting, is it?"

"Oh, yeah. Yeah, it is. If you're into synthesizers and drum machines."

"Let me guess. You've got a band." She glanced down at his long fingers. "And you play the keyboard."

He grinned and shook his head. "Nope." He raised the magazine. "This is the closest I've got to a real musical instrument."

She nodded in the direction of the corner booth. "Thanks for sticking up for me. But that was strange, wasn't it?"

He looked around. "What was strange?"

"The way that guy's voice just cut out. Sudden onset of laryngitis or something."

The boy shrugged. "Could be the flu. Nearly everyone else has it."

Abby considered this. "Right." *Better not push him*, she decided. *If he did do something to that guy's voice then he's not going to admit it.*

The boy suddenly sat upright, looked up toward the TV in the corner. The sound was off, but the picture showed the newly constructed power plant twelve miles away.

A line of scrolling text across the bottom of the screen read ". . . superhero Max Dalton believed to be one of the hostages. Police have cordoned off the area and are . . ."

The boy jumped to his feet, tossed a twenty-dollar bill on the counter. "Got to go. Keep the change."

Before Abby could even respond, he was out the door and running down the street. Mandy appeared next to Abby and made a grab for the twenty. "Oh, big tipper!"

Normally Abby would have snatched the money out of her hand. Instead, she was staring at the TV screen. "What is all this?"

"Oh yeah. It was on the radio. Bunch of terrorists attacked the new power plant. Cops all over the place. And the guy said that Max Dalton got captured or something."

"Dave's out back, right?" Abby pulled off her apron and pushed through the double doors. The manager was sitting on the back step sipping out of a mug. "Dave? I've got to go home for a couple of hours."

"Aw, you're kidding, right? Abby, we're *swamped*! All the

46

kids are coming in tonight because their parents are too sick to make dinner."

She folded her arms and glared at him. "Swamped? Dave, you've been out here for ages, and Mandy only works about twenty minutes out of every hour. I've been going for eleven straight hours—I haven't even had my lunch yet!"

Dave sighed, pushed himself to his feet, and carried his mug back into the kitchen. Over his shoulder, he said, "All right, all right. Be back by . . . nine, OK?"

"I'll do my best." She closed the door on him.

Abby looked around to make sure that no one could see her, then made her way to the far side of the yard. An old wooden shed was slowly rotting in the corner, half-hidden among the piles of junk. She pulled open the door and ducked inside. Under a large, paint-spattered plastic sheet was a rusty oil drum with its lid hammered into place so tightly that nothing short of a crowbar would be able to open it.

She popped the lid with her fingers, and one by one removed the items she'd been storing for exactly this sort of situation.

First came the heavy boots she'd bought at the local army surplus store. Next the builders' gloves. Then the extra-thick black denim jeans and the leather biker's jacket that the would-be robber had left behind.

She quickly stripped off her uniform and pulled everything on. She'd spent months modifying the jacket and jeans. A visit to the local hardware store and almost a whole week's tips had provided her with hundreds of steel washers, each about the size of a quarter. A scavenging session at the local dump had yielded a dozen yards of piano wire.

She'd threaded the washers onto the jacket and jeans with the wire to create her own homemade chain mail.

When she zipped up the jacket, Abby took a moment to consider what she was about to do. Her heart was thumping like crazy and she'd already broken out in a sweat.

She was a superhuman. She was stronger and faster than an ordinary person, she had tremendous stamina, and she had some sort of strange ability to manipulate metal—even though she didn't quite understand that part herself.

I've got to do this, she told herself. *If Max Dalton really has been captured, I might be able to help.*

Her hands trembled with anticipation and no small amount of fear as she reached into the oil drum and removed the last two items.

The first was a secondhand full-face motorcycle helmet.

The second had once been a three-foot-long solid steel bar. Abby had spent a week hammering it flat so that its cross section was a narrow ellipse rather than a circle. She'd fashioned a handgrip from a strip of rubber cut from a car tire and bound it to one end of the bar with piano wire. Then she'd sharpened one edge, brought it to a point at the top.

She slung the heavy sword into the specially made sheath on the back of her jacket, then pulled on her helmet.

She opened the door to the shed, peeked out to make sure that there was still no one watching, then closed the door behind her.

The back wall was seven feet high. Abby vaulted over it, landed lightly on her feet in the alley, and ran.

CHAPTER 6

Lance McKendrick knocked on the door of his parents' bedroom and pushed it open.

His mother was asleep, the blankets pulled right up to her neck. His father was hunched over on the side of the bed in his pajamas and the thick dressing gown he'd stolen from a hotel, blowing his nose on a tissue.

"How are you doing, Dad?"

Albert McKendrick turned dark-rimmed, bloodshot eyes toward his son and shrugged. "Lousy. Feel like I've been run over by a truck delivering bowling balls." He sniffed. "Back's killing me, and when I try to stand up I get dizzy. Half the time I'm freezing; the other half I'm soaked with sweat." He wiped his mouth with a fresh tissue. It shredded on his two-day stubble and left his chin and upper lip covered with tiny particles of paper. "Where's Cody?"

"Training. He should be back in about an hour. Will you guys be OK on your own until then?"

His father nodded, then sneezed. "God, I *hate* being sick."

Lance returned to his own room and pulled the small briefcase out from under the bed. It had been locked, but that had been easily sorted out with his homemade tension wrench and half-diamond pick.

He was disappointed to discover that the briefcase was almost empty. All it contained was two sheets of paper filled with dense columns of numbers and a small envelope holding an electronic keycard. The envelope had a local address written on the front, and a seven-digit phone number on the back.

Lance had spent the past couple of hours wondering what to do next. He was almost certain that the briefcase was what Paragon had been looking for. *But why? Who was the guy driving the car?*

I should hand this stuff over to the cops. But if I do that now, they'll want to know why I didn't do it earlier. And if they guess I picked the locks, I'll be in real trouble.

I could say I just found it. I went back to Jade Avenue and I spotted the briefcase in the Sternhams' hedge.

But he knew that wouldn't work: The police would have thoroughly searched the area.

He went downstairs, grabbed the local phone directory, and brought it back to his room. The back cover folded out into a map: Lance found the address in the middle of the business park. He knew the area quite well—he'd run a couple of scams on some of the businesses there.

From the direction the car had been heading, the driver must have been leaving the park when Paragon spotted him.

Does that mean that Paragon didn't know where the place is?
Would the guy have told him by now?

Lance realized that deep down he'd already decided what he was going to do. He put the empty briefcase back under the bed, stuffed the pages into his backpack, then put the keycard and the envelope into his jacket pocket.

It was an easy ten-minute cycle to the business park. As Lance passed through the entrance, he told himself, *I'm just going to go past and look at the building. The place could be swarming with cops.*

The building was on a narrow side road. Lance pedaled past it and risked a quick glance. There was no sign of life.

It was a two-story office that looked just like dozens of others surrounding it, with the exception that there was no company name on the front, not even a brass plaque beside the door.

He went around the block three times before he worked up the courage to steer into the building's four-car parking lot. There was still no one around.

The electronic lock on the door bore the same manufacturer's stamp as the keycard. There was no buzzer or any other obvious way for a caller to get the attention of whoever might be inside, so he simply knocked on the door and waited. He decided that, if anyone answered, he'd pretend he was looking for Complete Office Solutions. That was a company on the far side of the business park.

There was no answer. He knocked again, louder this time. The only response was the echo of his knock.

Lance hesitated for a moment, then thought, *What the heck. Let's see what's in there.*

He swiped the keycard through the lock, and the door clicked open. He quickly stepped through and used his elbow to push the door closed—he didn't want to leave any fingerprints. In his backpack he had a pair of latex gloves he'd stolen during his last visit to the dentist, but he was reluctant to use them just yet—all of his "Wait, this isn't what it looks like!" excuses would fall apart if it was obvious that he'd come prepared.

The small lobby was dark and bare, and the air smelled dry and stale. There was a single desk facing the door, but its light coating of dust told Lance that it had been a long time since anyone had used it.

Beyond the desk was an ordinary wooden door, and Lance was just about to open it when he spotted a small red flashing light on the side of the desk: an alarm box with a keypad.

Oh man. . . . Does that mean I've already triggered the alarm? No, can't be that. Anyone who's supposed to be here will need time to enter the code.

He bit his lip. The alarm box wasn't a model he recognized. *So what is the code? And how much time do I have?*

He shifted closer to the alarm box to see whether any of the keys showed signs of wear, but they all looked the same.

No good. Get out. Bad idea from the start.

Lance was halfway to the door when he remembered the seven-digit number on the back of the envelope. *Maybe it's not a phone number.*

He dashed back to the alarm box, pulled the envelope out of his pocket, and keyed in the number using the knuckle on his index finger—the cops could pull fingerprints from almost anything.

The red light stopped flashing, and there was a soft *click* from the wooden door.

Lance pushed the door open with his shoulder, and stepped through into a wide, windowless storage room. The overhead fluorescent lights were on, giving him enough light to see a wide garage door at the far end, shelving units on each side, and twin workbenches—each the size of a Ping-Pong table— in the middle of the room.

On the nearest workbench was a large, curved metal box that very much resembled something he'd seen earlier that day: Paragon's jetpack.

Lance swallowed as he slowly circled the bench, unable to keep his eyes off the jetpack.

This has to be one of Paragon's hideouts. The guy in the Pinto must have stolen his keycard or something.

He reached out his hand and ran it along the jetpack's cold, smooth surface, then realized what he'd done and used the sleeve of his jacket to wipe off his fingerprints. From his backpack he took out the latex gloves and pulled them on.

But if the guy stole the keycard, how did he get the number for the alarm?

Lance stepped back and looked around. The shelving units were loaded with identical blue plastic storage boxes. He picked one at random and popped the lid. Inside was a pair of severed hands.

He yelped and dropped the box. It fell on its side and spilled out its contents—not a pair of hands after all, just a set of gloves. They looked like something a knight would wear: strong leather covered in small hinged plates that allowed the fingers to move. But the plates were made of some sort

53

of hard plastic, not metal. Lance picked them up and pulled them on over his latex gloves, flexed his fingers, and punched his right fist into his left palm.

Lance grinned. *Nice! They've got to be worth a few bucks!*

He put the armored gloves in his backpack and opened the next box. It contained a half-dismantled complex-looking mechanical device. *Too heavy to take, and I don't know what it is anyway.*

The next three boxes housed similar devices, but on the next shelf the boxes contained what looked like sections of Paragon's armor: lightweight arm, leg, and chest pieces, all highly polished silver or chrome. Lance pulled out one of the chest-plates and turned it over in his hands. Like the gloves, it was composed of hinged sections and padded on the inside. He held it up against his chest, but it was way too big for him.

On the next row down he found something else he had seen that day: Paragon's grappling gun—or something very much like it. The gun was bulky and heavier than it looked, made of a thick black plastic. A red gas cylinder was fixed to the back, and a three-pronged hook protruded from the muzzle. A thin steel cable trailed from the hook into a spool beneath the barrel.

Lance just had to try it out. He hefted the gun in his hand and aimed it at the far wall. His eyes half-closed, he squeezed the trigger. Nothing happened. *Probably needs to be charged up or something.* He put it into his backpack anyway, and resumed looking around.

The backpack was getting full now, so he knew that he couldn't take much more. He felt a little disappointed at that. *I'm not going to get another chance to come back here.*

He walked back to the workbench and stared at the jetpack. He knew that if he took it, it would be missed a lot sooner than the gloves and grappling gun.

It's got to be worth a fortune. Lance remembered a newspaper article about Paragon that had said no one knew exactly how it worked, but dozens of engineering companies all over the world were trying to duplicate it.

He reached out and picked it up. It was very heavy, but not unbearable.

He couldn't stop himself: He slung the jetpack onto his back and fastened the clips across his chest. It didn't seem quite so heavy with the weight distributed across his shoulders.

Lance grinned as he pictured himself soaring and swooping through the air. *Man, that would be so cool!*

From the other side of the garage door there was a loud clunk. Lance froze. *That was a car door being closed.*

A motor whined into life and the garage door began to rattle upward. Lance looked around for somewhere to hide. *Oh God . . . Paragon's gonna beat the crap out of me!*

He wasted three seconds trying to unclasp the jetpack, then gave up. He grabbed his backpack and ducked down under the workbench.

He heard a man's voice say, "Marcus ain't gonna talk, but that don't mean we're safe. They'll have their forensics guys all over him."

Another man's voice, much quieter: "So . . . What, we're taking *everything*? That's gonna take hours!"

"Go a lot quicker if you ain't complaining. Start loading the truck."

"But what's the point? We're not gonna *need* mosta this stuff now!"

From his position underneath the workbench Lance could see their legs, so he was able to tell which way they were facing as they moved about the warehouse.

The door to the front office was still slightly open, and it was only a few feet away. He figured he'd need five seconds at most to get through the door. *Come on, turn around, turn around!*

Minutes passed, and Lance's right leg began to cramp. The two men had made several trips out to their truck, but only one at a time.

Eventually, the one with the softer voice said, "Listen. . . . About Marcus."

"What about him?"

"If the cops *can* get him to talk . . . we're toast."

"All the more reason to stop shirking and start working. If the cops find this place with us still in it, The Helotry are gonna come down on us like a ton of lead bricks."

The other man muttered, "I'm more worried about Paragon finding us."

"He won't. Marcus's stuff all got burned up with his car."

"How do you know that?"

"Because we're here and Paragon ain't."

"Yeah, well, I'm just sayin'. It's taken our guys years to reverse-engineer his armor and jetpack and I didn't even get a chance to try it out. If the schedule hadn'ta been moved up we coulda all had jetpacks and armor and everything."

"Yeah, well, if Marcus hadn't been dumb enough to take the thing out for a test flight, then Paragon wouldn't have

noticed him and he wouldn't have got caught. So . . . Hey—
where *is* the jetpack?"

Under the workbench, Lance cringed.

"I just loaded the crate inta the truck," the other man
replied.

"Not that one. The one Marcus was working on earlier. It
was right here on the bench."

CHAPTER 7

Right now, Roz Dalton despised the "one thing at a time" limitation on her telekinesis. If she'd been able to control more than one object, she might have had a chance to get away.

Instead, she'd been captured. The gray men had rushed at her, knocked her to the ground. At gunpoint they'd cuffed her wrists and ankles, and carried her inside the power plant.

Now she was sitting on the unfinished concrete floor of a large room. Except for a single large wooden desk at one end, the room was devoid of furniture. The gray man who'd been wounded by his colleagues was now sitting on the desk as one of them bandaged his arm.

Roz's brother and the Rangers were on the ground close to her, similarly cuffed. Whatever these guys had hit the men with, it was still affecting them. Max was lying on his side, moaning slightly, his legs twitching every few moments.

Ox and Lash looked to be completely unconscious. They too were on their sides. Lash's mouth and nose were leaking a puddle of saliva and thick mucus onto the floor. His breathing was ragged, uneven.

Ollie French was awake, but not in good condition. He sat with his knees drawn up to his chest and his arms wrapped around his legs. He was shivering uncontrollably.

What did they do to them? Roz wondered. Whatever it was, it had disabled two of the world's most powerful superhumans and three highly trained former U.S. Army Rangers.

Roz's wrists and ankles chafed from the cuffs, and her backside was numb from sitting on the hard floor, but aside from that she felt fine.

Her telekinesis was still working too, but there was no way it could help her now: Five of the gray men were watching her at all times. Like the Rangers, these men had also been well-trained: They said nothing, kept to the shadows so that she couldn't get a good look at them.

A door opened somewhere behind her, and she heard soft footsteps approaching. A woman's voice said, "Do not turn around. Understood?" Roz nodded.

"How are you feeling?"

Roz wasn't quite sure how to answer that. She'd been expecting something more along the lines of "Who are you?" or "What are you doing here?"

"Well?"

"A little uncomfortable," Roz said.

The woman asked, "Is that all?"

"A bit scared too. Is that what you want to hear?"

"No dizziness, nausea, muscle aches?"

"No. Aside from the bruises your friends gave me. And I need to use the bathroom."

Roz heard the woman move closer. "So you are Rosalyn, daughter of the late Malcolm and Roberta Dalton. Sister to the famous Maxwell and ten-year-old Joshua. Max is a mind-reader; you appear to have psychokinetic abilities.... It will be interesting to see what powers—if any—Josh will develop."

Without turning her head, Roz looked around, hoping to catch the woman's reflection in a window or door. "Josh can create illusions so convincing that you can't tell what's real from what's fake." She forced a smile. "Like the illusion that you are still inside the Midway power plant and that your men have captured me. But the truth is that you've already been arrested. You're in jail. Everything you think you see and hear is just a fantasy created by Josh."

"Very clever. But you haven't thought that one through, have you? Josh is too young for any superhuman abilities to have developed."

It was worth a shot, Roz thought. "What are you people *doing* here? The power plant isn't even operational yet. There's nothing to steal. And you can't escape—the whole area is surrounded." But the fading footsteps told her that the woman was walking away.

Roz slumped forward with her head lowered, trying to give the impression that she felt defeated. But the gray men had cuffed her hands in front of her, not behind: She could see the cuffs, and if she could see something she could manipulate it telekinetically.

But there was a problem: She had no idea how the cuffs'

locking mechanism worked. She could see the outside of the cuffs, the strong double-chain linking them, but that was all. She concentrated on splitting one of the chain's links. It wasn't working. She could move the individual links, but not twist them out of shape or break them.

Physically Roz was no stronger than an ordinary human, and now she began to understand why she wasn't able to use her telekinesis to lift very heavy objects: It was somehow tied to her physical strength. *Maybe that'll change,* she thought. *When Max was my age he was only able to read minds. It took him a couple of years to learn how to control them too. Maybe my power will get stronger as I get older.* She let out a sigh. *A lot of good that does me right now.*

I could be an Olympic runner. If I don't tell anyone I'm a superhuman, I could be the world champion.

Abby de Luyando had kept to the alleyways and side streets as she ran, then increased her speed when she reached the open road. The nuclear power plant was twelve miles from the diner—less than twenty minutes after she left, she could see it high on a hill a mile away, its massive cooling towers tinted orange by the setting sun.

But she couldn't get much closer. The police and army had set up roadblocks, and a dozen helicopters were hovering in place encircling the plant. Another two army trucks came roaring up the road behind her. Abby vaulted over the low fence on her left and ducked down in the long grass.

A voice right beside her said, "You know, you're pretty fast, but I could hear you coming a mile away."

She whirled around, but there was no one there.

The voice said, "All that jangling and clinking. It sounds like you've got a pile of loose change in every pocket."

Abby raised the visor on her helmet. "Are you . . . Are you invisible or something?" Even as she asked that, she knew it couldn't be true—the grass around her was undamaged. Anything invisible would have left a mark.

"No. Look to your left."

Abby looked. She couldn't see anything but fields and trees.

"I'm right here," the voice said. "I'm waving. Look."

Then she spotted it: At the far side of the field an arm was waving back and forth.

"I see you. Who are you and what are you doing here?"

"I'm here for the same reason you are, I think. I want to help out."

"Stay put. I'm coming over." Keeping low, Abby ran across the field. She was all too aware now that her chain mail made a lot of noise. *I'll have to glue it all down or something.*

"A little closer," the voice said.

Then Abby saw him. A tall figure dressed in a skintight black and green costume. He was masked and gloved, but didn't look that much older than she was. They stared at each other for a moment. "So . . . ," she said. "Who are you, then?"

"Who are *you*?"

"I'm not telling you until you tell me."

He paused. "Well, how do I know you're not one of the bad guys?"

"How do I know *you're* not?" She moved a little closer and peered at his face. "You're the guy from Leftover's, aren't you? The one reading the *Record Collector* magazine."

He bit his lip. "Well, if I am, then that means you can only be the waitress."

Aw, rats! "Maybe I've got a power that lets me know things . . . sort of magically. You know, psychic stuff."

"In that case, what's my name?"

Abby sighed. "All right. I'm the waitress from the diner."

"And I'm the guy with the magazine. So what can you do?"

"I'm strong, fast, and I've got this." Abby removed the sword from her back.

"Can you use it, though?"

She shrugged, and held out the sword. "I don't know how to fence, but it's heavy and it's sharp."

He gently pushed the sword aside. "Well, keep the pointy end away from me. So what *is* your name? Your superhero name, I mean."

"I haven't actually thought of one yet. What about you?"

"Thunder. I can control sound waves."

"Oh. Is that all?"

"It's not enough?"

"Well, it doesn't sound especially useful." She took a step back and looked at his costume. It was a one-piece, skintight rubber, mostly black with wide green stripes down the arms and outside of the legs. A large zipper ran from his throat to his navel. "Wait, is that a *wet suit*?"

He looked a little defensive. "Well, yeah. But at least I *look* like a superhero. Yours looks like you made it yourself."

"I *did* make it myself! And I'd rather look like this than some guy who looks like he can't find his snorkel and flippers."

Thunder put up his hand. "Hold on. . . . There's more trucks coming. Five . . . no, six. And they sound bigger than the others. Reinforcements—it's the National Guard."

Abby looked around. All she could hear was the constant hum of the helicopters. She turned back to him. "Can you hear, like, *everything*?"

"Up to a distance of about five or six miles, yeah, usually. But right now there's too much noise from the cops and the army and the helicopters for me to hear what's going on inside the power plant. So . . . What's your plan?"

"Don't really have one. I just wanted to see if I could help. They said that Max Dalton got captured. I was sort of thinking of offering my services to the police."

Thunder rubbed his chin. "Yeah, same here. But now I'm not so sure. They don't know who we are."

"We should sneak closer and maybe you can hear the guys inside the plant. Then we could tell the cops and they'd know we're on their side."

"And what'll *you* do?"

"I don't know yet."

Thunder sneered. "Oh, good plan! You really are a newbie, aren't you? First time out, is it?"

Abby ignored that. "We're not helping anyone by sniping at each other. Let's just get closer and see what happens."

With Thunder leading the way, they crept forward through the long grass. After a few minutes, he said, "OK. . . . I can hear the army guy in charge—Colonel Morgan. He's saying that Dalton's helicopter pilot told them that Dalton's sister is in there too. She went in after the others were captured, and got captured herself. Idiot."

"Keep the noise down," Abby said.

"They won't hear us. We could set off a bomb here and they wouldn't know unless they were looking. I'm stopping our sounds from reaching them."

Abby wasn't about to admit that that was a very useful ability. "So what are they planning?"

"I think they don't know what to do. There's supposed to be sixteen hostages. Eleven workers and Dalton and his crew."

"Can you stop *any* sounds?"

"Pretty much, yeah."

"So you could, like, block out every sound inside the power plant?"

"I could, but then they'd know something was up. We're going to have to do something, though. Sounds like half of the cops and most of the army guys are coming down with the flu. Come on, we'll see if we can get closer."

It's the perfect time to attack something, Abby thought. *Seems like nearly everyone has the flu these days.* She froze. *Unless it's not the flu. Maybe it's something else.*

She ran to catch up with Thunder. "Hey!"

"What?"

"Anyone you know got the flu?"

"Sure. Most of the teachers at school, my folks, most of my neighbors. Why?"

"Same here. My mother, my aunts. Four of the guys from work. Lots of the regular customers. The guy who lives in the apartment next door to mine was up all night coughing his guts up. . . . I don't think this is the ordinary flu. There's always some epidemic or other going around, but they take time to spread. This one is happening all over the world at the same time. That's just not possible, unless it was done deliberately. Someone has created a plague."

CHAPTER 8

"I swear I left it right here," the man with the deeper voice said.

Lance swallowed. *Please don't let them find me!* He peeled off the latex gloves and tried once more to open the jetpack's clasps, but couldn't find a catch or a button.

The other man said, "You musta already loaded it inta the truck with the other one."

"I didn't."

"Well, check anyway. It's not like anyone woulda took it. Hey, you don't think that Marcus had it on him when he got arrested, do ya?"

"We would have heard."

Seconds later, the man's muffled voice came from outside. "I toldja, it ain't in the truck."

I'm outta here! Lance darted out from under the workbench and made a dive for the door.

One of the men said, "What . . . *Hey!*"

Lance slammed the door behind him, ran through the musty office and out to the front. He jumped onto his bike, slung the backpack onto the handlebars, and began pedaling like crazy. He couldn't help grinning. *I did it! I got away!*

He zoomed around the corner and onto the main road, shifted up a gear, and increased his speed. It was tough going with the heavy jetpack on his back, but he wasn't going to stop for anything.

Then he heard the roar of an engine coming up fast behind.

He risked a glance back: A large white panel truck was bearing down on him. Two black-suited men were in the cab, the passenger gesturing wildly while the driver sat with a grim, determined look on his face.

Lance took a sudden right into another narrow side road, almost coming off the bike. The driver had to hit the brakes to make the turn.

The road was closed off at the end, with only a narrow pedestrian passage leading through the gap between two buildings. *They'll never be able to follow me through!* He mentally pictured his route home. *If I cut through the church grounds I can . . .* He stopped himself. *No, can't go home. Not with all this stuff. I have to hide it somewhere.*

As he was considering the best place to stash his stolen goods where they wouldn't be found, he cycled out of the business park and onto the street. The rush-hour traffic was long gone, but the street was still busy.

He slowed a little as he approached the crossroads, weaved in and out of the waiting cars, then turned right, heading toward the mall. There was a dense clump of bushes at one end of the eastern parking lot—he'd often hidden stuff there before, and it had never been discovered.

At the next junction he jumped the red light and almost collided with a white truck that was turning the corner. He pulled hard on the brakes, put his foot down to steady himself, and glared at the driver. His face fell. *Oh no. . . .*

The two black-suited men looked as surprised as Lance did. The passenger shouted, "That's *him*! An' he's the same kid from the accident! He musta got Marcus's briefcase!"

Lance jumped back onto the bike, darted around the truck and down the road, knowing that they'd have to make a U-turn to follow him.

He heard a loud *bang* and something shattered a mailbox as he passed. "They've got guns? Oh, this just gets better and better!"

Another *bang*, and Lance felt like something had thumped him in the back. *They hit the jetpack! OK, that's it. I quit.* He slowed a little, steered the bike onto the pavement. *I'll say I'm sorry and hand it all back and when their hands are full I'll run like mad.* A hundred yards ahead was the pedestrian entrance to a housing estate. *Perfect. Stop there and—*

There was a third gunshot. Lance changed his mind about stopping. He hunched forward, keeping his head low, and pushed as hard on the pedals as he could. There were two more shots, and before he even heard the second Lance found himself racing forward, as though he had just crested a steep hill.

But the road was almost flat, and still his speed was increasing. It felt like someone was pushing him from behind.

Then a familiar whine reached his ears, and he knew what had happened: The last gunshot had somehow activated the jetpack.

He zoomed out onto the road, his knuckles white on the juddering handlebars. *I'm gonna die!*

He knew that he couldn't slow down or jump off the bike. With the jetpack still thrusting him forward he'd have no way of stopping. He couldn't even lift his head more than a couple of inches.

Lance rocketed across an intersection, overtook a guy on a motorbike, narrowly missed a deep pothole. He could steer the bike, but it wasn't easy—at this speed, the slightest nudge on the handlebars sent him weaving all over the road. *The fuel in this thing has to run out sometime. Need a good long stretch of road . . .*

Ahead, the road branched to the right: the on-ramp for the freeway. He knew that bicycles weren't allowed on the freeway, but figured that in this case the traffic cops might make an exception. Besides, he didn't have any other option.

There was a line of cars at the end of the ramp waiting to pull out into the busy traffic. Lance zoomed past the surprised drivers and cut in ahead of a white Toyota.

The speed limit on the freeway was sixty-five miles per hour. Lance knew from being in the car with his dad that most drivers regarded sixty-five as the minimum speed, not the maximum. He didn't know how fast he was going now, but he was overtaking everything else on the freeway. The bike shuddered and rattled over the asphalt and he prayed to the god of cycling that he didn't blow a tire.

He tried to remember exactly what the newspaper article on Paragon's jetpack had said about its range. He had a horrible feeling that there had been something about Paragon being able to make it all the way from New York to Chicago without the need to refuel. *And he's a lot bigger than me too. Plus he's got all that armor. This thing might not run out before I reach the end of the freeway!*

Lance's back and shoulders were aching from the strain, and he desperately wanted to sit back. He knew that if he did, the jetpack would launch him into the air, bike and all.

Paragon had spent years developing his jetpack. He knew how to control it, how to land safely.

Lance didn't even know how to undo the clasps.

"I can hear breathing," Thunder said. "Lots of it. A couple of dozen people. Most of them are struggling—their breath is all wheezy and bubbly."

Special Agent Lloyd Rosenfield—a gruff middle-aged man with thinning hair and little patience—turned to the military officer. "Colonel, explain to me again why we're taking advice from a couple of kids who think it's Halloween."

"Because we're superhuman," Abby said. "We can do stuff your soldiers can't." She'd disliked this man from the moment his shiny rented car had screeched to a stop and he'd bounded out brandishing his FBI badge.

They were half a mile downhill from the power plant, surrounded by armed police officers, soldiers, and FBI agents, standing on the narrow road next to the FBI's operations truck. The power plant was now completely encircled by soldiers, but none closer than five hundred yards.

Rosenfield looked at Abby. "What? You want to say that again with the visor up so we can actually *hear* you?"

Colonel Morgan said, "They seem to be the real deal, Agent Rosenfield. At least, the boy does. He can hear stuff from miles away, block sounds, project his voice, all that sort of thing." Morgan was a short, squat man in his forties with buzz-cut white hair.

Abby and Thunder looked at each other. It had been her idea to talk to the police—Thunder had wanted to find a way into the power plant without their help.

Rosenfield considered them for a moment, then nodded. "All right." He extended his hand to Thunder. "Welcome aboard." As Thunder reached out to shake it, Rosenfield said, "Whoa, wait a second. Where I come from we believe it's disrespectful to shake hands wearing gloves."

Thunder started to pull off his right glove but Abby put her hand on his arm. "Don't. Then he'll have your DNA on his hand and he'll be able to find out your secret identity."

The agent rolled his eyes. "Secret identity? Are you *kidding* me? This isn't a game, kids. Go on home before your mommies miss you."

The colonel said, "We're wasting time here." He looked to the west. "And we're losing light. Sun's almost down. These guys haven't made any demands that we know of. So what do they want? Thunder?"

Thunder closed his eyes for a moment. "There's a woman, sounds like she could be in charge. She's talking to one of the men. . . . Telling him that they have to keep waiting." He opened his eyes. "They're getting restless. Hungry too."

"I don't believe this," Rosenfield said. "Colonel, we need to take charge of this situation. You've got half the able-bodied cops in the state hanging around here scratching their butts. We can't even get hold of any grown-up superheroes because Max Dalton is our only point of contact. I say we storm the place."

"And risk the hostages? No. If we knew exactly where they were, we might be able to take a chance on that. But we're operating blind here."

Thunder asked, "You've got blueprints for the power plant, right?"

The colonel nodded. "Of course. Our analysts are going over them in the truck. We've got several possible access points, but like I said, we'd need to know exactly where they're keeping the hostages."

"I can help you with that. I can tell by the echoes where everyone is. I might not be able to tell the difference between the terrorists and the hostages, though."

Colonel Morgan looked to Rosenfield, who grudgingly nodded and said, "Worth a shot."

Thunder followed the colonel into the truck, leaving Abby facing the FBI agent. After a moment's awkward silence, he said, "And what good are you?"

"I'm strong and fast," Abby said.

"So's Tylenol. Difference is Tylenol takes headaches away; it doesn't create them."

Abby glared at him, then reached over her shoulder and withdrew her sword. "And I've got this."

"You have a sword. Great. I'll definitely call you if it turns out that the bad guys are Athos, Porthos, and Aramis."

Abby didn't know what those names meant, but she wasn't about to admit that. "You want a demonstration, is that it?"

He smirked. "Be my guest."

"All right. The demo comes in two parts." Holding the sword by its blade, she offered him the hilt. "Take this."

He grabbed hold of the hilt, and Abby let go.

The sword slammed to the ground, almost pulling Rosenfield over with it.

"Heavy, isn't it?" She reached down and took it from his hand, then slowly walked over to his rented car. "The FBI is insured, right?"

Before he could answer, Abby swung the sword single-handed straight down on the hood of the car. The blade moved faster than anyone could see, but everyone jumped at the earsplitting *bang*. Rosenfield stared. His mouth dropped open. "My car! You dented the hood!"

Inside her helmet, Abby was grinning. "Dented the hood? Oh please! Is that all the credit I get?" She reached out to the hood and peeled it back as though it was nothing more rigid than a cotton bedsheet. The metal creaked and snapped. The FBI agent's mouth dropped even farther.

The sword had sliced straight through the engine block.

"Yeah. . . . You might want to get that patched up before you bring it back to the rental place," Abby said.

"Willful destruction of government property," Rosenfield muttered, his eyes still on the ruined car. "That's a federal offense."

"Sue me."

Colonel Morgan climbed out of the truck, followed by

Thunder. They slowed as they reached the car. The colonel whistled. "Bit of an oil leak there, Agent Rosenfield."

The agent pointed to Abby. "She—"

"Never mind that. Thunder here has given us our first break. We know where every hostage and every perp is. And we can get in without them realizing. We need your explosives guys with us to blow the main doors."

Rosenfield shook his head. "The hostiles would see you coming."

"Not if we come from above, drop down onto the roof from a chopper."

"Then they'd *hear* you coming."

Thunder smiled. "That's where I come in."

Roz lifted her head. *Something's changed. . . .*

The sun had set and the room was in almost total darkness now, but that wasn't what felt different. She slowly looked around the cavernous room. The gray men were still watching her from the shadows. Max and the Rangers were still on the floor. Max was curled up into a ball, quietly shivering. Ox was almost motionless, the only sign of life the gentle rise and fall of his chest. Ollie and Lash were both flat on their backs. Ollie's eyes were open, flicking rapidly back and forth, his breath rasping and uneven.

How long have we been here now? Three hours? Four? Why hasn't anyone come for us?

That was when she realized what was different: The constant sound of the helicopters was gone.

They can't have abandoned us. . . . They must be planning something.

Roz stretched out her legs and arms as much as the cuffs would allow her. With some difficulty, she got onto her knees, then pushed herself back onto her feet.

The gray men immediately raised their weapons.

"Just stretching," Roz said, rolling her head from side to side. *If something is going to happen, I have to be ready to go into action.* She began to shift from one foot to the other. "I need to use the bathroom. Badly."

If Titan is out there working on a way to get to us, he might be listening in. He's supposed to have really good hearing. "Look, what harm can it do? There's five of you guarding five of us, and I'm the only one conscious. Two of you can take me to the bathroom and the rest will be more than capable of guarding Max and the others."

One of the gray men took out a radio and muttered something into it. A minute later, she heard footsteps in the corridor outside the room.

"Do not turn around," the woman's voice said. "Eyes closed, head down."

Roz did as she was told, and a leather bag was dropped over her head. But it wasn't pulled tight: Looking down, she could see a woman's hand unlocking the cuffs around her ankles.

"Try anything and we'll kill your brother."

"I understand," Roz said.

She felt a hand grab her arm and she was led toward the door. She couldn't see much as she walked, other than her feet. She was brought into a bathroom and led to a stall.

"Go, and be quick about it," the woman said.

"I need my hands free to get out of my uniform."

There was a pause, then the woman reached for the handcuffs. Roz took a chance: She telekinetically lifted the bottom of the leather bag enough to see that the woman stored the handcuff key on a loop on her belt.

After Roz was done, she was handcuffed once more and led back to the center of the large room. She was ordered to sit down, and then the cuffs were placed on her ankles. Roz used her power to raise the bag again, just in time to see the woman clipping the key on to her belt.

She tried not to smile: Anything she could see, she could control. She quickly unclipped the key, allowed it to drop to an inch above the ground. After the woman pulled the bag from her head and walked away, Roz jumped the key into the lock on her handcuffs, and turned it.

There was a slight *click.*

She checked the gray men—they didn't seem to have noticed. She used the key to unlock the cuffs around her ankles.

All right. . . . I'm ready. If someone outside is planning to get in, I'll be able to help.

CHAPTER 9

Lance didn't know how far he'd gone—the road signs were streaking by too fast. A bug slammed into his forehead. *That's sixteen.*

He was amazed that the bike had held together, but knew that it was only a matter of time before it had a puncture or hit a bump and one of the wheels buckled. When that happened, it was all over.

His whole body ached from the constant pressure of the jetpack on his back, and he thanked his younger self for spending all that time wrapping SureGrip Friction Tape around the handlebars.

He zoomed past a camper and then there was nothing ahead of him for as far as he could see. The freeway was straight and flat. *Maybe it's worth trying the brakes now. . . . Might slow me down a little.* He slid his fingers onto the lever for the back brakes, gave it a tentative squeeze. It didn't make any noticeable difference to his speed. He pulled harder. Still nothing.

All right. Front brakes. Using the front brakes at such a high speed was incredibly dangerous—if the bike stopped too suddenly he'd end up as a mile-long red smear on the asphalt. He gave the lever the slightest pull. He could see the twin rubber pads move in toward the wheel's rim. *Little more . . .* The rubber pads touched the rim and instantly disintegrated. *Oh man . . .*

By staring down at his chest Lance had already figured out how to open the clasps on the jetpack's shoulder straps, but that required using both hands. There was no way he was going to let go of the handlebars.

Another bug collided into his right cheek. *Seventeen. All I need is one to hit me in the eye and then I'm in serious trouble.*

Ahead, the back of a police car was rapidly approaching. It began to accelerate as Lance neared it, and in seconds he and the police car were traveling side by side. The uniformed officer in the passenger seat had a megaphone. "Pull over!"

"I can't!" Lance shouted, praying that the cop was able to hear him. "I don't know how to shut this thing down!"

"Pull over! *Now!*"

"I wish I could!"

"There's a roadblock eight miles ahead. If you don't pull that thing over before you reach it, we'll be forced to open fire!"

That's not fair! This isn't my fault! But even as the words ran through his mind, Lance knew that wasn't exactly true. It *was* his fault. He was the one who'd taken the briefcase, broken into the warehouse, and stolen the jetpack.

The police car was struggling to keep up with him. "You are traveling in excess of one hundred forty miles per hour, kid!" the officer said. "You have any idea how much that comes to in speeding fines? Now pull over!"

"Yeah, right!" Lance shouted back.

Then the police car fell behind. Lance noticed for the first time that the hard shoulder was lined with cars and trucks—the police had obviously cleared the way. He couldn't help wondering whether there was a news helicopter overhead, broadcasting the chase.

The freeway crested a low hill, and when he reached the top, Lance could see the roadblock a couple of miles away. He would reach it in less than a minute.

Then a voice to his right said, "So what's this? Science project? Couldn't you have made a volcano like everyone else?"

He risked a quick glance: Paragon was flying alongside him.

"Help me! I can't stop it!"

Ahead, illuminated by an array of portable spotlights, Lance saw the armed police officers duck down behind the line of cars spread out across all four lanes of the freeway. In seconds, Lance was close enough to see their faces.

Paragon reached out an arm and hit something on the side of the jetpack, then grabbed hold of Lance's collar and lifted him off the bike, which slammed into the side of one of the cars, showering the area with spokes and lumps of rubber. Paragon floated down to the ground on the far side of the blockade and let go of Lance.

"Oh, thank God!" Lance collapsed to the ground, his head spinning. He felt like he was going to throw up.

The armored superhero hauled him to his feet. "Get that thing off." Lance undid the jetpack's clasps—it was infuriatingly easy now—and it dropped to the ground with a loud *clank*.

A policeman with sergeants' stripes yelled, "Awright, get these cars out of here and get the traffic moving again! And someone clear up these bike parts!" He strode over to Lance and Paragon. "Mind filling me in?"

Lance started to explain everything. He knew that there was no point in lying. But he had only reached the part with the car crash on Jade Avenue when the sergeant interrupted him.

"Skip it. Paragon, I'm going to leave this in your hands. He's clearly a minor. You sort it out, send me a full report."

Paragon nodded. "First chance I get."

The sergeant glared at Lance. "And then we can decide how we're going to prosecute." He started to turn away, stopped, and handed Lance a white handkerchief. Lance looked at it.

"Uh, thanks?" Lance said.

"You got bugs all over you, kid."

As Lance wiped his face Paragon took him by the arm and steered him to the freeway's median. "What did you think you were doing?" He held up the jetpack. "Where did you even *get* this thing?"

Lance swallowed. "The guy you were chasing earlier, the guy in the car? He had a briefcase. There was an address and a keycard. It was a warehouse. I, uh . . ." Lance looked down at his feet. He had never felt so ashamed. "I thought there might be something there I could sell. I broke in, found the jetpack. But they came back. I made a run for it, but they shot at me."

He pointed to the bullet-hole in the back of the jetpack. "I was on the bike when it happened. I couldn't turn it off."

Paragon shook his head slowly. "Unbelievable."

"It's true!"

"Oh, I can see that it's true. What's unbelievable is that these people—whoever they are—have managed to duplicate the jetpack." He thrust it back into Lance's hands. "You hold on to that."

Lance's eyes grew wide. "I can *keep* it?"

"No. You're coming with me and I'll be carrying you, so you need to carry that."

"What about my backpack? It was on the handlebars."

"You have twenty seconds to find it."

Lance found his backpack—still attached to the handlebars—wedged into the framework of the car his bike had hit. Two police officers glowered at him as he struggled to pull it free. "Sorry about this. Really."

"Got it?" Paragon asked. "Then strap the jetpack on, and hold tight to your bag. We've got a long way to go."

"Are you taking me back home?"

"Not yet. I've got too many questions and I don't trust you not to run away. There's a situation up north and they need my help." Then he added, "I'd be there by now if it wasn't for you."

"Yeah, well if it wasn't for me you wouldn't know about those guys duplicating your jetpack." As soon as he said that, Lance felt a surge of guilt. "Sorry. I . . . Thanks for saving my life."

"You're welcome. Now prepare yourself. You thought you were traveling fast before? That was a Sunday stroll."

He stepped behind Lance, grabbed hold of the jetpack's shoulder straps, and suddenly they were rocketing into the night sky.

Half a mile from the power plant Abby and Thunder stood to one side trying to look innocent as they listened in on Agent Rosenfield's conversation with Colonel Morgan. Thunder was using his sound-manipulating ability to channel the conversation from almost a hundred yards away.

"So who are these people?" Morgan asked.

"We honestly don't know much." Rosenfield glanced back over toward Thunder. "Kid says they used the word *helotry* a couple of times to describe themselves."

Morgan said, "A helot is a slave, right?"

"So I'm told. And a helotry is a bunch of slaves. Slaves to what, we don't know."

"You trust those kids, Agent Rosenfield?"

"Doesn't look like we have much choice. The girl is very strong, very fast. I don't know if the boy has any physical powers, but his ability to muffle sounds will be a great boon in getting in. The doors and walls are strong enough to withstand a standard charge, and anything stronger will attract the terrorists' attention. We're going to have to use shaped explosives to take out the superstructure. That means ripping out pretty much the entire wall."

Abby turned to Thunder. "How *are* you doing that, exactly?"

He put up his hand. "Shh. They're still talking."

Rosenfield said, "Paragon's on the way, but I don't think we can wait much longer. Thunder says the hostages are really suffering." He blew his nose. "Hope I'm not coming down with it too. Your men up to the task, Colonel?"

"I trained them myself, Agent Rosenfield. They can handle anything." The colonel sounded almost offended that the FBI agent was questioning his men's abilities.

Thunder said to Abby, "That's it. Are *you* ready for this?"

She nodded. "The sooner the better. I've still got to get back to work. And after that I've got to go home and fake doing my homework for an hour."

Thunder frowned. "Fake it?"

"Long story."

Colonel Morgan approached Thunder carrying a flak jacket and two helmets. "Put these on. You're going in with the troops. Do you understand what that means? We don't like putting civilians in harm's way, but we're running out of time. Ordinarily we'd just wait out a situation like this, but if the hostages are sick, we can't take that chance."

Abby nodded, and turned her helmet over in her hands. "I can't wear this. You'd see my face!"

"It's dark. No one will recognize you. And that motorcycle helmet won't stop a bullet." He rapped the army helmet with his knuckles. "This will."

Abby pulled off her motorbike helmet and lowered the army helmet onto her head. "Have you got one in a smaller size?"

Five minutes later a Sikorsky S-70 copter plummeted from three thousand feet straight toward the roof of the power plant's largest building.

Abby was securely strapped in and holding so tight on to the edge of her seat that her fingers left impressions in the metal. Beside her, Thunder seemed to be thoroughly enjoying himself. He was leaning past her and staring out through the open hatch, a wide grin spread across his face.

Colonel Morgan stood in front of them, hanging out of a strap fixed to the ceiling and swaying gently from side to side. "Thunder, when I give the word I want the noise of this craft blocked out. You sure you can do that?"

"Yeah," Thunder said, not taking his eyes off the rapidly approaching scenery. "Only . . . It'll block out *all* the sounds. We won't be able to hear each other."

"We understand that. When we get inside, you two keep to the rear at all times, got it?" Morgan looked over to a lieutenant standing next to the pilot, who held up his hand with his fingers splayed. The lieutenant dropped one finger, then another.

"Ready . . . ," Morgan said. "Now!"

Abby saw Thunder close his eyes and frown in concentration, then suddenly she was completely deaf. She couldn't even hear her own breathing.

Thunder smiled and gave her a thumbs-up.

Colonel Morgan moved over to the open hatch and leaned out for a few seconds, then Abby felt the copter lurch and sway. Morgan turned back to his men and nodded, then pointed to Abby's seat harness and mouthed the words, "Let's go."

She unclipped the seat harness and stood up, holding on to Thunder's shoulder to steady herself. *OK. Here we go. First-ever mission.* She wondered whether it would have been a good idea to tell Agent Rosenfield her name, just in case something happened.

The seven soldiers had already leaped out of the copter,

then it was Thunder's turn. Abby felt a little resentful that he didn't seem to be even the slightest bit worried, whereas she was almost shaking with fear.

Thunder jumped out, and Abby stepped over to the hatch. The copter was hovering two yards above the flat roof. She knew that she could cover that distance with no problem if they were on the ground, but now she hesitated. *Do it! Jump!*

Then she felt the colonel's hand in the small of her back gently pushing her forward. She jumped, landed heavily on the roof next to Thunder. He mouthed, "You OK?"

Abby nodded. A queasy excitement churned her insides.

Colonel Morgan dropped down, withdrew a handgun from the holster on his hip, and led his men toward the edge of the roof. The copter's ferocious downdraft eased as it rose another twenty yards.

Two of the soldiers quickly fixed black nylon ropes from the copter to their chest harnesses and dropped themselves over the edge. Abby cautiously stepped forward and looked down. Ten yards below the two soldiers were attaching something to the wide double doors. One of them gave Colonel Morgan a thumbs-up, and he relayed the signal to the copter's pilot. The ropes began to reel in, dragging the men back up the side of the building.

Then Morgan put his hand on Abby's shoulder and hauled her back from the edge, shaking his head.

For a second she didn't know what he meant, then there was a brief flash, the roof trembled slightly, and a strong, acrid smell reached her nostrils. The colonel let go and gestured for her to look.

Thunder joined her as she peered over the edge again. The building's entire front wall was gone, shattered into a pile of bricks, glass, and wood. Colonel Morgan allowed them a few seconds, then pulled them back and signaled to his men.

Abby could guess what that meant: Begin.

CHAPTER 10

Roz Dalton realized she'd been dozing and lifted her head. *What woke me?* She looked toward the gray-clad men, but they seemed to be as stoic as ever. Beside her, Max coughed silently. *He's getting worse. They all are. I can't even hear their breathing.*

Then she realized she couldn't hear anything at all. Even the low hum of the building's air conditioner had stopped. She scraped her boot heel on the concrete floor. Nothing.

She gently pulled at the handcuffs, knowing that they should make a clicking sound as they opened. Still nothing. The cuffs noiselessly dropped to the concrete floor. *Either I've gone deaf, or something's blocking out all the sound.*

Then a movement caught her eye: A door behind one of the gray men silently burst open—the man didn't even notice. A pair of U.S. Army soldiers rushed at him, slammed him to the ground. The other gray men had seen this—they dived for cover.

There was a flash from somewhere behind Roz, then another. *Muzzle flare! They're shooting!* She ripped the cuffs from her feet as the room erupted in noiseless gunfire.

She scrambled over to her brother, grabbed hold of his legs, and kept low as she dragged him to the side. She was about to go back for one of the Rangers when more soldiers spilled into the room, all with their rifles firing. Roz saw one of the gray men hit in the shoulder, another in the abdomen.

The remaining two had knocked over the large wooden desk and taken refuge behind it. Their weapons protruded from the top and sides, firing blindly.

Roz jumped as a small crater appeared in the floor only inches away from her left foot. To her right, she could see that the soldiers had spread out, but there was no other cover on their side of the room. *We're sitting ducks here! Maybe I can use my telekinesis to create a sort of shield. . . . I can move only one thing at a time, but if I can figure out when they're going to fire I can—*

She realized that there was a much simpler approach: She concentrated on the heavy desk. It wobbled, then toppled forward, exposing the gray men. They immediately dropped their weapons.

A U.S. colonel strode into the room, gesturing to his men to take care of Max and the Rangers. He was followed by two teenagers, a boy and a girl. The boy appeared to be wearing a flak jacket over a wet suit. The girl was wearing what looked like a leather jacket covered in coins. The colonel saluted Roz and pointed toward the door.

He wants me to go with the others. Roz shook her head and said, "No way," but no sound came out.

He nodded as though he'd been expecting this, and turned to the teenage boy. He ran his finger across his throat. Instantly, Roz could hear again.

The boy said, "I've released only this room, is that right? The rest of the building is still muffled."

"Perfect. Ms. Dalton, I'm Colonel Morgan. My men are going to take the rest of your team to the infirmary. Is there anything you can tell us that might help us free the other hostages?"

"I don't even know where they're being kept."

"We do. All right, I want you to stick to the rear with these two, but don't be embarrassed to use your power if you think it might save lives. Thunder, has anyone else noticed the attack?"

"I can't tell—I'm blocking the sounds."

"All right. We'll play it safe. By the numbers, people. Morales and Goodman, take point. Thunder, let's bring on the silence."

The sound evaporated once more.

Colonel Morgan signaled to his men, and they rushed forward. The other doors to the room were locked—one of the men shot out the lock and kicked open the door.

The corridor was dark and empty. Moving in twos, the soldiers cautiously approached each room, burst open the door, and rushed in, one marine crouched low and moving left, his colleague standing and moving right. All of the rooms were empty.

Roz watched from behind with the other teenagers. The boy seemed confident and calm, but the girl with the sword on her back looked nervous.

She briefly wondered if they were brother and sister: They were both—presumably—superhuman, and they were both African-American. Aside from her own family, she'd never heard of any other superhuman siblings.

The soldiers slowed and spread out as they approached a set of steel double doors at the end of the corridor. Two of them dashed forward and crouched down in front of the lock. A minute later they turned back. Roz saw one of them mouth the words, "Can't open it."

Colonel Morgan frowned for a moment. One of the other soldiers approached him with an explosive charge in his hand and a questioning look on his face. Morgan shook his head.

Of course, Roz thought. *The other hostages must be inside. If we blow the doors, they could be hurt or even killed.*

Then the girl in the homemade chain mail stepped past Roz, brandishing her heavy-looking sword.

She walked up to the doors, stared at them for a second, then reached as high as she could and swung the sword at the doors, slicing straight through the metal. Two more quick strokes, one on either side, and the doors collapsed inward. The girl ducked aside as the soldiers rushed into the room.

Roz could see the hostages lying on the floor, their hands and feet bound, their mouths gagged. *I have to help them!* She started forward, but the boy called Thunder grabbed her arm and held her back.

It was over in seconds. The remaining gray men dropped their weapons and raised their arms. Thunder allowed the sound to return, and the air was filled with moans and shouts.

"It's done. Get these terrorists out of here!" Morgan roared into his radio. "I want them stripped and searched and taken back in *separate* vehicles, full armed escort, understood?"

One of his men said, "Medics are on the way, Colonel. But these people aren't doing so good. They've got it bad."

The girl with the sword said, "Colonel Morgan? Only the hostages are sick. The terrorists are all fine. Well, apart from the ones that got shot."

He looked at her for a moment. "You're right. Which means you could also be right about the plague being artificial." Into his radio he said, "Run a complete medical on each of the terrorists. I want to know what makes them immune."

Morgan turned to the teenagers. "All right. Good work, you three. Now get out of here and report to Agent Rosenfield." They lingered for a second, but the look on Morgan's face told them he wasn't kidding.

Roz led the others back into the corridor. "I'm Roz Dalton, by the way."

"We know," Thunder said. "You OK?"

"Hungry and tired and worried about my brother, but aside from that, yeah, I'm fine. Who are you guys?"

"I'm Thunder. But this one won't tell us her name."

Roz said, "Well, thanks for the save. You did that thing with the sound, right?"

He nodded. "I can control almost any kind of sound waves."

"And what about you?" Roz asked the girl with the sword. "We have to call you *something*." They reached the large room in which Roz had been kept. It was now filled with dozens of soldiers.

"I'm not sure I should tell anyone my name," the girl said.

"It's Abigail," Thunder said. He smiled at her shocked expression. "I've been eating at your diner for months."

"Shut up! People will hear!" She looked around at the soldiers.

"No they won't," Thunder said. "I'm blocking the sound."

She sighed. "All right. I'm Abigail de Luyando. Call me Abby. But what's *your* real name?"

The boy bit his lip. "Um . . ."

"Um? What's that short for?" Roz said, failing to hold back a smile. "Well, it's a good thing you were there, Um. That's a very handy power you have."

Abby said, "I just wish *I'd* had more to do. All I did was slice open a door."

They walked outside, stepping over piles of shattered bricks and broken glass. Roz took in deep lungfuls of the night air. "God, that feels good!" She stopped and watched as two medics carried out one of the hostages on a stretcher. The man was clearly in distress, moaning and convulsing. "So . . . It was the flu that knocked out Max and the others?"

"That's what it looks like," Abby said.

"But one minute they were fine, the next they were in trouble. Max thought it was a weapon."

Thunder shrugged. "It is. A biological weapon. The terrorists must be immune. How are you guys feeling?"

"Fine so far," Abby said. "You?"

"No sign of it yet," Thunder replied.

They stepped aside as another stretcher was carried out, this one carrying a pale-skinned, shivering woman in her early twenties.

"So what did they want in there, anyway?" Roz asked. "There couldn't have been anything worth stealing."

"No one knows yet. They didn't make any demands," Abby said. She checked her watch and sighed. "Great. It's past nine. I'm probably going to be fired. And when I get home I'll be grounded." To Thunder, she said, "So what about you? What time do you have to get back to Atlantis?"

He looked at her. "What?"

"Forget it."

Roz said, "I'll need to know how to contact the two of you."

Abby asked, "Why?"

"Well, this isn't over. That woman escaped."

"What woman?"

"There was a woman in charge of the terrorists. I didn't get to see her face but I definitely heard her voice. She wasn't with the others when we found the hostages. How did she escape?"

"No one escaped," Thunder said. "The whole place has been surrounded for hours."

They looked at each other, then down the hill toward the two medics ahead of them carrying the stretcher.

Abby shouted, "Hey! Wait! That's not—"

The young woman rolled off the stretcher, landed on her feet. In one swift movement she jabbed her left fist into one medic's chest while kicking back with her right foot at the other's head.

Abby began to run.

She heard Roz shout, "Abby, no!" but she didn't turn back: Roz and Thunder had already played their part—now it was her turn to go into action. She pulled her sword from her back as she ran.

CHAPTER 11

Abby raced down the hill, but the woman was waiting for her: She snatched up the aluminum stretcher and swung it at Abby. Abby blocked it with the blunt edge of her sword. They stood for a moment, their weapons locked against each other.

"You're strong, little one," the woman said through gritted teeth. "Stronger than I am, perhaps." She had pale skin, shoulder-length brown hair, and green eyes.

"Who *are* you?"

The woman took a step to the left. "Someone who isn't dumb enough to stay in Roz Dalton's line of sight." She suddenly let go of the stretcher, and Abby staggered to the side, the sword slipping from her hand. Abby ducked down as the woman swung a punch at her face, and made a grab for her legs.

The woman jumped, somersaulted over Abby, and twisted as she landed. Abby rolled to her feet, but the woman was faster: She suddenly pivoted on her right foot—her left flicked out and clipped Abby across the chin. Abby reeled backward, spotted her sword, and made a dive for it.

Then Thunder came charging down the hill, straight for the woman. She didn't hear him coming: He slammed into her back and sent her sprawling.

But she recovered much faster than he did. She hit the ground face-first and kicked her legs backward, flipping over on her hands. She landed on her feet and bounced again, spinning around to face him.

Thunder had landed on his back and was pushing himself up when the woman came down feetfirst on his stomach.

Abby jumped for her, but the woman—still with one foot on Thunder's stomach—simply smiled and waited.

Abby swung her sword. The woman threw herself backward and kicked up, knocking the sword out of Abby's grip, sending it straight into the air. *I need a wrist strap!* Abby thought.

The sword reached its peak and began to fall—Thunder was directly in its path. *I can catch it! I—*

The woman threw herself at Abby, knocking her to the ground, then rolled off before Abby could grab hold of her. Abby stared upward. *No! The sword!*

Less than two feet above Thunder's chest, the sword suddenly shifted to one side. It landed point-first next to his right arm, its great weight driving it more than six inches into the dirt. Abby jumped up, looked around, but the woman wasn't there. "What . . . ? Where is she?"

Roz skidded to a stop next to Thunder. "You two all right?"

Thunder groaned, sat up clutching his stomach. His voice weak and wheezing, he said, "Yeah, I think so. Thought I was dead meat there. Thanks. Where'd she go?"

Roz pointed straight up—the woman was a shrinking dot against the night sky.

"Who is she?" Abby asked.

"I've never met her before, but Max has. She's dangerous. Completely psychotic. Very fast and very strong. And she's absolutely merciless. She's also one of the few people whose mind Max can't read or control. She calls herself Slaughter."

Lance McKendrick clenched his teeth to prevent them from chattering with the cold.

Though Paragon had flown in a straight line and at a relatively constant speed, Lance had been battered repeatedly by turbulence that left him swaying wildly from side to side. His armpits chafed from the jetpack's shoulder straps and cold wind brought stinging tears to his eyes.

The armored hero hadn't spoken during the flight, and Lance started to wonder what was on his mind. *Maybe he's thinking that looking after me is the last thing he needs. For all I know, he's got a wife and kids at home.*

That made him think about his own family again. He prayed that his brother Cody had made it home OK from practice, because if he hadn't, then their parents were home alone. *I'm going to be grounded until the end of time for this.*

After more than an hour, Paragon's amplified voice said, "How are you holding up?"

Lance shouted back, "I'm kinda more concerned about how *you're* holding *me* up!"

Paragon laughed. "I'm not going to drop you, don't worry."

"Are we there yet?"

"Almost. Look straight ahead."

In the distance Lance saw a thin ring of light on the ground, rapidly growing as they approached. At the center of the ring was what looked like a nuclear power plant. Paragon slowed, dropped down to a height of about eight yards. Lance could now see that the ring was formed from the headlights of dozens of army vehicles and police cars.

Paragon said, "Hey, kid. Do me a favor. There's a switch on the left side of my helmet, just below the jaw. See if you can reach it."

Lance awkwardly stretched up his left arm and found the switch. "That it?"

"Yeah, it's my radio. Hit it, will you? And then shut it off when I'm done."

Lance pressed the switch, then heard Paragon say, "This is Paragon contacting FBI Special Agent Rosenfield." A pause. "Understood. Put me through to whoever's taken over the operation." There was another, longer pause. "Colonel Morgan? This is Paragon. I'm approaching your position from the southeast. ETA one-zero-zero seconds. Paragon out."

Lance hit the switch again, and Paragon dropped even closer to the ground—Lance didn't want to know how near they were to the treetops, but he could imagine the branches and leaves brushing the soles of his sneakers. When they were close enough for Lance to make out individual people, Paragon slowed almost to a stop, and drifted down.

Lance felt the asphalt under his feet. His knees buckled

and he would have collapsed if Paragon hadn't been holding on to him.

"You OK?" Paragon asked.

Lance nodded. They had landed between two covered army trucks and were now surrounded by soldiers.

A middle-aged man in uniform came running. "Paragon? Colonel Morgan." He looked briefly at Lance, then turned back to the armored hero. "Good news is the situation here has been dealt with."

"So I just flew hundreds of miles for nothing?" He didn't sound happy.

"Not exactly. Come with me—I want to fill you in on the latest development. You're not going to like it." He looked at Lance once again. "Did someone forget to tell me it's Bring Your Kid to Work Day?"

"How old do you think I *am*?" Paragon asked. "No, he's not mine. He's a stray I picked up along the way. Long story." To Lance, Paragon said, "Stay put. Touch nothing. Talk to no one. Got that?"

"OK. . . . Only, how am I going to get home? My folks have no idea where I am. And they're sick. They need me."

"Should have considered the consequences before you decided to go breaking and entering, shouldn't you?"

"Then someone has to let them know where I am!"

Paragon leaned closer. "That'd be a lot easier if you told me your real name. Now stay put."

Lance watched him follow the officer into a large, dark, unmarked truck. *Now what do I do?* He stopped a passing soldier. "Is there anywhere I can make a phone call?"

"I look like a tour guide or something?" The man pointed back over his shoulder. "Ask one of those cops back there. Most of them are local."

Great. More cops. Like I haven't spoken to enough of them already today. Lance started toward the police officers when he spotted a trio of people who were much more approachable: teenagers.

They were walking down the hill from the power plant, and from the look of their clothing Lance could see that they were superheroes. Or wanted to be, at least.

The pale-skinned girl stopped in front of him. "You're the one who came in with Paragon?"

"That's right."

The boy gestured toward the jetpack on Lance's back. "You his sidekick or something?"

Lance resisted the temptation to pretend that he and Paragon were equal partners. "Not really. Do you know where I can find a phone?"

"Try a phone booth," the boy said. "They're famous for that."

"Yeah, very helpful," Lance said. He turned to the girls in the hope that they'd be more friendly. "Where would I find a phone booth?"

The shorter, dark-skinned girl said, "Nearest one I can think of is on the edge of town. About ten miles away. But if it's an emergency, you could ask one of the cops to put a call through on his radio."

"Thanks. I'll . . . Maybe I'll wait."

Then she said, "Hey, can you fly me back to town? I'm

kind of in a hurry. The colonel told me to get a lift from one of the army trucks but they can't turn around 'cos the road is so narrow."

"Out of gas," Lance said. "Sorry."

"Thanks anyway."

As they moved on, the girl smiled at Lance and he felt his knees weaken. *Wow. . . .* He ran after them. "Hey, hold up. Why don't you get the guy on the motorbike to give you a lift? He'd be able to get through the traffic no problem."

The girl looked around. "I didn't see anyone with a bike."

"Well, there's one around here somewhere. I saw a helmet on the side of the road back there."

"Ah. That's mine, actually." She removed her army helmet and ran one hand through her hair.

"So you've got a bike but no helmet?" Lance asked. "I mean . . . You have a helmet but you don't have a bike." In his head, a small voice was reminding him of his pledge to never make any friends. He mentally told the voice to shut up.

"Yeah. . . ."

Then the other boy said, "Abby, I thought you were in a hurry?"

"Thunder, what did I say about not using my real name?"

Paragon's voice boomed out. "I told you to stay put and not talk to anyone!"

Lance cringed and turned to see the armored hero striding toward him. "Sorry. I just need to get in touch with my folks."

Paragon stopped in front of Roz. "Good to see you again, Ms. Dalton. Your brother's in good hands, but they still don't know exactly what they're dealing with. The virus is still spreading and it's almost certainly artificial."

"What's the prognosis?" Roz asked.

"There is none, at the moment. According to Colonel Morgan's people, it's looking like it has a communicable rate of about eighty percent. But they're still collating the data, so that figure could be way off. Could be that some of the infected just have the ordinary flu, or even just a cold. And it's not just America: It's broken out in Europe, Africa, and Asia." He paused. "I won't lie to you. At least four people who contracted it have died, but again we're not entirely sure whether there's a direct connection. The medics are trying to isolate whatever it is that's keeping the terrorists immune. If they can do that, they might be able to construct a vaccine or even a cure."

"Did the colonel tell you about Slaughter?"

"He did. You three were lucky she didn't kill you on the spot. The first rule of dealing with Slaughter is that you do *not* run toward her. You run away. She's too strong and too fast for all of you put together."

Abby began, "Yeah, but—"

"But what?" Paragon's visor swiveled toward her. "I doubt any of you even laid a hand on her. She's way out of your league, understand? She didn't have to face any of you—she could have just flown away. She chose to let you fight her. She was testing you. You failed."

The boy called Thunder said, "I tackled her to the ground. I blocked the sound so that she couldn't hear me coming."

"Well, good for you. Let's just hope she doesn't remember that."

"And she said that I was probably stronger than she was," Abby said.

Paragon sighed. "All right, kids. It's time to close your mouths and open your ears. A few months back Slaughter threw Titan through a moving train. Before he could recover she picked up one of the cars and smashed it down on top of him. The car wasn't empty. It was a miracle that none of the passengers were killed. Last time I tangled with her was in Manhattan: She got away when she started throwing civilians a hundred feet into the air. She didn't care where they landed, but she knew that I'd have to let her escape so I could catch them. That's the sort of person we're dealing with here. She is a cold-blooded killer, and if she discovered your identities she wouldn't hesitate to murder every single member of your families. Don't go patting yourselves on the back because you faced down Slaughter and survived. You didn't win. She let you live. There's a huge difference, and if you can't see that then you should go home, throw away your costumes, and abandon the idea of being a superhero forever." To Roz, he added, "That includes you too. You do not mess with Slaughter. Even Max wouldn't tackle her on his own." He turned to Lance. "What's your name? And don't tell me it's Jason Myers. I want your real name."

"Lance McKendrick."

"Good. I'll get the police to call your house and let your folks know that you're all right."

"I'm not going home?"

"Not yet. I want you to tell me everything about that warehouse and the men who chased you. The colonel's scheduled a meeting in fifteen minutes. So get some rest because it's going to be a long night."

"Can you do me a favor first?" Lance asked. "Abby here needs to get back home. . . . Can you take her?"

Paragon nodded. "All right. What about you?" he asked Thunder.

"I'm cool. I'm not expected home for another hour."

"OK. Lance, you better be here when I get back. I mean it."

Paragon scooped Abby up in his arms and launched himself into the air.

Lance glanced at the others and then turned in a slow circle, taking in the military vehicles and dozens of soldiers. "So . . . What exactly is going on here?" he asked Thunder.

The boy ignored him, and passed a slip of paper to Roz. "My number. I'm guessing that this isn't over. You need me, just call."

"What about Abby?"

"I can contact her. I know where she lives."

Roz nodded, then Thunder vaulted easily over the low fence and ran across the field.

After a couple of seconds, Lance asked Roz, "Was that guy wearing a wet suit? What a dweeb!"

"He can hear you, you know," Roz said. "Super-hearing."

Lance smirked. "Yeah, right."

Thunder's voice appeared out of nowhere: "She *is* right. I can hear everything."

"Now that's just creepy," Lance said. "So, uh, Ms. Dalton? What's happening here?"

"Call me Roz," she said. She told Lance about the attack on the power plant, and the fight with Slaughter.

"And the other two just showed up?" Lance asked. "Scuba-boy and the cute chick just decided they were superheroes?"

Roz's eyes narrowed a little. "The cute chick?"

"Um . . . I mean, the cute babe." He saw her expression of distaste and hastily suggested, "Girl?"

"It's the *cute* part that I find objectionable. But, yes, they just turned up. Thunder was able to listen in on the terrorists—they referred to something called The Helotry, but we don't know exactly what that means."

"I've heard that word before," Lance said. "Recently, I mean. . . ." He shrugged. "So what were they after?"

"We don't know."

"But you said that the power plant isn't even operational yet, right? That means they can't have been after the uranium."

"Plutonium," Roz corrected. "The plant was finished ahead of schedule . . . ," Roz said. A frown line appeared on her forehead. "So that could mean that they had to move their plans up."

"Right. They took advantage of everyone getting the flu and they . . . Wait, how did the bad guys know that *they* wouldn't get sick?"

"We think they caused it," Roz said.

"Nah. . . . They wouldn't make the whole world sick just to distract everyone's attention from the attack on the power plant." It was his turn to frown. "Thunder was right—this isn't over, is it? They're planning something much bigger

than this. And they want everyone out of the way because . . .
I've no idea."

A passing soldier sneezed violently, and Lance flinched.
"Oh great. Now we probably have it too."

Roz stared at him.

"What?"

"You go to school, right?"

"When the mood strikes me. Why? Don't you?"

"No, I'm homeschooled. But is anyone in your school sick?"

"Sure. Lots of them. So many that school was actually
canceled today. My math teacher got it first, then the social
studies teacher, then . . . Huh. That's odd. . . ."

"Only the teachers, right?" Roz asked.

"Yeah. . . . My folks are sick, so are most of my aunts and
uncles. But not me or my brother or any of my cousins, that I
know of."

Roz nodded. "That's what I thought. The plague is only
affecting the adults."

CHAPTER 12

Abby pointed toward the yard at the back of Leftover's Finer Diner. "Down there. Can you land in the alley?"

Paragon descended, the down-thrust from his jetpack scattering the litter and debris from the alley floor. "You live here?"

"No, I work here. But I need to change back into my work clothes before I go home."

"And how far is home?"

"About a mile."

"All right. Get changed and I'll take you."

Abby vaulted over the wall, and landed silently. The diner was still open, but the back door was closed so there was no one to see her. She felt a little guilty for having run out on Dave on such a busy night, but reminded herself that such was the life of a superhero.

She ducked into the shed and began to quickly change out

of her costume. *I'm a superhero.* She realized she was grinning but couldn't help herself. *I helped rescue Max Dalton and all those other people! I even fought Slaughter!* She shook herself. *No, can't think like that. Paragon was right. We were lucky. She could have ripped my head off.*

She pulled on her shoes, put away her costume and sword—and the U.S. Army helmet she'd forgotten to give back—then returned to the yard. She quickly scaled the wall and dropped down next to Paragon.

He was talking to someone on his radio. "Yeah . . . Got it. All right, Colonel. Understood. One hour, then." He disconnected the call. "There's no rush. The colonel's delayed the meeting until we can get more data from the CDC. Probably just as well, because we're going to have to walk to your place. Some local superhero-spotters saw us flying over the town and they're searching for us. You know the back routes?"

"Sure. Back this way and then we can turn right." She had to almost run to keep up with Paragon's long strides. "Can I ask you a question? Why 'Paragon'? I mean, that's kind of an arrogant name. And you don't seem like the arrogant type. If you were, you wouldn't be hiding your face. Paragon means 'the very best,' right?"

"Close. It means 'a model of perfection.' I didn't choose the name. I never even thought about needing a name when I started out. Then there was a newspaper article that said my armor was the paragon of home-built engineering, and the name just stuck."

"How long *have* you been doing this?"

"A few years. You?"

"This was my first time."

"You made your own armor?"

"Yeah," Abby said. "And my sword. It's a bit crude, though. I saw a sword in the antiques shop but it looked too, y'know, flimsy. Plus it was way expensive."

"The armor is impressive. Probably wouldn't stop a bullet, but it'd provide you with a lot of protection otherwise. Do your folks know that you're superhuman?"

"No. There's only my mother. Dad left when I was six, just after the four twins were born."

"The *four* twins? You mean, quads?"

"No. Two sets of twins, all boys. The second set were born ten months after the first, so right now they're all the same age."

"And you're the eldest?"

"Second eldest. My sister is nineteen. Hardly ever see her, though. She works all the time. My mom can't work much because she's in a wheelchair."

"So that's why you're working at a diner at your age. How old are you, anyway?"

"Fourteen."

"I see. Well, that's the sort of age most of you superhumans get your powers."

"But you're not one of us?"

"No. I'm just a normal person. But like you, I make all my own armor and equipment."

"What about the jetpack? You could sell that idea and make billions."

"Abby, most people can barely drive a car along the street without crashing. I'm not going to be the one responsible for giving them an extra dimension to mess up in."

A few moments later they emerged from the network of alleyways. Abby pointed to a large tenement building across the street. "That's my place there. Thanks. And thanks for the lift too. I've never flown before. Apart from being in the helicopter earlier."

Then a voice came screeching out of the doorway to Abby's building. "Abigail de Luyando! Where have you been? Do you *know* what time it is?"

Abby sighed. "Great. It's my sister."

The girl darted out into the street. "Mom's been worried sick. Sick*er*. And your manager said you told him you were coming home for an hour and that was ages ago. And he said you'd been there since 8:30 this morning! Why weren't you in school? How long has this been going on? And who is this guy?" She glanced at Paragon, looked back at Abby, then paused. She bit her lip, then slowly her eyes turned back to Paragon. "Oh."

"Nice to meet you, Ms. de Luyando. Your sister here was witness to a crime and she very kindly offered to help the police with their enquiries."

"I see. . . ."

Abby recognized the look on her sister's face: She was considering some sort of plan. *What's she up to now?*

"That's all very well, Mr. Superhero, but how am I supposed to explain this to our mother?"

"I could come inside and talk to her myself, if that'll help."

"Yes. That might be for the best."

Oh, very good! Abby tried not to catch her sister's eye—if she did, they'd both end up grinning.

Abby led them into the building and up the stairs toward

her apartment. She felt a little ashamed at how rundown everything was. The wallpaper was long gone, the stairs bare and creaking—especially under Paragon's weight—and the only light came from a couple of flyspecked yellow bulbs. Abby pushed open the door to the apartment. "Mom?"

She was greeted with another torrent of "Where have you been?" and "What time do you call this?" then her mother saw Paragon and immediately shifted into "important visitor" mode. "Well, look who it is!"

Mrs. de Luyando pulled her blanket tighter around her shoulders, then expertly steered her chair around the room, fluffing up cushions and straightening the pile of *TV Guides* on the coffee table. "Will you have something to drink? There's a beer in the fridge."

"I don't drink, but thanks."

"Coffee?"

"Thanks again, but nothing for me, Mrs. de Luyando. Can't really drink wearing this armor."

Abby's mother nodded. "Of course. You don't want to remove your visor."

"It's not just that," he said. "More that I don't like flying on a full bladder."

"I understand completely!" she said cheerfully, then hissed at Abby's sister, "Go wake the boys. They'll be mad if they find out they missed meeting the famous Paragon!" She turned back to him, all smiles again. "You don't mind, do you?"

He lowered himself into the sofa. "Not at all, no. Actually, it's been a long time since I had a chance to just sit down for a minute and take it easy. As I was telling your other daughter,

Abby's late because she witnessed a crime. Unfortunately we're not allowed to talk about the details, but I can tell you that she was extremely brave. If it hadn't been for her, a lot of innocent people would have been hurt."

Feeling slightly uncomfortable, Abby sat down opposite Paragon. This wasn't a scene she'd ever pictured happening.

"Brave she might be," her mother said, "but I've just found out she's been skipping school to go to work." Her shoulders sagged. "Abby, you should have talked to me."

Abby rolled her eyes. "Not *now*, Mom!"

Then Paragon said, "Forgive me for asking, Mrs. de Luyando—"

"Call me Alison."

"Alison." He gestured toward her wheelchair. "You live on the fourth floor. On the way up I saw that the elevator was out of commission, and it looks like it's been that way for a long time. How do you leave the apartment? If that's not too personal a question."

Abby's mother covered her mouth with her hand and coughed. "Excuse me. I don't go out often, Mr. Paragon. My girls carry me down. Sometimes our neighbor helps too. But it's not so bad. Abby's pretty strong for her age."

There was a moment of awkward silence, which was broken by the return of Abby's sister and her brothers. The boys—all dressed in identical pajamas—clustered around Paragon, staring at him with their mouths open.

Abby said, "From left to right: Tyler, James, Elvis, and Stefan."

"Elvis?" Paragon asked.

Mrs. de Luyando said, "It was that or The Beatles."

113

Abby's sister groaned as she sat down on the arm of the sofa next to Paragon. "Mom, that joke is so old it should be put into a nursing home."

Abby said, "Oh, and you've already met our big sister, Vienna."

Half an hour later Abby accompanied Paragon out of the apartment. The superhero's presence had not gone unnoticed: It seemed that everyone in the building was in the hallways as they passed, many of them shivering and wrapped in blankets but still not willing to miss a chance to see a superhero so close. Some of the people reached out to touch his armor as he passed.

When Abby opened the main door, there was a sudden cheer: The street was packed with people all craning for a better look. They quickly broke into a chant: "Par-a-gon! Par-a-gon!"

"I hate this part of the job," Paragon said to Abby, keeping his voice low.

A horn blared, and the crowd grudgingly parted to allow a new cherry-red BMW to pull up in front of the building. A thin white woman in her early thirties climbed out. She was dressed for a romantic night out: little black dress, heels, expensive platinum-blonde hairdo. For a moment Abby thought that the woman must be an actress or a pop star.

Oblivious to the crowd, the woman glided over to Paragon. "Mr. Paragon. When I heard you were here I just *had* to come and see you!"

"Thank you," Paragon said, moving to step around her.

She blocked his way. "You must allow me to introduce myself. Catherine-Jane Avery."

"Nice to meet you, Ms. Avery. Now, I must—"

The woman put her hand on his chest. "No, really. One of his tenants told Daddy you were here and I have to say he's very excited. He wanted to come and meet you in person but he's a little under the weather at the moment."

Paragon tilted his head toward her. "His tenants? Your father owns these buildings?"

"Oh yes. Daddy owns a *lot* of properties. Terribly wealthy. Self-made man, like yourself of course!" She laughed at her own joke.

"And is your father a *good* man, Ms. Avery?"

"Certainly. Generous to a fault." She gestured toward her car. "My birthday present. Gorgeous, isn't she? Now, Daddy's told me that he'd love to meet you. A sort of man-to-man thing, I suppose. Two influential men sitting down to solve the problems of the world, I would expect." She handed him a business card. "I'm sure you'd have plenty to talk about—you have so much in common. And he'd be willing to pay you handsomely for your time, of course."

Without even looking at the card, Paragon passed it to Abby. "Ms. Avery, did you know that there is a woman living on the fourth floor of this building who is in a wheelchair?"

Avery's perfect smile slipped a little.

"And did you also know that the elevator has been broken for over two years? Your father has apparently refused to have it fixed because he claims that it's not cost-effective." He moved closer to the woman. She stepped back. "Instead of buying you a new car—which I imagine it's safe to say you didn't actually need—he could have spent those thousands of dollars repairing the elevators in all of these buildings. He could have fixed the heating, replaced the antiquated wiring, repaired the plumbing, installed wheelchair ramps . . . or sorted out any of a hundred other areas of neglect."

She looked down at her feet. "I'm sure that any oversights can be explained."

"Explained?"

"I mean, rectified. Fixed."

"They can. And they should have been fixed years ago. Ms. Avery, your father is *not* a good man. He is a selfish, greedy, uncaring man. Please do not compare me to him."

The apartment room was small and dark. The windows' heavy blinds were down, the only light coming from their rectangular outlines. The air was warm and stale, tinged with the lingering scent of bitter incense. There were no pictures, ornaments, or any fixtures. The floor was bare wooden boards.

At the center of the room, an old woman sat on the only piece of furniture: a basic wooden chair. Her hands were clasped together in her lap, and she sat straight upright. Her face was mostly in shadow, but there was just enough light coming from the windows to see that she was skeleton-thin.

"So. It is done. Everything that you were instructed to do has been accomplished." The woman's voice was rough, but strong. Slaughter nodded.

"Speak up, girl."

"It's done. Just as you instructed."

"The men performed adequately?"

She nodded again. "Considering that they were under-equipped and didn't even have the new body armor, yes. I still think we should have waited."

"Your opinions have little value, Slaughter. Do not waste my time with them. The early completion of the power plant forced our hand. There was superhuman interference?"

"Maxwell Dalton and his sister, then two others. Both in their early teens. Dalton has been incapacitated."

The old woman paused. "This is not expected." Another pause. "I see. These children—could they pose a threat?"

"It's unlikely. They have very little experience."

"Unlikely, but not impossible. You will disable them."

"As you wish," Slaughter said.

Again, the woman paused as though she were listening to a voice no one else could hear. "There is another matter. A human boy witnessed the capture of Marcus by Paragon and later broke into the warehouse in Fairview. We believe he may have stolen information that could undo our plans. The boy is with Paragon now. His name is Lance McKendrick. You will find him and kill him."

CHAPTER 13

Inside the cramped FBI operations truck, Lance leaned back in the padded swivel chair. He felt like he'd been telling the same story for hours. *Do they think I'm lying; is that it?* "I was running for my life. They were shooting at me."

Colonel Morgan looked away from Lance and cleared his throat. "We don't have time for this, Paragon. What makes you think there's a connection with the attack here?"

"Because Lance said that the men in the warehouse talked about their plans being moved forward." Paragon had his back to them. On a desk in front of him was the stolen jetpack. He had removed its cover and was doing something to the circuits inside. Over his shoulder he added, "Could be just a coincidence that the power plant was finished ahead of schedule, but . . ." He stopped what he was doing and turned to face the colonel. "Two secret organizations discovered on the same day? We have to assume there's a connection—and we don't have much else to go on. Lance, is there anything else you can remember that might be useful? Sure they didn't call each other by name?"

"Not that I remember." He yawned. "When can I go home?"

"That's not up to me," Paragon said. He returned his attention to the jetpack. "Kid, you're lucky to be alive. I'm not even sure how those guys managed to get this thing to fly at all. The afterburner control looks like it was put together by someone working in the dark and wearing boxing gloves. This thing is a death trap."

Lance looked at the colonel. "Am I under arrest?"

"No. You're helping us with our investigation." The colonel sighed, and rubbed his neck. "From the top, Lance. . . . The only name they mentioned was Marcus, you said."

Lance began to swivel back and forth in the chair. "Yep. One guy said something about how the plan was a wash-out if the cops could get Marcus to talk, and the other guy said something about how they're going to be in big trouble." He stopped swiveling and slightly chewed on his lower lip while he tried to remember the men's exact words.

The most important skill when running a con wasn't sleight of hand but the art of cold-reading, the ability to instantly evaluate a mark and pick up on tiny clues about his or her personality. Lance had practiced this over and over: He was now almost always able to tell just how far he could push someone. The key to cold-reading was observation: watching and listening.

Now, Lance felt certain that back at the warehouse he had heard and dismissed something vital. *OK, think. . . . What was it they said? A mixed metaphor—one of the guys said something and got it wrong. . . . Lead bricks, that was it!* "'Like a ton of lead bricks,'" Lance said aloud.

He looked up to see the colonel's puzzled face staring back. "What?"

"Yeah. As if a ton of lead bricks is going to be any heavier than a ton of *ordinary* bricks. That's why that stood out. One of them said, 'If the cops find this place with us still in it, The Helotry are gonna come down on us like a ton of lead bricks.'"

"You're certain?" Paragon asked.

Lance nodded. "Yep. I knew I'd heard that word before."

"So it's the same people," Colonel Morgan said. "There's more than a few secret organizations around, and the FBI always knows at least *something* about them. But that's not the case with The Helotry. We've never even heard of them before. Which makes them potentially very dangerous. Anything you can tell us will help."

Lance shrugged.

"All right, Lance, let's start again at the beginning," Colonel Morgan said. "You were walking home when you heard the car, right?"

"Oh, come on! How many times do we have to go over this? Look, I've told you all I know. Now you tell *me*. What's going on?"

Without looking up from his work, Paragon said, "Colonel, I think you should tell him."

After a moment's hesitation, the colonel said, "One of the terrorists said something. Most of them have remained absolutely tight-lipped, but this one guy . . . He was in a lot of pain—shot in the shoulder by one of his colleagues, apparently—and the medics had to put him under to operate. He started to talk before the anesthetic knocked him out. He said, 'We're bringing him back. We're bringing back the Fifth King.' "

"What does that mean?"

The colonel shrugged. "We're not completely sure. I consulted with a colleague who has a Ph.D. in history—he said that the Fifth King was a warrior from somewhere around the Mediterranean who lived over four thousand years ago. He was said to be a demigod, stronger than a hundred men, able to run faster than a horse. No one knows where he came from, but according to my colleague he once fought for the Assyrian empire and defeated an entire Egyptian army almost single-handedly. His followers called themselves The Helotry of the Fifth King and they worshipped him as a god. His real name is long forgotten, but some scholars—my friend included—think that his story was later absorbed into the legend of Gilgamesh."

"Gilgamesh? My history teacher said—"

Colonel Morgan held up his hand. "Much of Egypt is desert now, but there's some evidence to suggest that it was all once a thriving, fertile land. That ties in with the stories of the Fifth King. After he defeated the Egyptian army, he took control of the survivors and marched on Egypt. They burned down the forests, poisoned the fields, slaughtered most of the population. He established himself as the ruler of Egypt *and* Assyria. His goal was to enslave the whole world. He probably would have succeeded too, but something stopped him. There are conflicting legends about that. Some of them say that his arrogance had angered the gods and they banished him to the underworld as punishment. Others say that his own son—or maybe his nephew—killed him in his sleep. One legend has it that he was consumed in a pillar of fire. Another claims he was turned to stone and imprisoned inside one of the Egyptian pyramids."

Lance said, "Could he have been a superhuman?"

"That's what we're thinking. That's if he ever really existed—there's no firm evidence. But even if he *didn't* exist, it's likely that The Helotry think he did. Lance, there's nothing more dangerous than a religious fanatic. According to our research, one of the Fifth King's methods was to sneak plague victims into his enemies' cities—some of his followers even volunteered to be infected—then when the plague began to spread, the rest of his warriors would swarm into the cities and slaughter everyone left who was capable of fighting."

"And now this flu thing is everywhere. . . ." Lance thought about this. "Maybe . . . Maybe the Fifth King was the first superhuman, the distant ancestor of all the others. If The Helotry *are* trying to bring him back to life, it could be that they released the plague because they don't want any other superhumans to be as powerful as he is." He stared at the colonel. "Your nose is running."

Morgan wiped the back of his hand across his nose. "Aw no. . . . Two-thirds of my men are sick already." His whole body convulsed with a violent sneeze, and when he looked up, Lance saw that his eyes were bloodshot and his face had gone pale.

Paragon pushed open the door. "We need a medic in here!" To Lance, he said, "Get out." He picked up a flashlight and tossed it to him. "Go into the middle of that field and wait there until I come for you. *Now*, Lance!"

Lance grabbed his backpack and dashed between Paragon and the colonel. He leaped from the truck and scrambled over the fence.

He'd never been out of the city at night before, and once he'd left the glare of the portable spotlights, the darkness seemed to wrap around him like a thick blanket. He switched on the flashlight. The beam swayed and juddered as he ran.

He slowed to a stop after a couple of minutes and looked back. Soldiers were running toward the FBI truck and Paragon was bellowing orders at them.

I could be infected too. He practically sneezed all over me! Lance remembered a teacher telling him that when the symptoms showed up, the infected person was no longer contagious. *Was that the flu, or just a cold? Is it even true, or just one of those things that people always say?*

A few minutes later, Paragon flew over the field, the down-thrust from his jetpack leaving a wide circle in the grass as he touched down. "More than three-quarters of them are infected now, Lance. And we've checked with CDC—they're getting reports from all over the world."

"CDC?" Lance asked.

"The Centers for Disease Control and Prevention. They have the facilities to monitor things like this. Their experts are saying that it's definitely an artificial virus, but they've never seen anything quite like it. They figure it could take weeks just to unravel its RNA and create a vaccine. The only positive news is that the virus doesn't appear to be immediately fatal." Paragon hesitated for a moment. "Lance, I have to leave you here. I know that so far the virus is infecting only adults, but we can't take that risk. I've contacted Roz Dalton. She's going to pick you up. She's also going to get in touch with Thunder and Abby. They'll take care of you."

Lance stepped closer, and stared up at his reflection in Paragon's visor. "What about you?"

"I've got a place not too far from here. I'm going straight there now. I've got it too, Lance. I started feeling the effects a few minutes ago."

Lance dry-swallowed. "But . . ."

"For all we know, Roz, Abby, and Thunder are the only superhumans who haven't been infected. It'll be up to you four to find out who created the virus."

For a moment, Lance was silent, then he took a deep breath, and let it out slowly. "Why me? I mean, I'm just ordinary."

"Ordinary? No, you're not. You're resourceful, and you've got guts. Heck, you rode a jet-propelled bike for almost two hundred miles and managed to stay on. Not many people could do something like that. I know you don't have any superhuman abilities, but then neither do I. I have to go, Lance. Pretty soon I won't have the strength to stand. Tell Roz everything I told you, OK?"

"Wait! Paragon, I need to know more! That guy who crashed his car—why were you chasing him in the first place?"

"The jetpack they built . . ." Paragon's voice was weakening. "They did a few test flights ten days ago and were spotted by a military satellite. I was told about it, went looking for them. The fuel is a combination of dinitrogen tetroxide and ultra-concentrated hydrogen peroxide, compressed into a viscous liquid. When the jetpack is active it leaves a faint trace that can be detected if you know what to look for. I spent the past week checking out every place in Fairview where the jetpack could have been built. My scanner picked up traces of the fuel on that guy's car. Enough to let me know that he was involved." Paragon swayed slightly once more. "I just . . . I didn't know who these people were. I just wanted to talk to them. You know. Talk shop. That was all. And then he saw me coming and made a run for it. That's when I knew . . ." His shoulders sagged. "I've got to . . ."

Lance nodded. "I know. Go. I'll talk to Roz."

Paragon wished him luck, then took a few steps back and activated his jetpack. He roared into the air and left Lance standing in the field. Alone.

CHAPTER 14

4,491 years ago . . .

The throne room was enormous, immaculate, glorious. Visitors first noticed the polished obsidian floor inlaid with intricate gold patterns around its borders. Then their attention was drawn to the twenty-three white tree trunks on each of the room's three sides. Curious, the visitors would approach the trunks and reach out to touch them, only to feel not warm bark but cold, hard marble. Then they would look up and gape openmouthed at the exquisitely painted ceiling.

The painting showed five scenes. In the center, Lord Krodin—rendered almost true to life—stood with his sword in his left hand, and the world in his right. The surrounding images showed Krodin slaying the kings of Egypt, Assyria, Sumeria, and Khamazi.

And then the visitors would look to the center of the room. Seventeen wide steps led up to the dais on which the throne itself rested. The throne had been carved from a single piece of oak. It was taller than a man and wider than his outstretched arms, polished smooth and black, inlaid with thumb-sized rubies and emeralds.

Krodin rarely used the throne. It had been built to his exact specifications, but the carpenter—an annoying but talented man—had been very pleased with his work, and Krodin didn't like the humans to have a pride in their work that was stronger than their devotion to their leader. So when the carpenter was present, Krodin would often sit on the top step to the left of the throne as he conducted the matters of his empire.

But today he had chosen to stand among his people on the main floor. His advisers—most Egyptian, some Assyrian, some Greek, and one each from Thule and Iberia—waited in turn to impart their news and receive their instructions.

The senior adviser—the former Egyptian general called Imkhamun—ushered forward a slender young woman dressed in white robes. "Envoy Alexandria of Assyria, Lord."

Alexandria bowed as she approached. "Lord Krodin, I bring news from Assyria."

The woman had flawless ebony skin and pale blue eyes that would not look into his.

"Raise your head, Alexandria. Speak to my face, not my feet."

With some hesitancy she said, "Lord. Our forces will reach Harappa within the week. But our scouts inform us that the people of the Indus have tripled their defenses. They are said to have powerful engines of war, metal dragons that can breathe devastating pillars of flame."

"I have heard of such things," Krodin said. "Their dragons use a flammable liquid extracted from the black oil beneath the Arabian sands. But the engines are large, cumbersome. A score of men is required to move them into position." He thought for a moment. "Under a flag of truce you will send a small party—a dozen men, no more—into the Indus' camp. They will offer the commanders ten thousand slaves in exchange for one of the dragons."

The woman nodded. "As you say, Lord, it will be done."

"The Indus are not fools, and will not accept the offer. But they will be boastful. They will display their dragons' great power. *That* is when our armies will strike—when the dragons have breathed their fire and their steel bellies are empty. The dragons are to be destroyed."

Alexandria bowed once more, and backed away into the crowd.

A large, pale-skinned, bearded man approached. Krodin recognized him as Ambassador Heriko. The man's knowledge of the Assyrian and Egyptian languages was poor, but he was said to be the greatest warrior in all the Northern Lands. He was almost a head taller than Krodin, broad across the shoulders and with arms thicker than a normal man's legs.

Despite the heat of the afternoon, Heriko was dressed as always in his layers of leather and fur. A wooden shield was slung across his back and a heavy sword hung from his belt. "Heriko bring news to you, Lord Krodin. The warriors of Germania did greet our envoy with smiles but returned only their lifeless bodies. They warn that Germania will never weaken before your power."

Krodin raised an eyebrow. "Is that so? Ambassador, you

will send word to our forces in the North that Germania and its outposts are to be left alone for now."

"As you say, Lord Krodin."

"One thousand of your men will disguise themselves as Germanians and sail to the kingdoms of Albion. Lay waste to the land, but kill only one man out of every three."

"Lord, with ease the warriors of Heriko's land could—"

Krodin raised his left hand, and Heriko fell silent. "I am sure that they could. But enough of Albion's men must be left alive to wage war on Germania."

Ambassador Heriko nodded. "As you say, Lord Krodin. But—"

"Twice you would contradict me, Ambassador Heriko?"

The ambassador's heavy brow furrowed. "Lord?"

"I do not like that. Remove your sword from its sheath."

The other ambassadors, envoys, and servants formed a wide, murmuring circle as Heriko slowly withdrew his heavy, double-edged sword.

"You northern warriors claim to fear nothing, not even death. Let us put that to the test. Fall on your sword."

Heriko lowered his sword, resting its point on the floor. With his free hand he scratched at his beard as he stared at Krodin.

"Do you not understand?" Krodin asked. "Or do you hesitate out of cowardice?"

The scratching stopped. "Heriko fears nothing," the man said. He stepped closer to Krodin, looked down at him. "Not even the little king all others fear."

Without taking his eyes off the warrior, Krodin said, "Imkhamun. Show this man your hand."

The Egyptian shuffled forward, and raised his right hand so that Heriko could see the scarred stump where he once had a thumb.

Krodin said to Heriko, "Fall on your sword. If you do not, I will kill you myself. Then I will remove your thumbs. Your people believe that a warrior must do battle with demons to gain entry to the Hall of the Slain, but a man without thumbs cannot hold a weapon."

Heriko stared unblinking at Krodin. His grip on the sword tightened a little. His muscles tensed.

The sword swung.

Krodin caught the blade in his left hand. He spun on one foot, planted the other in Heriko's chest, and pulled the sword from the warrior's hand.

Moving faster than anyone could see, Krodin continued the spin, shifted his grip on the sword so that he was holding the hilt. He stretched out his arms.

Krodin's spin ended with the edge of the sword buried in Heriko's chest.

The warrior's eyes grew wide. His body shook. He made a weak, uncoordinated grab for the weapon with both hands, then toppled, crashing heavily backward to the floor.

"Imkhamun? Take him away. Have his thumbs removed *before* he dies. I want him to see—and feel—what's being done to him. And inform Heriko's first general that he is the new ambassador." Krodin looked around, spotted the Assyrian envoy. "Everyone but the Lady Alexandria will leave."

In seconds the throne room was empty but for Krodin and the dark-skinned woman. Krodin approached her from the side, then circled slowly around her. "Raise your right arm. Outstretched, level with the floor. Palm down."

Nervously, the woman did as she was ordered. Krodin circled her twice more before he stopped at her side and spoke again. "Where are you from?"

"Ta Netjeru, Lord."

"You are a long way from home. Ta Netjeru—The Land of the Gods," Krodin mused. "Do you believe in the gods, Lady Alexandria? In the paradise rewarded to the virtuous? In the underworld that is the fate of the reprobates?"

"Lord, I . . ." She stared at her outstretched hand. "I do not know. I did, once."

"But now you have met me," Krodin said. "Many people believe that *I* am a god. A demigod at the least. This is not so, but it amuses me to allow such a folly to thrive." He resumed circling. "I know that some call me the Fifth King. Not the *first* king, which would imply that I am the best, but the fifth, to suggest that I am only one among many." He smiled. "It is intended as a disguised insult, I think. A . . . what would Imkhamun call it? . . . a compliment laced with irony. The Egyptians excel at such things. They are a remarkable people with a mastery of words that few can match. I have listened to Imkhamun's woman speak many such things to her husband. Hemlock dipped in honey. The people of Hibernia call them 'backhanded slurs.'"

Krodin stopped in front of Alexandria. "Backhanded. The back of *your* hand carries a mark, I see. You have disguised it with paint that closely matches the color of your skin. A normal man would not see this. But I am not a normal man."

The woman was trembling now, her hand shaking as Krodin took hold of it with his left. He licked his right thumb and rubbed it over the dark paint, revealing a small tattoo of a cobalt blue eye encircled by a golden sun.

"An eye inside the sun. I have seen this before. Many times. I am somewhat older than I look, Lady Alexandria, and I have a perfect memory. The symbol indicates that you belong to the Azurite Order. A century ago your forebears attempted to assassinate me in Eritrea. I thought I had killed them all and destroyed the Order forever. Clearly I was mistaken." He stared into her ocean-blue eyes for a long time. "You may speak. And speak freely."

"Four escaped your massacre of the Azurite Order. Four out of seven hundred. They swore vengeance. They continued in secret, rebuilt their numbers."

"And now? How many?"

"More than you can count."

Krodin laughed. "Indeed? Perhaps that is so. Perhaps the new Azurite Order does have more agents than I can count. But tell me this, Lady Alexandria . . . Does it have more agents than I can kill?"

She looked away.

"You may lower your arm." Krodin walked around her once more. "You will return to your superiors. Tell them that the Fifth King forgives them for their attack in Eritrea. They may move freely and openly. There will be no reprisals."

"Lord . . . ?"

"Yes, I know. Strange, is it not? Such compassion is surely not expected of the man called the Butcher of Uruk, the Devastator of Empires, the Fifth King. You will tell the leaders of your organization that they need not fear me. This is my gift to the Azurite Order, and I know that your people's custom dictates that a gift cannot be accepted without one given in return."

Alexandria raised her head again, turned to follow him as he walked in his slow circle.

"I was born more than five hundred years ago, Lady Alexandria. I have seen much. I have traveled to places your people do not even know exist. I do not age, and I cannot be killed. I will be here in a hundred years, a thousand, ten thousand. You humans can never know nor fully understand immortality, so you instead try to achieve a semblance of it by erecting statues, by carving your names on the entrances of your tombs. And by having children in the hope that they will remember you well, pass on your story to *their* offspring. I have never taken a wife. It has always seemed . . . pointless. The beauty of even the most glorious woman will fade with time. She will wither and die. I could never allow myself to love something that could not last. . . . Until today." Krodin reached out his hand and brushed Alexandria's cheek with the backs of his fingers. "In exchange for my pardon of the Azurite Order, their gift to me will be a wife."

CHAPTER 15

The pilot—Ernie Wieberg—sat bleary-eyed in the copilot seat of the Bell 222B helicopter. He was wrapped in a thick blanket and every few seconds he shivered violently. His nostrils had been stuffed with wads of tissue paper and when he sneezed, the wads would shoot out and he would have to replace them.

Roz Dalton sat next to him with her hands gripping the joystick so tightly that her knuckles were white. Her eyes darted across the instrument board: radar, altitude, artificial horizon, airspeed, back to the radar.

"Gedly," Wieberg said, then noisily snorted and cleared his throat. "Gently. Wodge—*watch*—the altimeter."

"I know, I know," Roz said. She hated flying, and hated helicopters even more. The only thing keeping them in the air was the powerful engine. At least an airplane had wings and could glide if the engine cut out. If that happened in a helicopter, the craft could fly in only one direction: down.

When her telekinetic powers first appeared, Max—already an established superhero—had insisted that Roz was to receive full training. By the time she'd reached her fourteenth birthday she could drive an armored car, fly a Cessna, and disassemble, clean, and reassemble an assault rifle blindfolded. Monday to Wednesday Roz was tutored in standard school subjects. Thursday and Friday were for military training. Saturdays she was expected to practice using her powers. Sundays were supposed to be for relaxing, but somehow Max always found something for her to do, from looking after their younger brother Joshua to answering his mountains of fan mail.

Roz didn't mind most of it. She was solitary by nature and understood that Max was trying to do his best as a surrogate parent. Sometimes, though, she wondered whether she accepted every order he gave because he was manipulating her thoughts. He had assured her many times that his mind control didn't work on her, but how would she know whether that was true?

"All ride, sed her dowd," Wieberg said. He removed the wads of tissue and loudly blew his nose on a handkerchief.

As Roz eased the copter's joystick forward, Wieberg said, "Slowly . . . Tage her dowd to fibe yards . . ." Another snort. "Five yards."

"Take *it* down, not her," Roz said automatically. It really bugged her when men talked about machines using the feminine pronoun. She checked the radar again, then looked out through the cockpit's windshield. "OK . . . I think I see him. Hit the spotlight, will you?"

Ahead, a flashlight beam swayed back and forth as Lance McKendrick—standing alone in a field of long grass—

waved both arms above his head to attract the copter's attention.

"The spotlight, Ernie," Roz repeated. She glanced at him: The shivering was much worse now, and a film of sweat had broken out on his forehead.

Roz flipped the switch telekinetically, and the spotlight attached to the Bell's undercarriage blazed a beam of light down on Lance. *OK, got to do this without any help.* Roz frowned in concentration, the tip of her tongue protruding from the side of her mouth. She'd landed the copter only once before without instruction, but Wieberg had been right beside her at the time, ready to take over if she got into trouble.

The copter set down with a heavy *thump*, bounced once, and settled again. Roz felt a little embarrassed about that, but then remembered something Ox had often said: Any landing you walk away from is a good one.

She shut down the engine, unclipped her harness, and—on legs that were still shaking a little—climbed down and strode through the grass toward Lance.

He was saying something to her but she couldn't hear him over the roar of the copter's rotors. He pointed toward the road. Roz turned to see headlights bouncing their way across the field.

She followed Lance toward the jeep as it came to a stop. It was being driven by a soldier—a private—who didn't look that much older than she was. The two medics in the back jumped out and ran to the copter.

"It's everywhere!" the driver shouted to Roz and Lance. "Been on the news. There's like, *millions* of people all across the States already infected!" He beckoned them closer.

"Get in. There's only about ten of our guys left who haven't caught it."

Lance jumped into the back, and Roz climbed in beside the driver. "Where are you taking us?" Roz asked.

"Have to pick up that guy Thunder and the girl with the sword." The soldier steered the jeep in a tight arc and headed back the way he had come. "The guys at the CDC are saying that maybe one adult out of every five has already caught it for sure. Luckily most of them have it pretty mild right now. We've had to clamp down on the media reports to stop the civilians panicking, so the official word is that it's just the flu and everything's under control." The jeep hit a furrow and bounced. "Name's Frankie Nazzaro, by the way. So you guys are superhumans, right?"

"She is; I'm not," Lance said.

"You two all right?" Nazzaro asked. "Any symptoms?"

"I'm fine," Roz said.

Lance said, "Me too. Hungry, though. I haven't eaten in hours."

"We'll get you something after we pick up the others." With a final bump, the jeep left the field and steered onto the road. Most of the army trucks and police cars had been cleared away—Roz saw three men climbing into one of the trucks. They were wearing what looked like silver space suits.

"That's the guys from the CDC," Private Nazzaro explained. "Near as anyone can figure, the terrorists blanketed this whole area with the virus sometime during their attack. Don't know how they did it, though."

Roz said, "I left Quantum at Max's safe house. I was hoping that his fast metabolism would have helped him burn through the infection by now, but he's in a really bad way. He was the first of us to be hit with it."

Lance asked, "Do you know what those guys were doing here yet?"

The young man shrugged. "Not a clue. There wasn't anything to steal." He slowed the jeep to a crawl as he eased it past a truck that was parked diagonally across the narrow road. "But these guys, The Helotry or whatever they call themselves . . . The medics are still trying to find out what makes them immune from the plague."

"Why aren't *you* infected?" Roz asked.

"Reckon I'm too young." He flashed a crooked-toothed grin. "I'm eighteen, but I'm a bit of a late developer. Never thought I'd be pleased about that—the other guys are all, y'know, muscles and stubble and everything. I'm a coupla years behind them. Man, they always give me such a hard time about that. Not anymore, though."

"Is there any word from Paragon?" Roz asked.

Nazzaro shook his head. "I haven't heard. But they don't tell me more than I need to know. Colonel Morgan's been hit pretty bad and the whole chain of command is messed up—we're just trying to do the best we can with what we have left."

Roz decided not to ask him anything else: He was one of those drivers who had to look at their passenger when talking to them.

It was close to midnight, and the roads were almost empty. Nazzaro roared the jeep through the town as though traffic laws didn't apply to him. He cruised through the red light on Main Street, screeched around the corner onto Gardner—

taking the turn so wide the jeep ended up on the other side of the road and almost demolished a phone booth—then hit the accelerator.

As they reached the town's outskirts they passed four army trucks going in the opposite direction. Nazzaro honked the horn and waved, but they didn't return his greeting.

"Jerks," Nazzaro muttered. "All right, guys," he shouted. "Keep an eye out for a place called Maple Towers. Should be coming up on the left."

"We already passed it," Lance said, "way back there." He was holding on to the back of Nazzaro's seat.

"OK, hold tight!" Nazzaro slammed on the brakes and spun the wheel at the same time. Roz and Lance were almost thrown out of the jeep as it left curved skid marks across the road.

They roared back the way they had come and eventually turned right into a wide, tree-lined avenue. After a quarter-mile Nazzaro slowed the jeep to a crawl.

Roz and Lance looked around as they waited. It seemed to be a fairly wealthy neighborhood—large houses, plenty of space between them, lawns so perfectly clipped and level they could have been used as pool tables.

After a few moments Lance said, "Now what?"

"Should be around here somewhere," Nazzaro said. "You guys have the exact address?"

Before Roz or Lance could reply, a disembodied voice said, "Stop there. I heard you coming ages ago. I'll be there in a couple of minutes."

Softly, Roz said, "Can you actually hear us right now?"

"Yep," Thunder's voice said.

Nazzaro whistled. "That is one freaky power you have there, kid."

"It's pretty useful at the movies, though," Thunder said. "I can shut out all the sounds around me and concentrate on the show." As he spoke, it sounded to the others like his voice was slowly circling them.

"How *are* you doing that?" Lance asked.

Thunder's reply came from the left sleeve of Lance's jacket. "I'm agitating the air molecules. Or something. I don't understand the physics of it myself. I just know I can do it."

The location of the sound jumped again, this time coming from Roz's mouth: "I've already spoken to Abby. She's on the way—has to pick up her costume first."

Roz jumped. "OK, never do *that* again!"

"Sorry. But if you look to your left . . ."

They looked.

"Your *other* left," Thunder's voice said directly to Lance.

Thunder came running around a corner, dressed in his makeshift superhero costume.

"Abby's on the other side of town," his voice said, though Roz could see that he wasn't moving his lips.

Thunder clambered into the jeep next to Lance. Private Nazzaro fired up the engine again and returned to the main road. This time, however, no matter how heavy Nazzaro's foot was on the accelerator, the engine was completely silent. "I don't want you waking up the whole neighborhood," Thunder explained. "Don't you people ever service your vehicles?"

The soldier shrugged. "Not my department."

"I was watching the news," Thunder said after a few

140

minutes. "People are beginning to panic about the plague. There's going to be riots, looting, murder. . . ."

Lance said, "No there won't. They'll all be too sick to riot."

The older boy gave him a withering look. "Yeah? What if the plague kills all the adults and there's only kids and teenagers left? Imagine a whole bunch of guys just like *you* trying to run things. The country wouldn't last a week."

"Strange," Lance said. "You'd think that someone who had the superhuman ability to manipulate sound wouldn't need such a big mouth."

"Why are *you* here, exactly?" Thunder asked. "What can you actually do, apart from steal things and get a whole freeway closed? That was on the news too. Skinny kid on a jet-propelled bike doing two hundred on the freeway and crying his eyes out."

"I was *not* crying," Lance said. "The wind was in my eyes."

"That's enough," Roz said. "Look, we don't know what The Helotry are up to, but we're probably the only ones who have a chance of stopping them. All the adult superheroes are out of commission. Max has files on almost all of them— each of their hometowns has been targeted with the plague. There's been no reported sightings of *any* of them since this afternoon. So we're going to have to work together. Start acting like a team."

The others fell silent for a while, then Thunder said, "When you say 'team,' you're not counting this guy, right?" He turned to Lance. "I mean, no offense, kid, but you *can't* do anything, can you?"

Before Lance could protest, Roz said, "Give it a rest, Thunder! I'm in charge here. I make the decisions."

"Who says you're in charge? I'm the eldest."

Private Nazzaro muttered, "Actually, *I'm* the eldest."

The others looked at him, then Roz said, "Right. But . . . you're not really on the team."

Another red light was fast approaching—Nazzaro pressed harder on the accelerator. "Why not? I've got military training." He jerked his thumb over his shoulder toward Lance. "I'm more useful than this guy. No offense, McKendrick."

"None taken," Lance said. "You make a good point. We're going to need all the help we can get."

Roz considered this. *He could be right. Max never had any problems working with the Rangers.* "All right," she said. "You'll need to check with your superiors, but if they're happy with that, you're in."

Nazzaro turned to her and grinned. "Yes! Always wanted to be a superhero!" He twisted around and smiled at Thunder and Lance. "So what are we going to call ourselves? We need a cool name like The Sensations. Maybe not that, though. Sounds like a sixties beat combo."

Roz grabbed his arm. "Will you watch where you're going?"

"Right, right . . ." The private returned his attention to the road. "My old man's always giving me grief about that." He turned toward Roz again, grinning. "This one time I was—"

"The road!"

"Gotcha. Anyway, I was—"

Something dark and heavy crashed down onto the jeep's hood. Nazzaro screamed and stamped down on the brake. The jeep skidded to a stop and the body kept moving—it hit the ground hard, rolled a good twenty yards, and lay still.

Lance was out of the jeep and running for the body before it had stopped rolling. Roz leaped out after him, slowed as she approached. Lance was in the way, and it was pretty dark. She couldn't see much, but the closer she got the tighter the knot in her stomach became. "Oh no. . . ."

Without turning around, Lance softly said, "It's Abby."

CHAPTER 16

Twenty-five minutes earlier, Abigail de Luyando had silently pushed open the window of the bedroom she shared with her sister and climbed out onto the fire escape. Instead of descending the creaking metal steps and taking the risk of waking up old Mr. Sutcliffe two floors down, she'd vaulted over the rail and landed in the alley.

Her conversation with Thunder had been odd. She'd been half asleep, going over the day's events in her head, when a voice whispered her name. She'd jumped up and flicked on the light, but the only other person in the room was Vienna, softly snoring to herself.

Then the voice had come again. "It's me, Abby. Thunder." He'd told her how he'd been contacted by Roz and that she was coming to pick them up.

Now, Abby ran along the town's deserted streets. Leftover's—normally open until two in the morning—was dark and empty. She darted past, ducked down the side street, and three minutes later was back on Main Street dressed in her homemade costume. Thunder had told her where he lived, so she started running in that direction.

She was still pulling on her gloves as she reached the front of the diner when she saw the woman standing in the middle of the street, watching her.

Abby stopped.

The woman was now wearing a close-fitting bloodred costume, with purple gloves, belt, and boots, but Abby still recognized her: Slaughter.

Abby's mouth suddenly dried. *Oh God.*

Slaughter walked forward slowly, almost casually, her hips swaying as though she was stepping onto a dance floor.

Abby had seen enough TV shows and movies to know what was coming next. Slaughter would sneer, boast a little, threaten to kill her, and then the battle would begin.

All right, Abby thought, her hand slowly rising toward the sword on her back. *Don't give her the chance. As soon as she starts talking—*

Slaughter darted forward, leaped, spun in midair. She landed on one foot in front of Abby, still spinning. Her other foot slammed into the side of Abby's face, knocking the army helmet from her head. Abby staggered to the right, almost losing her balance.

Still spinning, Slaughter struck Abby's face in the same spot with her left fist, then her right. Abby reeled backward.

Slaughter dropped to the ground, pivoted on her arms, crashed her legs into Abby's. Abby felt herself hit the ground hard. *Got to move—*

The woman pushed herself up and flipped over in one movement. She came down with one foot on either side of Abby's head, the toes of her boots almost brushing Abby's shoulders. Abby stared up at her, not knowing what to do.

Slaughter reached down and took hold of Abby's belt, effortlessly hoisted her into the air.

Dangling upside down, Abby made a grab for Slaughter's left leg, but the woman was too fast: She jabbed upward with her right knee, hitting Abby in the stomach and letting go of her belt at the same time.

Abby tumbled as she sailed through the air and had a brief moment to see a large painted *O* approaching—then she crashed through the plate glass window of Leftover's.

She skidded on her back across table seven and hit the floor hard. *Move! Get out of here!*

Abby jumped to her feet and grabbed her sword from its sheath on her back, and in the half-light noticed that her right glove was glistening red. *Blood! I'm cut!* Then an all-too-familiar tang reached her nostrils. It wasn't blood—it was the cheap ketchup that Dave the manager bought by the gallon and decanted into genuine Heinz bottles.

Then Slaughter was leaping through the shattered window.

Abby jumped backward, felt the edge of the countertop pressing against her back, and slashed at Slaughter with her sword.

But the woman was already two yards to the left, having turned her leap into a short flight and changed direction. Abby lunged toward her and slashed again.

Slaughter cartwheeled over the counter and passed feetfirst through the rectangular window into the pitch-dark kitchen.

Abby ran for the kitchen's double doors, jumped at the last moment and hit the doors with her shoulder, crashed through and rolled to her feet.

In the triangle of weak light from the doorway, Abby saw the cook's largest knife thud into the tiled floor an inch away from her right boot. She ducked to the left as a second knife whizzed past her head so close she felt the wind. At the same time a third knife clipped the shoulder of her jacket and spun away to clatter across the floor. *No fair! She can see in the dark!*

She ran for the back door. *Can't take her on in here. Not with all these things she can use as weapons!*

A heavy steel frying pan embedded itself in the back door, followed almost instantly by a horizontal hail of razor-sharp steak knives.

Abby ducked down behind the largest oven, and as she did so she caught a faint glimpse of Slaughter. The woman was standing in the corner next to the well-stocked cutlery drawers. Tiny points of light glinted off the knives in her hands—at least three in each—and from her eyes. Slaughter's pupils looked huge, wide, and dark.

Abby snatched up one of the fallen steak knives and threw it toward the far wall, to the left of the double doors. It spun as it flew. The wooden handle clipped the light switch.

The overhead lights came on instantly, and Slaughter finally made a sound: She gasped, let go of the knives, and covered her eyes with her hands.

Abby dropped her sword, grabbed the top edge of the oven with both hands, and hauled herself over it in one movement. She clenched her fists as she sailed through the air, slammed them both into Slaughter's unprotected stomach an inch above her wide belt. *Don't stop, don't stop! Don't give her a chance to recover!*

As the woman doubled over, Abby put all of her strength into her right fist. It collided with Slaughter's chin, knocking her back against the wall. Abby swung her left fist at Slaughter's temple, and at the same time stamped down on the woman's right foot with her heavy boots.

Slaughter screamed, swung her fists wildly. Abby dodged the clumsy blows, aimed another punch at Slaughter's stomach.

Slaughter suddenly lashed out with clawed fingers toward Abby's throat. Abby saw it coming: She caught the woman's hand, planted her right fist into Slaughter's face.

Slaughter screamed again, and launched a frenzied barrage of punches, kicks, and head-butts. Abby found herself staggering backward under the assault.

Then one of Slaughter's blows hit its target: Abby's jaw.

A burst of pain—greater than anything she had ever imagined—flared through Abby's skull. She reeled back, hit the corner of the oven, and lost her footing. Dizzy and nauseated, she collapsed to the floor.

Slaughter stood over her, fists clenched and eyes blazing. Through gritted teeth, she said, "You . . . You *hurt* me!" She wiped the back of her glove across her mouth. It came away streaked with red. "This is *my own blood*! No one has ever made me bleed before!"

Abby tried to scramble out of Slaughter's reach, but the enraged woman struck out with her foot, the heel catching Abby in the jaw. Another kick, and another. Abby felt the back of her head slamming against the floor.

She made a grab for another of the steak knives, but Slaughter kicked the knife out of reach and stamped heavily on her hand. Abby felt like her whole world was made of pain.

She felt Slaughter's hands roughly grab her shoulders, and she was hoisted to her feet. Half-carrying, half-dragging Abby across the kitchen floor, the woman launched a vicious kick at the kitchen's back door, snapping the heavy lock. She pulled Abby out into the yard. "You think you're hurting now? You don't *know* what hurt is. But I'm going to show you."

Still dazed, Abby was aware of a floating, rushing sensation. She was sure she was moving, but Slaughter's strong hands were still holding on to the shoulders of her jacket.

Then she recovered a little, and realized that her feet were swinging freely.

She looked down. The backyard of Leftover's was shrinking away.

Oh dear God! She's going to—

Eight hundred feet above Main Street, Slaughter opened her hands, and Abby fell.

The last thing she saw as she tumbled through the air was a rapidly approaching jeep.

CHAPTER 17

"She's alive," Lance said, turning to look at Roz. "You know any first aid?"

"A little. But the soldier . . ."

They looked back toward the jeep. Private Nazzaro was still sitting behind the wheel, mouth and eyes wide. All the color had drained from his face.

"He's not going to be much use," Lance said. For the second time in twenty-four hours, he wished he'd paid attention during the first-aid classes at school. *Recovery position. No, wait. . . . Can't move her in case she's hurt her back or her neck. What's the first thing?*

"She's breathing OK," Thunder said, crouching down on the other side of Abby. He pulled off his right glove and placed his index finger on her neck. "And her pulse is strong." He gently pulled back on Abby's eyelids. "Pupils are fine. Abby? Abby, can you hear me?"

The only response was a low moan.

"My God, how did this happen?" Roz asked. "She just fell out of the sky!"

Lance looked up. The sky was overcast, thick clouds tinted orange from the town's sodium lights. "She's not able to fly. If she was, she wouldn't have asked Paragon for a lift. So—"

"Go home," a woman's voice called.

They looked up to see Slaughter standing across the street, arms folded, almost daring them to attack. "Go home," she repeated. "That's the only way you're going to survive this night."

Thunder and Roz stood up, faced her.

Lance said, "Guys, if she can do this to Abby—"

Roz cut him off. "Thunder? Use your power. Pop her eardrums."

Then Abby's weak voice said, "No . . . Don't . . ."

Slaughter suddenly screamed, staggered, placed her hands over her ears.

"Pain makes her mad," Abby said softly—but Lance was sure he was the only one who heard her.

Slaughter launched herself at Thunder. He ducked to the side—but Slaughter twisted in mid-flight and clipped him across the jaw with her elbow. Thunder stumbled back, received another punch to the jaw, then a kick to his stomach.

He dropped to the ground, rolled aside as Slaughter's boot came down hard where his head had been. He made a grab for her foot, but the woman easily pulled herself free.

Her fists clenched, she threw herself toward him—

—and stopped in midair, her body quivering.

Lance took a second to see Roz staring at Slaughter, the exertion of using her telekinesis clear on her contorted face, then he grabbed Abby's arms and started to drag her toward the jeep. Abby was kicking feebly. "Let me . . ."

"No!" Lance said. "We can't take her on. You heard what Paragon said. We need to get away from here!"

Then Abby pulled her arms away, rolled onto her side. "My sword . . . It's in the diner. The kitchen. Get it."

Lance hesitated for a second. Nearby, Slaughter was screaming at Roz, but the teenage girl was still holding her suspended above the ground. Thunder was getting to his feet. *I don't think the others have superhuman strength*, Lance thought. *From what Paragon told me, Abby's the only one who comes close to matching Slaughter.*

"Someone help me!" Roz said, her teeth gritted. "I can't hold her back much longer!"

Lance ran for the diner. The doors were clearly locked— the only way in was through the broken window, past razor-sharp shards of glass.

Oh man. . . . Maybe if I jump I can sort of roll through and not get sliced up. He dismissed that idea instantly. *Get real. You're not a superhuman.*

He began to pull off his jacket, with the idea of wrapping it around his hands to protect them, but he was still wearing his backpack. He stopped. *How dumb can you get?* Lance removed the backpack and took out the armored gloves he'd stolen from The Helotry's warehouse. They certainly looked capable of knocking out the worst of the window's jagged shards.

It took a moment to punch out enough of the glass, then he grabbed the window frames and pulled himself through the window and onto the debris-covered table.

The diner's kitchen lights were on, and Abby's sword stood out clearly on the tiled floor. He grabbed the hilt and almost wrenched his arm out of its socket in the process—the sword was too heavy for him to lift with one hand.

With some effort he hoisted it onto his shoulder, then returned to the main part of the diner. Outside, he could see Slaughter silently tumbling, spinning, kicking—Roz and Thunder didn't stand a chance.

Abby was on her feet now, swaying slightly. She began to move toward the fight.

Lance shouted, "Wait! The sword!"

She didn't react.

Thunder's blocking out the sound—she can't hear me!

He clambered back onto the table, then threw the sword out onto the street and jumped after it.

The heavy sword had landed next to his backpack, and Lance spotted the hook of the grappling gun protruding from it. *I should have told Paragon about that—he might have been able to charge up the gas cylinder.*

In the middle of the street Abby threw herself at Slaughter—the woman didn't hear her coming. She struck Slaughter in the small of the back with her shoulder, knocked her off her feet.

Slaughter recovered almost instantly, rolled and pushed herself upright, grabbed hold of Abby's left arm and pulled. Abby was lifted into the air, spun, thrown into Roz and

Thunder. Thunder collapsed to the ground, his head slamming off the asphalt.

The sound instantly returned.

Lance snatched up his backpack and ran for the jeep. "Hey! You!" He had forgotten the soldier's name. "Start it up! Ram her with the car!"

But Private Nazzaro was still in shock. Lance pulled the man out of the driver's seat, left him lying stunned on the ground.

Lance knew the principles of driving, but he'd never done it. More than once, his brother Cody had offered to teach him. *Should have taken him up on that,* Lance thought.

He looked back toward the fight: Abby was making a run for her sword. Slaughter was right behind her.

Lance pounded down on the jeep's horn—the noise blasted through the street, and Slaughter turned to look in his direction.

Lance felt his blood chill. The look on Slaughter's face told him that he would be next.

Something exploded beside him—Lance turned to see Private Nazzaro half-crouched, smoke rising from the barrel of the pistol aimed at Slaughter.

"Did you hit—?"

Nazzaro turned and ran. Then Slaughter was crashing into the front of the jeep. The vehicle shunted six feet backward. Lance felt it tip over as she lifted up the front.

He had a sudden image of what would happen when the open-topped vehicle landed upside down—he'd be crushed.

But there wasn't enough time to get out. Lance ducked

down into the foot-well. His gloved hands brushed something heavy and hard—the grappling gun. He had a brief moment to again wish that he'd asked Paragon to charge the gas cylinder, then the jeep toppled over and crashed heavily to the ground.

Lance found himself facedown on the road, scratched and scraped, but otherwise unhurt. *OK. I'm better off under here. She's not going to—*

A purple-gloved fist punched through the jeep's door.

Grappling gun's heavy—hit her in the face with it!

He knew that he was going to die in the next few seconds, but all he cared about was hurting Slaughter enough to give the others a chance to get away.

The door was wrenched free and thrown aside. Lance grabbed the grappling gun—but it was stuck, wedged between the dashboard and ground. *Oh no.*

His fingers brushed against the gun's hook as strong hands grabbed hold of his upper arms and pulled him out. Lifting him as though he was no heavier than a toddler, Slaughter held him in front of her. Through gritted teeth she growled, "You shot me!"

Lance saw a thin black streak across the woman's forehead. "Wasn't me!" The grappling gun's hook was in his hand, but he couldn't move his arms enough to swing it at her.

"I'm going to save you for last," Slaughter hissed. She threw Lance back over the jeep. He landed on his feet, stumbled, and almost fell.

In front of the diner, Abby was holding on to her sword. Lance watched Slaughter streak toward her.

Slaughter was less than three yards away from Abby when she suddenly shuddered and stopped. The jeep scraped a few feet along the ground, towed by the grappling gun's cable.

Lance had attached the hook to Slaughter's belt.

Slaughter dropped to the ground, and Abby swung her sword.

CHAPTER 18

Roz got to her feet in time to see Abby's sword slam into the side of Slaughter's head.

The blow was strong enough to knock the woman halfway across the street. She rolled along the ground, tangled up in the grappling gun's cable.

Please don't let her be . . . Roz ran, skidded to a stop two yards away from Slaughter. "Thank God!" Roz said aloud. "She's alive. Unconscious, I think."

Cautiously, Abby, Thunder, and Lance approached.

"I thought you were going to kill her," Roz said.

Abby slung the sword into its sheath on her back. "I used the blunt edge."

They peered down at Slaughter. She was lying on her back, breathing heavily. The left side of her face was already blossoming into a mess of purple bruises.

"What do we do with her?" Thunder asked.

Lance said, "Use the cable. Tie her up."

"She's strong enough to snap it like it was thread," Roz said.

Private Nazzaro limped toward them. "Finish her."

Roz stared at him. "You better not be saying what I think you're saying."

"I am. Which of you is the strongest?" He looked at Abby. "You. Wrap the cable around her neck. Strangle her. It's the only way to be sure."

"We're *not* doing that!" Roz snapped. "Anyone else got any ideas?"

"If you don't want to strangle her . . ." Nazzaro slightly raised his right hand, and Roz noticed that he was still holding his gun.

Thunder said, "Don't do it! The U.S. military does *not* execute prisoners!"

"Anyway, her skin is invulnerable, you idiot," Lance said. "You already shot her in the head."

The soldier crouched down next to Slaughter. "Skin's invulnerable. Right." With his free hand he pulled open her mouth. Then he pushed the muzzle of the gun between her lips. "Let's see how invulnerable she is with a hole in the back of her head."

Abby withdrew her sword. "I can move faster than you can pull the trigger. Now back away or you're going to lose your arm."

Nazzaro shouted, "What is *wrong* with you kids? She already nearly killed all of us, and when she wakes up she's not going to be grateful that we spared her life! You think she's called Slaughter just because it's a cool name? She will murder every one of us!"

"Even if you're right, we need her alive!" Lance said. "She's connected with The Helotry—she can tell us where they are!"

"You think that, then you're a moron, kid. She'd never talk."

Then Roz said, "You're going to let go of the gun and back away. Right now."

"Never gonna happen!"

"That wasn't a suggestion." Roz concentrated on the soldier's right index finger, used her telekinesis to pull it away from the trigger.

She could feel him straining to keep the finger in place. "Stop fighting me," Roz said. "I'll break it if I have to."

Nazzaro opened his hand, and fell backward.

Thunder grabbed hold of Nazzaro's arm and hauled him to his feet. "Go back to the jeep. If the radio's working, call for assistance. Got it?"

"You're making a mistake."

"No. We just stopped you from making a bigger one. And you're off the team, by the way." He pushed the soldier in the direction of the jeep. To the others, he said, "What do we do?"

"I have an idea," Abby said.

A little over fifteen minutes later an army truck screeched to a stop in front of the diner. Roz greeted a young soldier as he jumped down from the cab.

"Corporal Redmond, National Guard 109th Engineer Group," the soldier said. "Where is she?"

"Over there," Roz said. "We've got her tied up. Sort of."

"Sort of?" The man frowned. "Oh."

Slaughter was lying on the ground tightly wrapped in a thick cocoon of green and silver metal strips: Abby had used her sword to slice through the jeep's hood and side panels, its interior framework, its fenders and bumpers, and even one of the axles.

The corporal walked around Slaughter. "Still unconscious?"

"She is," Roz said. "Unless she's a world-champion faker."

"What are we supposed to do with her?"

"Take her with us. We need her to tell us how to find the rest of The Helotry."

Corporal Redmond nodded. "Take her with us. Right. . . . So, where are we going?"

Thunder said, "Good question. We don't know yet." He pointed to Private Nazzaro, who was standing at the side of the street. "And we want *him* out of here. He's a liability."

"What did he do?" Redmond asked.

"Stuck his gun in Slaughter's mouth when she was unconscious and wanted to shoot her. I'm pretty sure that's not the way you people do things."

"Not even close." The corporal's voice was suddenly cold. "I'll see to it that he's dealt with appropriately. But I've got to tell you, there's only a handful of us who haven't been infected yet."

"What about you?" Roz asked. "How old are you?"

"Twenty-one. I just got over a serious bout of the flu and the medics tell me that's what's keeping me clear so far—I've been taking a heavy course of Amantadine for three weeks. No idea how long that's going to last."

The corporal climbed back into the truck, turned it around in the road, and reversed it as close to Slaughter as possible.

Abby's great strength wasn't enough to lift her into the back of the truck. It took all six of them—even Private Nazzaro helped.

When they were done, the corporal asked, "So where are we going?"

Roz shrugged. Lance had told them about The Helotry's plan to bring back the Fifth King. *But what does that even mean? Where do we begin looking?*

"We need to get to the terrorists," Abby said. "They're immune to the plague and surely they must know something about what's going on."

Thunder shook his head. "Unlikely. They'd have been told only the bare minimum in case they got captured. And they're certainly conditioned to resist interrogation."

"Agreed," Roz said. *What would Max do?* But she knew the answer to that: Her brother would read the terrorists' minds and find out everything they knew, then he'd work from there. She turned to the corporal. "Is there any word on my brother's condition?"

"No change, last I heard."

Lance asked, "What about the other superhumans?"

"Nothing," the corporal said. "But most of the real news is blocked, anyway. SOP in a situation like this."

Lance and Abby exchanged a glance. "SOP?" Abby asked.

"Standard Operating Procedure," Thunder explained.

"But everyone knows by now what's going on," Abby said.

Corporal Redmond said, "No, they don't. If they did,

161

there'd be mass panic, and that would cause at least as much damage as the plague itself."

From inside the back of the truck came the sound of creaking metal.

"She's awake!" Roz shouted. She had a brief glimpse of the metal cocoon bursting apart. A plate-sized chunk of steel streaked toward her head—and then Lance slammed into her side, knocking her out of its path. She recovered almost instantly, pushed Lance away from her, and jumped to her feet.

The others were standing still, staring up at the sky. Slaughter was gone.

"Blast!" Roz reached her hand down to Lance, helped him up. "Thanks."

Abby said, "What do we do now? Oh God, if she comes back . . ."

"She *will* come back," Thunder said. "And we should get well away from here before she does."

Roz bit her lip. "We don't have the raw power or speed to stop her. Quantum's not too far from here, in one of Max's safe houses. But he was the first one to get sick. . . . And without Max I don't know how to get in touch with anyone else. Thunder, can you use your power as a weapon?"

He shrugged. "How?"

"I don't know. My telekinesis works up to a point, but she's just too strong. She's been doing this for years, and she's absolutely merciless."

"Right. We need an edge," Abby said. "But what can we do? All the adult superheroes are out of commission! There aren't any other teenage superheroes that we know of."

Then Lance suddenly grinned. "Right. Absolutely right. I'm sure Slaughter knows that too. And *that's* our edge."

"What are you talking about?" Thunder asked.

"Not everyone who gets superhuman powers is going to be one of the good guys. There's a prison just outside a town called Oak Grove. There was a documentary about it a few months back. Any of you guys see that? It's where they keep some of the supervillains. . . . And there's one there who's pretty powerful. I think it was Titan who caught him, 'bout a year ago. He's supposed to have some sort of weird control over matter on an atomic level. Basically, he's a fire-starter. Pyrokine, the guy calls himself."

Roz suddenly shuddered. She felt her stomach clench and her heartbeat quicken. *That name* . . . It was like a half-remembered dream, a sense that somehow she had heard the name before, and that it was important.

Abby said, "That's crazy! We can't recruit a supervillain!"

"We might not have a choice," Roz said. "But there is one flaw in your idea, Lance. The plague, remember? All the adults are infected."

Lance's grin spread wider. "Right. But that's what part of the documentary was about. The prison is the only place strong enough to hold Pyrokine, even though he really should be in a juvenile detention center instead. Y'see, he's only fifteen."

CHAPTER 19

"You failed," the old woman said to Slaughter. "They are mere children. Inexperienced. Weak. And yet they defeated you."

The old woman was, as ever, sitting in the shadows in her dark, unfurnished room.

Slaughter stood still, arms clasped behind her back. She kept her expression grim—she didn't want to give anything away—though the cuts and bruises on her face and her ripped uniform were clear signs of her defeat.

"Well?"

Slaughter began, "I did my part. The failure started with Marcus. He allowed himself to be captured. The next time—"

"The *next* time?" The woman pushed herself out of her chair.

Slaughter bit down on the inside of her cheek to keep her teeth from chattering. She felt a sick churning in her stomach and prayed that it was caused by fear and nothing else.

The woman stopped in front of Slaughter. She wanted to look away, but knew that to do so would be a sign of weakness.

The old woman's face was shrouded in pale, translucent skin—shot through with thin red and blue veins—that hung loose around her jaw and neck. Her teeth were yellow-brown, chipped and cracked. Her eyes were so heavily bloodshot they were pink. The sockets were deep, dark-rimmed, half-covered by the sagging flesh from her brow. The eyelids were deformed, covered in styes that constantly seeped thin lines of yellow and white fluid.

The woman's breath was stale and hot, and when she spoke, tiny drops of spittle landed on Slaughter's face.

It took every ounce of Slaughter's will not to flinch.

"Not one of these children has the power to stop you, yet you *fled*. Like a craven, beaten wretch."

Carefully, Slaughter said, "I was ill prepared. I allowed my anger to take control."

"All you *are* is anger, girl! Do you forget that? You are bile and hatred and fury personified. That is your strength, your very being. The first child, the strong one. You toyed with her like a cat with a vole. Why did you not simply tear out her throat?"

"She—"

"The others. Dalton's sister. Her power could be formidable, but she lacks the experience and the imagination to use it to the greatest effect. What she does *not* lack is empathy for her colleagues. She can be defeated simply by threatening to kill one of the others. And the boy called Thunder? He has little physical strength. You should have swatted him as though he were a wasp." The old woman's eyes narrowed. "Above all, your task was to kill the human boy. Even in this, you failed." She turned away, walked slowly back to her chair. "You disappoint me, Slaughter. For four thousand years, The Helotry have been preparing for this time." She lowered herself into the chair, and resumed her stiff-backed pose. "The Fifth King will rise again."

Slaughter stared at the woman, thankful that she was now back in shadow. "I will stop the children."

"Only a fool repeats the same actions in the hope of obtaining a different outcome. The children have now worked together. They were a collection of individuals, now they are becoming a team. You thought you were fighting them, but because you let them live, the result is that you were training them, teaching them to defeat you." The woman leaned forward slightly. "Our plans have been put in motion and cannot be stopped. The Fifth King will—*must*—rise again. We have set loose the plague. On *your* recommendation, the plague was designed to affect only adults. You assured us that the young would not be a danger, that it would be to our advantage to have them healthy, strong enough to rebuild the Earth to the Fifth King's requirements."

"I couldn't have known that Roz Dalton would—"

"Silence! The young humans are fickle, you told us. Aimless, easily distracted. They will accept the Fifth King with less resistance than the adults. Now I no longer think that this is so." She fell silent for a moment. "I think that you lied. There are consequences for deceit." Another pause. "You of all people know what I can do. What I *will* do, should you fail again."

"I—"

The woman raised a hand. "Your punishment must wait. You will proceed with the preparations for the resurrection of the Fifth King. The children are a nuisance, but they know little of our plans. Leave them for now. It is unlikely that they can interfere at this stage. The Fifth King will rise again. Hail the Fifth King."

Slaughter nodded, and waited to be dismissed.

Then in a voice colder and harder than before, the old woman repeated, "*Hail* the Fifth King."

"Hail the Fifth King," Slaughter recited. "The Earth is his plaything, the humans his property. His rightful place as sovereign of the Earth will be restored. His day is coming."

The woman shifted a little, and her right hand fell into the light, allowing Slaughter to see the tattoo on the back of her hand: a blue eye inside a golden sun.

Slaughter couldn't see the old woman's face, but she knew she was smiling.

"Midnight has passed," the old woman said. "His day is today."

They drove through the night. Even the freeways—usually busy at any time of the day—were almost deserted.

The back of the truck contained nothing but small twisted fragments of jeep left behind following Slaughter's escape. Lance and Thunder—trying to be gentlemen—had insisted that Roz and Abby ride in the cab with the corporal. Now, three hours later, Lance was regretting the act of chivalry. He felt like he'd fallen butt-first onto a pile of gravel from a height of at least twenty feet.

He shuffled about again, trying to get comfortable. *Should have told the girls that we'd take* turns *in the cab.*

Thunder was lying on his back at the other side of the truck, eyes closed, breathing softly. He was wearing a too-big army jacket that he'd found in the cab. Lance wanted it for himself, but Thunder had shouted, "Dibs on the jacket!" before Lance had even spotted it.

Lance couldn't understand how Thunder could sleep with the truck bouncing around so much. As if on cue, the truck hit another pothole. Lance's head smacked against the side wall. "I *hate* this truck!"

Then Thunder said, "For crying out loud! Will you quit whining? You've done nothing but mutter under your breath and shift about for the whole time we've been in here. You're driving me crazy!"

"You've been awake all this time?"

"Yes."

"But . . . But you never said anything!"

Thunder turned toward him. "Didn't have anything to say. What, you think we're pals now or something? What would *we* have to talk about?"

Lance sneered. "Well, you could tell me all about those medals you've won for friendliness."

"Get real. You and I have nothing in common, Lance. I'm black; you're white. I'm a superhuman; you're a thief. I'm sixteen; you're, what, fourteen? I've got a near-genius IQ; you probably can't count to twenty without taking off your shoes and socks."

"Is that what you think? That I'm dumb just because I'm younger than you?"

"No, you're dumb because you're dumb." Thunder rolled onto his side. "You broke into that warehouse, stole the jetpack, got yourself shot at. Paragon was on the way to the power plant when he had to change course and save your life. He'd have had time to stop the terrorists—he might even have stopped Slaughter."

"Well, Mr. Near-Genius, if *you* hadn't . . ." Lance faltered. He tried to remember something stupid Thunder had done. "You blocked out the sound when we were fighting Slaughter and Abby couldn't hear me telling her I'd found her sword. She could have been killed."

"If she'd needed the sword that badly, she'd have got it herself."

"I'm the one who thought of going to Oak Grove."

Thunder nodded. "All right, I'll give you that." He rolled onto his back again. "That *was* good thinking. Assuming that it doesn't backfire and Pyrokine ends up killing us all. So what exactly can he do? You said he was a fire-starter, right?"

Lance stretched his arm over his head and scratched between his shoulder blades—he was more than a little concerned that the military weren't particularly conscientious about delousing their vehicles. "He can control energy."

"Like that girl who *calls* herself Energy?"

"Not really. She takes in heat and electricity and whatever and can channel it back out. Pyrokine sort of turns matter *into* energy. The documentary was mostly about the other prisoners—Texanimal, Brawn, Scarlet Slayer, The Gyrobot, a bunch of others—and how each one had to have a special cell. They only showed Pyrokine because he's a minor and he shouldn't really be in an adult prison, but there's nowhere else to put him." He scratched again. "I wonder what makes them turn bad. Somewhere along the way they must have made the decision to be evil. That's if they *know* they're evil."

"You're asking me?" Thunder said. "You're the thief. That makes you one of the bad guys."

"It's not like that," Lance said.

"You take things that don't belong to you. In what way does that make you *not* a bad guy?"

Lance couldn't think of a good reply. He'd always been able to justify his actions to himself, but now that someone was asking him, all of his answers seemed pretty weak.

"You know what I think?" Thunder asked. "You don't have the ability to put yourself in someone else's shoes. What's the worst thing you've ever done?"

Lance shrugged. "Nothing I've done has been really bad."

"In *your* opinion. All right, what's the best job you ever pulled? The most successful in terms of money."

"In one go? The sandwiches," Lance said. Just thinking of the word made his stomach growl. "I made just about six hundred dollars from that."

"So tell me about it."

"Right. Well, there's this industrial park on the edge of Fairview. Not a lot of companies, but some of them are huge and there's hundreds of people working there. The nearest place that sells food is like two miles away. I was going through on my bike one day about lunchtime and the traffic was really heavy. I realized that it was because pretty much everyone who worked in the park was going out for lunch. So I printed up a bunch of flyers listing lots of different types of sandwiches and how much they cost, and at the bottom it said that I'd be around every day at eleven to take orders. First thing the next morning I went around the entire park and left a bunch of flyers in every office and factory. I went around again at eleven and took all the orders. I made sure the prices were low enough that everyone would want them."

"And I suppose they all had to pay in advance?" Thunder asked. "You kept the money and never showed up again."

"Exactly."

Thunder sat up and faced Lance. "Don't you feel guilty about that?"

Lance shrugged. "Not really. No one lost more than a couple of bucks each."

"Imagine you were one of your victims, then. You're sick of having to go out for lunch every day, so when someone gives you the chance to have food brought to you, you jump at it. And then lunchtime comes around and you think, 'Sandwich guy's taking a long time,' but you wait anyway. You keep waiting. And half an hour later you're thinking, 'It's too late to go out for lunch now!' If you made six hundred dollars and the sandwiches were only two dollars each, that's three hundred people going hungry."

"I'm pretty sure no one died from missing one lunch."

"So they're hungry, and upset that they've been ripped off. How are they supposed to concentrate on their work? Suppose that one of them is on the edge. He's not doing too well in his job, trouble at home, whatever. Then you steal from him, make him go hungry, and the next day he comes into the office with a gun."

Lance couldn't help laughing at that. "If someone was that close to the edge I wouldn't be responsible for anything he did."

Thunder sighed. "I'm not getting through to you, am I? Look, let's see those gloves you stole from the warehouse."

Lance rooted through his backpack, fished out the gloves, and threw them to Thunder.

"Thanks," Thunder said. He removed his own gloves and pulled them on.

After a moment, Lance said, "Well?"

"Well what?"

"You're going to lecture me about the gloves, right?"

"No. I'm keeping them."

"But . . . They're mine!"

"They're mine now. In fact . . ." Thunder got to his feet. Holding on to the truck's side wall to steady himself, he walked over to Lance. "I want the backpack too."

Lance pulled his backpack closer. "Get stuffed."

"I'm bigger and stronger than you are. I'm going to take it anyway."

"All right. You've made your point."

"I made my point ages ago. You're just too dumb and too selfish to understand it." He suddenly straightened up, turned his head toward the front of the truck. "What was that?"

Lance looked. "I didn't hear anyth—"

Thunder reached down and grabbed hold of the backpack. "Sucker!"

Lance wasn't going to let go. They struggled for a moment.

"Man, what's *in* this thing?" Thunder asked. "It's heavy."

"Let go! My mom gave me this for my birthday!"

There was a long, slow *rip* and the backpack's contents spilled out onto the floor of the truck. The grappling gun slid toward the back of the truck and Lance made a dive for it. When he looked back Thunder was holding the two pages of numbers.

"Where did you get these?"

"Same place I got the keycard to get into The Helotry's warehouse. From that guy's briefcase. I think it's some sort of computer code or something like that."

Thunder pulled off the gloves and threw them aside— Lance snatched them up—then peered down at the pages in the semidarkness. "Oh man . . . You had this all along! You idiot!"

"What are you talking about?"

Thunder jabbed a finger at the first page. "These numbers here are the exact longitude and latitude of the Midway power plant! Look . . . Today's date, sunset and sunrise times. These are the road numbers leading to the plant. . . . God, this column here: They look like Social Security numbers. Could belong to the people who work there—and *these* are license plate numbers!"

He flipped to the next page. At first glance it was almost identical to the first, but the numbers were different. The lists of Social Security numbers and license plates were longer. Thunder frowned as he stared at the coordinates. "Windfield . . . That's only a few hours' drive from here, I think. There's a nuclear power plant there too. Went online a few months back."

Lance shrugged. "So . . . ?"

"So it means that the guy Paragon caught in Fairview wasn't just one of The Helotry's henchmen—he was way up at the top of the pile!" He slapped the first page down on the floor. "This is everything they needed to know to take over the Midway power plant. And this one about Windfield . . ." He thrust the second page at Lance. "It has *tomorrow's* sunset and sunrise times. Lance, this is where they're going to strike next!"

CHAPTER 20

4,456 years ago . . .

Shortly before dawn, Krodin strode out onto the balcony of his palace. The city was unmoving, the silence broken only by the gentle flap of flags in the morning breeze. Soon, the city would awaken and the humans would set about their daily routines.

He sometimes—though not often—wondered whether they were happy. There were no voices of dissent, but then such a lack can be caused by fear as much as contentment.

In the bedchamber behind him, his wife, Alexandria, stirred. She was lonely, Krodin knew. She could not connect with him and now that the children were grown and had families of their own, Alexandria spent her days working on her tapestries and pottery, tending to the palace's rare plants, or often just sitting on the balcony and staring at the city for hours at a time.

She had few friends, for almost no one was brave enough—or foolish enough—to put themselves in a position that might attract the notice of the king.

Alexandria was an old woman now, almost sixty. They had been together for thirty-five years, and she had borne him four strong sons and three beautiful daughters. She had been his constant companion and had done everything he asked without question.

But she had never loved him.

Krodin didn't know whether he was capable of loving or being loved. His parents had died when he was barely out of childhood, and his memories of them were tainted by the cruel, harsh time in which they lived. Every day had been a struggle against hunger, against the elements, and against the heartless, brutal despots who constantly battled over the land.

But that was a long time ago. There was no one left alive—save for Krodin—who remembered their names.

Krodin's older brother Kurgal had left home when Krodin was six, and the last Krodin heard, Kurgal had a wife and five children. By now, Kurgal's descendants would likely number in the hundreds.

For a moment, Krodin wondered how many of them he had killed in battle.

Below in the courtyard, the people of his citadel were gathering. They did this often: They stopped and simply stared at him. Sometimes they would kneel, praying to him. He had never requested this level of adoration, but it gave the humans some comfort to believe that they were in the presence of a god.

Alexandria approached him on the balcony. As always, she

kept her head lowered in his company. He turned to her. Her once-lustrous hair was now gray, her fine skin mottled and wrinkled, her slender frame now weak and bent with age.

"Good morning, Lady Alexandria. Did you sleep well?"

"I slept."

Krodin noted that she hadn't answered his question, but set it aside. The wife of a king should be allowed certain liberties. He turned once more toward the city. In the dark courtyard below, many more people had gathered, and still more were coming. He wondered whether today was another of their holy days. They seemed to have quite a lot of them.

The sky to the east was tinged with red. "This will be a fine day," he said to Alexandria.

"As you say."

Krodin considered her response. It was customary for his people to always address him as "Lord," but of late, Alexandria had taken to omitting that honorific. He didn't care about that, but it troubled him that he didn't know why her attitude had changed.

"Lady Alexandria . . . I have conquered the known world, united all the people under one banner." He gestured toward the flags adorning the square below: Each had a white background with a blue eye inside a golden sun, the old symbol of the Azurite Order that Krodin had adopted as his own. "I am immortal, unaging, wealthy beyond measure. No man can match my intellect. I am fluent in a dozen languages, a hundred dialects, and I have a perfect memory. I am the greatest warrior and the greatest king this Earth has ever known. Out of all the millions of people under my rule, I chose you—and *only* you—to be my companion. I have named this city in your honor. You have everything you could ever want, yet you are not happy."

"As you say."

He turned to face her again. "What can I do to *make* you happy?"

"There is nothing you can do now. But in the past . . ."

"And what could I have done?"

"You could have stopped," she said.

Krodin frowned.

Alexandria repeated, "Stopped. You *have* conquered the known world. But for what reason?"

"I . . . do not understand."

"You have butchered countless thousands of people, set nation against nation, people against people, brother against brother. You have terrorized the human race with your pointless bloodshed." She walked to the edge of the balcony and looked at the silent crowd in the shadows below. "It is very likely that every one of these people has lost a brother or a father or a son in one of your wars." She stepped back. "I would like to know why you have done these things."

Krodin's frown deepened. *"Why?* I am the strongest, the most powerful—"

"That does not explain why. What have you achieved but immeasurable pain and suffering?"

"I have united the world!"

"You have united the survivors of your conquests. But what of the dead? We humans did not ask for your rule, Krodin. We do not desire it. And we do not need it."

Krodin felt his heart quicken. "Be mindful of your words,

Alexandria. If any man spoke to me in such a manner I would—"

"Yes," she interrupted. She raised her head and looked into his eyes. "You would strike him down. Set your men on his family. Burn his village to the ground. You are strong, Krodin. Mighty. Fearless. Undefeated. But in so many ways you are weak."

He couldn't help but smile. "Weak?"

"Yes. Weak. You have taken so much, and it is not enough. But a man with a house full of gold that he does not spend is no richer than a man with no gold. You could have stopped when you took Egypt. None of the other nations would have dared to stand against you. They were not a threat, yet you still waged war on them. Whole nations have been destroyed simply because you feel that you must prove your strength. You are weak because you cannot exist without the reverence of the people. You cannot simply *be*."

"You are old, woman. Your mind fails you; you say things you cannot believe."

"No. I say things that *you* do not want to believe. But deep inside, you know, do you not? You know that every empire falls. Nothing is eternal, save death."

He turned his back, stared out at the lightening sky. "Leave."

Alexandria said, "Do not dismiss me. You are stronger than we are, this is true. But that does not make you better than us. Kill me for speaking and you will only prove my point." She hesitated for a moment. "There is a woman who lives on the edge of the city. Some say that she has a second sight. The people go to her for guidance at times. She tells them of her dreams of their future. Like you, she is more than human. You are not alone."

"Impossible. I would have heard of this woman before now."

"You hear only what your subjects allow you to hear. These people below do not worship you, Krodin. They despise you. When they kneel in prayer, they are not praying to you—they are praying to their gods for an end to your reign."

"And the people know of this woman, this future-teller?"

"Everyone knows, Krodin. She came to me months ago. She told me that there is an energy inside you—and inside herself—that makes you more than human. A sapphire glow that changes you, gives you your godlike powers. But you do not truly control this energy. One day it will break free. It will consume you. You will become a pillar of fire. The woman saw this in a dream, she told me. But it was a *true* dream. It will happen. You will die."

"And how will this supposed death occur? When?"

"She told me that one day the light of the breaking sun will strike your face, and then we will be free of you forever. It will be a day of great celebration. And the world *will* continue without you, Krodin. In time you will be all but forgotten. For all your conquests and carnage, you are not significant."

"It is superstitious nonsense, Alexandria. You should not believe such tales."

"But I *do* believe, Krodin. And you should too."

"Do *not* presume to tell me what I should believe, woman!"

"Ah, belief. . . . You once asked me if I believed in the gods, in the paradise to come and the underworld for the evil. I was uncertain then. But I have learned much in my time with you. *This* is the underworld, Krodin, a place where evil rules and the innocent suffer. An underworld created by your cruelty and selfishness and weakness. But the paradise will come, when you are gone."

"Enough!" Krodin bellowed, his voice echoing across the courtyard. He stepped toward her, raised a powerful fist.

Alexandria stepped back, though her face showed no sign of fear. "Our marriage is over, Krodin."

"*You* do not decide such things, woman!"

"No, it is not my decision. It is the decision of the fates." She looked away from him, and faced the east. "Good-bye."

Krodin stared at her, thinking that his wife had finally lost her mind. But her eyes glinted in the dawn light and there was a smile on her face, and he realized that he had never seen her smile before. Not once in thirty-five years.

For the first time in his long life Krodin felt something close to fear. He turned toward the city. The sun rose; its light spilled over his face. Far below, the crowds began to cheer.

And Krodin looked down at his body and saw that it was aflame.

CHAPTER 21

Something slammed nearby, and Abby opened her eyes. For a moment she had no idea where she was. She was looking through dust-streaked glass at a dark path that seemed to stretch off into an infinite blackness.

Then she felt the warm vinyl of the truck's seat beneath her and she remembered that she was a superhero on a mission.

The truck had been pulled over to the side of the road, and from the sounds outside, Thunder and Lance were arguing again.

Abby slid over to the door and groped for the lever, then pulled the door open and jumped out. The only real light came from the truck's headlights—the streetlights were out and the sky was overcast.

She followed the voices to the far side of the road. A pair of weaving flashlights showed the others beside a small car that had run into a streetlamp.

Lance was holding one of the flashlights on Thunder and Roz as they helped a middle-aged woman out of the driver's seat. The second flashlight was hovering a few inches above Roz's shoulder, its beam swiveling to point to wherever Roz looked.

They lowered the woman to the ground and Thunder checked her pulse and airway. The woman was moaning, her limbs flailing weakly. Her eyes and nose were streaming, and her skin was drenched in sweat. "I don't think she's injured," Thunder said. "She's sick, though. Got it pretty bad."

"She can't have been going fast, at least that's something. If she'd been speeding . . ." Lance shook his head, then aimed his flashlight at the hood of the car. "What do you think? Streetlights went out as she was driving and she couldn't see where she was going?"

"What about her car's lights, then?" Abby said.

Lance's flashlight swiveled in her direction. "Oh yeah."

Thunder took off his padded army jacket, wadded it up, and placed it under the woman's head. He unclipped a radio from his belt. "I'll see if I can raise anyone on this thing, but I'm not expecting much."

"We didn't want to wake you," Roz said to Abby. "This is the fourth one we've found. It's getting crazy. There were warnings all over the radio and TV not to drive, but when we were passing through the last town all the lights went out and the local radio station went off the air. One of the last things we heard was that the plague is still spreading and there's rioting and looting breaking out in all the worst-infected areas. The cops and the army are trying to keep order, but most of them are already infected and they—"

Abby interrupted her. "Wait, where's the army guy? Corporal Redmond?"

Roz and Lance looked at each other for a moment, then Roz said, "The infection got through to him. One minute he was fine, the next he was coughing his guts up. He told us to pull over, then he said we were to go on without him."

"You left him *behind*?"

"Abby, he insisted," Lance said. "He said that we were going to have enough to worry about without having to look after him too."

"So . . . who's driving the truck?"

"I am," Roz said. "We're about forty miles from the prison. We've been trying to contact them but no luck yet. The prison should have its own generators so it probably still has electricity." She led Abby around to the front of the car and unfolded a map on its crumpled hood. The flashlight floated away from her shoulder and hovered over the map, its beam directed at a long, winding line. "This is where we are now, roughly. The prison is here. . . ." The flashlight moved a few inches to the right. "And *this*"—the flashlight's beam zipped across the map to a circled area—"is a nuclear power plant."

"So *that's* what The Helotry are doing," Abby said. "Sabotaging the power plants."

"No, we don't think it's that," Lance said. "Not exactly." He explained about the pages he had found—stolen, Roz corrected—and how the final page seemed to indicate that the Windfield power plant was The Helotry's next target.

"They couldn't find what they wanted in the first one, so they're trying this one?" Abby asked. "That doesn't make much sense, though. If *this* power plant has been up and running for months, why wouldn't they just go there first?"

Roz said, "Clearly there was something in the Midway plant that this one doesn't have. But Midway wasn't operational. It didn't have a core." She shrugged. "It barely has a paint job."

"Ah, I think I've got it now!" Lance said, grinning. "It's not what the Midway plant had that this one doesn't, it's what Midway *didn't* have. They keep these places pretty secret, right? They don't want too many people to know exactly what they're like on the inside. So I'll bet you a million bucks that both of the power plants were built to the same plans. The Helotry waited until the Midway plant was mostly finished, and they attacked before it went online. It's an old trick: If you can't case the joint itself, you case an identical one. Now they know the layout of the place, what equipment will be used, the types of computers. They know everything they need to take over Windfield."

Abby said, "OK, *that* makes sense. But they must have known they couldn't get out again without being captured."

"They probably did," Lance said. "But Slaughter escaped. The rest of them were probably just . . . What's the phrase? Cannon fodder."

Roz nodded. "Yeah. . . . Yeah, you could be right. Slaughter learned all she needed to know from the Midway power plant. . . . But in this one they'll be facing much, much tougher security. There's no way they're going to get out of there."

"Maybe they're not *planning* to get out," Lance said. "Remember what Paragon told me about The Helotry believing they can resurrect the Fifth King? He was probably, like, the first-ever superhuman. If they *can* do something like that, they're going to need a lot of power."

"Then we have to warn them at the power plant," Abby said. "I mean, right now!"

Thunder came around to the front of the car. He held up the two-way radio. "First thing we tried. We're not getting anyone on this thing."

Roz said, "After we get Pyrokine we're going directly to the power plant. We just have to hope that The Helotry aren't already there." She gathered up the map. "Let's go."

Abby looked back toward the woman. "But what'll we do with her? We can't take her with us and we certainly can't leave her here like this."

No one responded.

"You said she was the fourth one, Roz. What did you do with the others?"

"We left them. There isn't any other option, Abby. We . . ." Her voice dropped to a whisper. "I know what you're thinking: She might die out here on her own. We've already gone over this. We have to stop The Helotry."

"But . . . This stuff about the Fifth King—it might not be true. I mean, they *can't* resurrect someone who's been dead for thousands of years."

Thunder said, "Maybe they can't. Could be that they're all just delusional nutcases. But *they* think that they can, and for whatever reason, they need an operational nuclear power plant to do it. We can't let them get that far. If something goes wrong and the reactor goes into meltdown . . . this whole state is toast."

Abby shook her head. *This is wrong, we can't leave the woman behind!* "What if it was one of us? What if it was me? Would you leave *me* to die alone at the side of the road?"

"Yes," Roz said. "You or me or any of us. This is bigger than any one person's life."

"Then I'll stay with her," Abby said. "You guys go, get to the prison and free Pyrokine. If you have him, you won't need me."

"We need you to *get* to him," Lance said.

"Then *you* stay!" Abby shouted. "You're not a superhuman anyway. We don't need you!"

Thunder took Abby's arm and led her away from the others. Softly, he said, "What could he do for her, Abby? Hold her hand and watch her get sicker and die? Annoying as Lance is, he *is*—and I wouldn't tell him this to his face—he *is* useful. He's got brains, and he's got guts. He's able to think around problems and see solutions quicker than the rest of us. He's the one who thought of recruiting Pyrokine. So we stick together. All four of us. OK?"

He's right, Abby thought. *We have to see this through to the end.* "All right. Let's do this."

They lifted the sick woman back into the backseat of her car, and wrapped her in a blanket Lance found in the trunk. Then Abby pushed the car a little farther into the ditch so that it wouldn't be hit by another car, but was still close enough to the road to be seen by any passing emergency vehicles.

Abby looked back as they returned to the truck. She couldn't help wondering whether they would be the last people ever to see the woman alive.

• • •

They were six miles away from the prison when a sign was caught in the truck's headlights: YOU ARE ENTERING OAK GROVE—A PLEASANT PLACE TO LIVE!

They crossed the town's outskirts a few minutes later. Ahead Roz could see the side of a building flickering orange, but otherwise the town was in almost complete darkness.

She slowed the truck to a crawl. "Abby? Better wake Lance and Thunder."

Sitting between them, the boys had fallen asleep and Lance's head ended up resting on Thunder's shoulder. Thunder pushed Lance away. "Get off! You're drooling all over me!"

"What are you complaining about?" Lance said, yawning. "Your costume's waterproof."

"Guys," Roz said. "The prison's on the other side of town a few miles out, but I think we might have trouble before we get there."

Ahead, the square at the center of the small town was blocked by a group of people, silhouetted against the light of a burning car. Roz couldn't be sure at this distance, but it looked like most of them were holding crude weapons— baseball bats, bicycle chains, hunting knives—as well as flashlights.

"We don't have time for this," Thunder said. "Is there any other way through the town?"

"Not unless we turn back and take the freeway. That's going to take even longer. I say we keep going, take it slow and easy."

At least a hundred people, almost all boys in their late teenage years, formed a line three deep across the town square, all staring at the truck as though daring it to keep coming. Four of them were sitting on large motorbikes.

Roz hit the brakes and the truck squealed to a stop. "Now what?"

After a moment, one of the bikers peeled away from the others and rode toward the truck. He was short and thin, wearing faded denims and an off-white T-shirt with a red fist crudely painted on the front. His hair was cropped so close he looked almost bald. He had a wooden baseball bat tucked into a loop on his belt.

As he reached the driver's side of the truck, Roz could see the look in his eyes that told her he was very much enjoying himself.

"Outta the truck," the skinhead said. He revved the bike's engine for emphasis.

"No."

"Don't think you get what's goin' on here, girl. The world's endin' or somethin'. Everyone over nineteen or twenty is sick. World belongs to the young now." He grinned. "We take what we want and no one is *ever* gonna tell us what to do again!"

A cheer rang out from the other teenagers.

"There's no law but what *we* make, and we say you get outta the truck!"

"Let's see how tough he talks after this," Lance whispered. He leaned past Roz and pushed his head out of the window. "You guys have worked out a system for the burials, right?"

A frown appeared on the biker's face. "What?"

"The burials. When the adults die, you have to bury them.

189

And go deep—at least ten feet. Otherwise the plague will hang around and when you guys get old enough, bam, *you're* dead too. Oh, and you have to bury them no more than twenty-four hours after they die. Any longer than that, and they'll start to decay. The bacteria eat the infected flesh, the maggots eat the bacteria and turn into flies. They'll spread the virus even further. You know how it goes: Birds eat the infected insects, the birds die and infect the soil, the plants start to die. In a few years the whole planet is a plague-ridden wasteland. Now, you're going to want to stock up on canned food, dry cereals, anything that doesn't easily perish. As much as you can get. And you'll need bottled water too. The virus can't be killed by boiling the water. Don't bother with frozen stuff, 'cos with the electricity gone it won't last more than a couple of days. You'll need to round up portable generators and all the batteries you can find. Do any of your people have any medical training?"

The skinhead numbly stared at him.

"No? That's not good. All right. . . . You can't help the plague victims, of course, but eventually some of you will be injured, or get sick. Now, the people in the last town we passed through back there . . . they're using the high school as a fortress. They're already boarding up the windows and filling the place up with supplies. They're planning to barricade the roads. And they're armed with more than just baseball bats, so don't get any ideas about raiding them. They've got half a dozen generators already wired up to spotlights and you wouldn't get near the place. From what we saw, they outnumber you by about three to one. For you guys, that's a bad thing in two ways. . . . First, if they come here and you're not ready, they will absolutely slaughter you. And second, because there's so many of them they're going to run out of supplies pretty soon."

Under his breath, Thunder muttered, "How the heck do you come up with stuff like that?"

The skinhead chewed on his lower lip for a moment. "All right. What you said could be true. If it is, we're gonna need everythin' we can get our hands on. We're takin' the truck and whatever you got in it. An' you guys are part of the team now." He grinned. "I mean, you guys know all this useful stuff, so it don't make sense to let you go tellin' everyone else." He slapped the bat against his palm. "Get outta the truck. Now."

Roz said to Lance, "Well, you got them scared all right. Well done."

"You have to the count of five to get outta the truck. Or we're gonna *take* you out."

"Back in a minute," Roz said to the others. She opened the passenger-side door and jumped out. She walked around the front of the truck and up to the skinhead. "You *are* going to let us through."

He laughed. "Or what?"

Roz stared at him, and concentrated. She didn't know exactly how her telekinesis worked, but at times she visualized it as an invisible, flexible tentacle that she could use to lift or move objects.

Now she slammed it into the skinhead's stomach. His body jerked and he toppled sideways off the motorbike—it crashed down with him, pinning his leg to the ground.

The mob started toward her. "Come on, then," Roz said.

She bent down and picked up the baseball bat. "Who's next for a set of broken ribs and ruptured intestines?"

The nearest teenagers stopped abruptly, and the ones at the back collided with them.

"I can take you all on. One at a time or in a bunch. I'm a superhuman, and so are my friends in the truck." To prove this, Roz let go of the bat; it remained floating in midair. "So if you people want to avoid the slow, agonizing death of the plague and instead have a quick, agonizing death right here and now, then we're happy to oblige. Otherwise, you'll get out of our way."

They didn't move any closer, and it took Roz a moment to realize that they weren't looking at her anymore. They were looking past her.

She spun around in time to see a dark-red human figure streak out of the sky and crash into the side of the truck.

She darted forward, but something impossibly bright flared on each side of the truck's cab, blinding her. Roz automatically covered her eyes and thought she heard one of the others—Abby, maybe, or Lance—scream, then she felt a small, hard fist slam into her jaw.

Still dazed, Roz staggered backward. She felt hands close around her neck, almost tight enough to choke her, then the sickening lurch of movement that told her she was being lifted into the air.

She grabbed for her assailant's arms, but the grip was too strong; the muscles were like concrete, the tendons like steel cables.

And she heard Slaughter's voice whisper, "No more games. You're all going to die."

CHAPTER 22

At first Lance thought the truck had been hit by a missile. There had been an earsplitting bang and the whole cab rocked.

For a second he saw Slaughter caught in the truck's headlights as she rocketed toward Roz, then the night turned to day as a sharp, agonizing glare burned through the cab's doors. Lance screamed—it felt like his eyes were on fire.

He felt Abby shift beside him, heard her kicking out at the windshield, then her hand grabbed his collar and suddenly he was moving up and forward. His knees smashed against the dashboard, then for a moment there was only the sensation of movement—until his left shoulder slammed into the ground. He collapsed onto his back and felt the particles of glass crunch under him.

Without waiting for the pain to subside he rolled onto his hands and knees. Then he heard Thunder shouting, "Lance! Get out of here!"

He scrambled to his feet and staggered forward, hands stretched out before him, unsure whether he was heading toward the truck or away from it. All he could see was a shifting green and red blur, a thousand times stronger than the afterimage of a camera flash.

There was a crash behind him, and Abby shouted, "Thunder, get down!"

Another crash—metal on metal—and a man roared in pain. Lance hoped it wasn't Thunder.

Lance's right foot hit the curb and he almost toppled over. *Which way am I going?* He jumped as someone or something brushed past him, but whatever it was didn't stop. Then his hands touched cool glass—a store window. Moving away from the sound of the battle, he felt the window's wooden frame, then a corner and a recessed doorway.

He stepped into the doorway, feeling for the door, but the recess seemed to go on for too long. It took him a moment to realize that the door was already open and he'd walked into the store. Over the sound of the battle, he heard something scrape along the floor ahead of him. "Who's there?"

A frightened voice—"Stay away!"—followed by more scuffling.

"I'm not going to hurt you," Lance said. "I . . . I can't see. Where are you?"

"Don't come any closer!" It was a girl's voice, or perhaps a very young boy.

Lance stopped moving. "Just tell me where I am. Please. The flash of light blinded me—I can't see anything."

A pause, then, "Bookshop."

The window behind him shattered and the voice screamed.

Lance dropped flat to the ground, his left elbow colliding painfully with the edge of a wooden display stand.

Lance slithered forward, hoping that he was going in the right direction. "What can you see outside?" His fingers brushed aside fallen paperbacks and shards of broken glass.

There was no reply.

He worked his way around another display stand. "Come on! What can you see?"

"Fighting. . . . There's a girl with a sword. A man in shiny armor."

Paragon! Lance thought. *No, can't be him. He was too sick— he couldn't have recovered yet.*

"Two men now . . . No, lots of them."

"The girl with the sword . . . is there a tall boy with her? He's wearing a costume—"

"There's a man on fire!" the voice said, high-pitched with panic. "He's burning but he's not hurt!"

"All right. Don't look out there anymore. Look at me instead. What's your name?"

"Dylan."

"How old are you, Dylan?"

"Seven."

"OK. Dylan, I'm one of the good guys, I promise you. I'll help you get away, but I can't see so you have to help *me*. Deal?" His right hand touched a sneaker, which was instantly pulled away.

"I'm scared."

"I know. Take my hand."

After a moment Lance felt a small trembling hand settle into his. "That's good. Dylan, where's your mom and dad?"

"At home. They're sick. I came out to get help. Then I saw the big boys and I got scared so I came in here."

I can't just leave him. "Dylan, is there a back way out?"

"Yeah, but I couldn't open the door."

Lance got to his feet. "Show me."

He felt the boy stand up and lead him through the shop. "You have to tell me if I'm going to bump into anything, OK?"

"OK," Dylan said.

Lance's knees clipped the seat of a chair. "Ouch! Like that chair."

"Sorry. It's back here."

He felt his left shoulder brush a doorjamb. "Is this a storeroom or something?"

"Yeah." Dylan pulled Lance's hand to the left. "Mind the boxes. The door is here. In front of you."

"I'm going to let go, but you stay next to me, all right?" Lance reached out carefully with both hands, and felt the varnished surface of a wooden door. He groped around for the handle, gave it an experimental tug. "Locked. Dylan, can you see any keys?"

"No. I already looked."

"Of course you did. Sorry. But is there a window?"

"Yeah, but it's too high. It's right up at the ceiling and it's very small."

"OK, forget that." *If I had my tools I might be able to pick the lock.* His fingers probed the handle and the surface of the lock. *Feels like a Solidsecure two-twenty.* "Dylan, I need some stiff metal wire. Can you see any paper clips or—"

From the main store came the sound of heavy footsteps crunching on the broken glass.

196

The boy gasped and ducked behind Lance.

Lance crouched down next to him and whispered, "What can you see?"

"Men. They have guns."

"Oh great. . . . OK, just stick close to me and play along with whatever I say, all right?" *They could be the army, or they could be working with Slaughter.*

Then Lance heard a voice from the far side of the room. "Who are you?"

"Jason Myers," Lance replied. "And this is Dylan. Who are *you*? What's going on?"

Another voice quietly said, "Not one of Dalton's crew."

"You sure?"

"*Look* at him. He's just about wet his pants."

Bingo! Lance thought. *We might just get out of this if I play the sympathy card.* Aloud, he said, "Help us, please. We came out to get help for our parents. They're sick. We got trapped in here. I . . . I'm blind. I lost my cane somewhere."

The second voice said, "Forget him. Let's go."

"No, wait!" Lance called. "Please! We can't get out!"

"We don't have time for this."

The first voice: "Listen, kid. The whole *world* is sick, understood? Just stay here until the fighting is over and you should be safe."

"Who are you? You sound like adults—how come *you're* not sick?" *They've got to be part of The Helotry,* Lance thought.

"We're the ones who are going to make everything better," the man said.

Lance heard the static-filled squawk of a radio voice: "Team eight, come in. What's your position?"

"Bookstore on Main, Mr. Remington," the second man replied. "All clear. Just civilians."

"Superhumans are on the run. Slaughter's got Dalton, and we're tracking two black kids. The white boy is still unaccounted for—he could be with the local teens. They've scattered, but they should be easy to round up. Secure the area in case the boy returns."

"Will do." The radio clicked off.

Lance heard the man approach, and felt Dylan shrink farther behind him. The boy was trembling.

"Did you see a guy about your age with the others?" The man asked.

"No. I can't see *anything.*"

"Oh. Right. Sorry. What about *you?*"

Lance sensed Dylan shaking his head, and said, "We've been hiding out here for hours." He decided to take a chance. "Are . . . Are you going to hurt us?"

"Now why would you think that?" The voice was gentle, sounding a little surprised at the question. "No, we'll take you someplace safe. Trust me: You have nothing to worry about."

Lance faked a sigh of relief. "Good, thank you." He put his arm around the boy's shoulders. "Me and my brother here were worried that the world was coming to an end or something. All the adults are sick but if you're OK then there must be a cure, right?"

The man didn't reply.

"Are you still there?" Lance asked.

"Oh, I'm still here." His voice was heavy with sarcasm. "I'm not going anywhere, Mr. McKendrick."

Lance stiffened. *How did he know?* "I'm Jason Myers. Who's this McWhatever guy?"

"So Dylan here is your brother?"

Aw no! Stupid, stupid, stupid! Should have asked him what he looked like! "Uh . . . Yeah," Lance said quickly. "We're adopted. Mom and Dad can't have kids of their own."

"Is that so?" There was the clear metallic *click* of a gun being cocked. "You look like a smart kid. But you're clearly not smart enough to tell when a name is androgynous. Dylan's a girl."

A few minutes earlier . . .

Abby threw Lance through the truck's shattered windshield, grabbed Thunder's arm, and pitched herself forward and out, dragging Thunder behind her.

She pushed Thunder aside and ducked as a long metal pole swung toward her head. It hit the truck hard enough to tear a gash in the radiator. She grabbed for the pole but the man on the other end let go and ran. She pulled her sword from its sheath on her back and quickly looked around. The teenagers had already fled, Roz was gone, Lance was on his hands and knees.

Beside her, Thunder said, "People coming . . . Dozens of them." He shouted, "Lance! Get out of here!"

Abby passed him the steel pole. "Back-to-back, OK? We've got to keep them busy, give Lance some time to get away."

A metal-clad man rushed at her out of the shadows. Abby swung her sword in a backhanded arc. Its blunt edge clanged against the man's armored chest and he collapsed to the side, smacked his head against the truck's remaining

199

headlight—cracking the headlight open—and toppled over. Almost total darkness flooded over them. *Oh great! OK, maybe we can't see them but then they can't see us either!*

She heard footsteps shuffling to her right, and in the faint orange light from the burning car in the town square she had a glimpse of a large metal weapon in the man's hands and twin glints reflected in a pair of thick goggles. *Night-vision goggles—they* can *see us!*

There was a muffled *ptooff* of compressed air, and a thick, short cable with steel spikes on each end thudded into the front of the truck only inches away from her right leg. The man cocked the cable-weapon and fired again, but this time Abby knew what to expect. She slashed out with her sword and sliced the cable in two.

Then in the half-light she saw four—maybe five—more armored men, all with the same kind of weapon.

Trying to pin us! "Thunder, get down!" She threw herself backward as the men fired in unison, collided with Thunder, and knocked him flat.

Take them a couple of seconds to reload . . . "You all right?"

Thunder was already getting to his feet, the steel pole still in his hands. "Yeah. We need to get out of here!"

She pulled the pole from his grip. "Stay behind me and keep low. I'm better with this sort of thing than you are."

"No arguments."

Abby slipped her sword back into its scabbard, and holding the pole like a quarterstaff she rushed at the armed men.

She spun, clipped one of the men in the side of his helmet, knocking off his goggles, jabbed another in the stomach. The remaining three backed away, and one of them fired.

Abby knocked the spiked cable out of the air, jumped, slammed the end of the pole into the ground, and vaulted over the men.

Their reactions were fast, but not fast enough: Abby whirled the pole over her head and brought it down hard on one man's shoulder—she heard something inside him *crack*—then whipped the other end about and struck one of his colleagues in the knees. The man screamed.

Abby moved toward the last of them, but he was already on the ground, whimpering, his body convulsing, his hands desperately scrabbling to pull off his helmet.

"Redirected that guy's screams," Thunder said as he ran toward her. There was something round and metal in his hands—one of the men's helmets. "Amplified them too." He pulled the helmet on over his mask. "OK, *now* I can see. . . . Y'know, the armor these guys are wearing is a lot like Paragon's. Let's pick up Lance and get out of here."

"But Roz . . ."

"She'll be OK." Thunder looked about. "More of them coming."

"You're sure about Roz?"

Thunder leaned down and grabbed the weapon from the screaming man's hands. "No. But we have to get to the prison, free Pyrokine. That's what she'd tell us to do." He tilted his head from side to side. "They're coming from *everywhere*!" He paused again. "We should leave Lance. If they all follow us he might be able to get away. How's your sense of direction?"

"I remember from the map which way the prison is," Abby said.

"Lead the way."

Abby handed the steel pole to Thunder and once more drew her sword. They ran past the truck and into the town square.

How did they find us? Abby wondered. *Could Slaughter have put a tracking device in the truck? No, more likely they followed the only truck that was moving.*

"Down!" Thunder shouted. Abby dropped flat to the ground as the store they were passing was bombarded with a dozen spiked cables. The store's windows and door shattered inward.

The square was suddenly filled with armored men, all aiming the same powerful-looking weapons.

Then a dark figure descended from the sky, settled gently on the hood of the burning car. As they watched, the fire began to grow. Flames licked at the dark figure's feet, quickly spread up his legs until his whole body was engulfed.

The burning man stepped off the car's hood and landed lightly on the ground.

He walked toward them, leaving a trail of fiery footprints.

Oh no. . . . Abby dry-swallowed. "Thunder . . . Run!"

Roz Dalton was dreaming. Shocking, violent dreams that made no sense but left her feeling sick, betrayed, hurt physically and emotionally. It was cold—as cold as last winter's holiday in Alaska—and there was a woolen scarf around her neck. But the scarf was too tight and she couldn't loosen it.

Unbidden and unwanted, an overwhelming sense of loss and abandonment filled her mind, and she realized that for the first time in as long as she could remember, she was crying for her parents, and . . . for someone else, but she couldn't remember who that was.

And then the scarf around her neck tightened once more, but the scarf was cold and hard and strong, and finally Roz came awake.

Slaughter had her hands around Roz's throat, and Roz knew that they were thousands of feet above the ground.

Slaughter had flown straight up. In seconds they had passed through the clouds and now—as Roz's vision finally began to clear—she realized she was looking up at the stars.

Slaughter was squeezing as hard as she could, and it was all Roz could do to keep up her telekinetic shield.

"Die!" Slaughter said. "Die, damn you!"

Roz clenched her fists and struck at the woman, but it was like punching a bronze statue.

"All right," Slaughter said through gritted teeth. "I can't strangle you, but I can hold you up here until you suffocate. Or maybe I'll do *this*." She let go of Roz's neck with one hand and slammed her fist into Roz's stomach. "Hurts, doesn't it? Here's another one." She punched again.

Roz twisted aside, deflecting most of the force. "Why are you doing this?" Her voice was weak, barely audible even to herself.

Slaughter's expression of fury faded into puzzlement, as though she had never encountered the question before. "What? Because you and your friends are in the way!"

"The Helotry—" Roz began.

Slaughter's grip loosened. "How do you know that word?"

"We know everything," Roz lied. "You're trying to bring back the Fifth King."

Slaughter stared at her. "*How do you know?*" she demanded.

"You have no telepathic powers—and not even your brother is strong enough to read my mind!"

"Your plan is going to fail. The Fifth King is a myth. And even if he *was* real, he's been dead for thousands of years. Nothing you do is going to change that."

"Little girl, you are so wrong it's almost funny. We *are* bringing him back."

"What are you going to do? Clone him or something?"

Slaughter sneered. "Clone him? No, cloning technology is years away from being feasible. Besides, we'd need a sample of his DNA, and he was destroyed in a pillar of fire. Maybe there aren't too many verifiable facts about the Fifth King, but that one we *do* know. His death was witnessed by thousands of people, and all their stories correlate. We know precisely where and when he died. And if you have that sort of information, and you've got the right sort of power source and the people smart enough to control it, you can do what we're going to do."

She paused, and Roz knew it was only for effect.

"And what's that? What *is* The Helotry's grand plan?"

"We're going to tear open a hole in space and time. In the last second before the Fifth King dies, we're going to snatch him out of the past."

CHAPTER 23

Abby knew she had no choice: She had to leave Thunder behind. He just wasn't fast enough to keep up with her.

As she raced along the tree-lined avenue she tried to console herself that it hadn't been her idea. When the armored men began to swarm after them, Thunder had told her to go on. She'd looked back, seen him standing in the road as the burning man approached, but his voice appeared next to her: "I'll be OK. Just go. Get to the prison."

That was only a few minutes ago, but now Abby felt like she'd never been so alone.

The Helotry's men were on the ground; at least that was something in her favor. If they'd been in an aircraft, she wouldn't have stood a chance of escaping them.

Now they were close behind, chasing her down in an eight-wheeled armored vehicle that wasn't much smaller than a school bus.

The streetlights were still out, but some of the houses on each side had candles in their windows and the vehicle's headlights behind her illuminated the road ahead. Abby chased her own shadow.

At least they're not trying to kill us, she thought, and then wondered why that was. *Probably Slaughter wants to kill us herself.*

Abby spotted a church coming up on the left: She vaulted its closed gates and ran through the empty parking lot. Behind her, she heard the armored car's brakes squeal, then its engine revved loudly, followed by a splintering crash as it rammed the gates.

There was a high wall at the back of the church. She quickly scaled it and found herself in someone's backyard.

"Abby? Can you hear me?" a disembodied voice said.

"I hear you, Thunder."

"Good. I've got that skinhead's motorbike and I'm heading back out of the town the way we came in. I've got two Boxers after me."

"Boxers?" Abby asked.

"Armored vehicles. Big, fast. Look like tanks but with wheels instead of tracks."

"There's one after me too."

"I've stopped one of them already," Thunder said. "Blasted it with sound waves."

Abby vaulted over a fence into another backyard and a friendly German Shepherd bounded up to her. She said, "There's a good boy!" and kept running.

"Uh. . . . Thanks, I think," Thunder said.

She leaped onto a low shed, over the wall, and into next-door's garden.

"You have to stop the Boxer, Abby. You're a lot faster than they are on foot. Get to the— Oh *man*! That burning guy is behind me. He's not chasing me, but he's pointing this way— letting the others know where I am! Who *is* he?"

"I don't know," Abby said. "Dioxin, maybe. Doesn't he burn?" *Lance would know,* she thought. *He knows them all.* "Thunder, if we don't make it . . ."

"If we don't make it, then we're going to take down as many of these guys as we can, all right?"

"That's exactly what I was going to say. Good luck."

"You too."

A few minutes later, Abby splashed across a shallow ornamental pond, crashed through a hedge, and found herself back on the road. She slowed to a stop. She was standing at a crossroads, and there was no sign of the armored car. *Yes! Lost them! OK. . . . Town's back that way, which means—*

She smiled. Off to the left, on the far side of a wide field, there was a point of light through the trees. *The prison. Roz said it would have its own generators.*

Abby left a long furrow in the high grass as she crossed the field, then she was standing in front of Oak Grove Prison.

Beyond a high razor-wire fence, its featureless stone walls were yellow-orange from lights placed just beneath the roof. The building was bigger than she'd expected: At least three hundred yards long, and maybe five stories high—though she couldn't be sure, as there were no windows by which to judge.

Her sword cut a vertical slash in the fence, and she climbed through, expecting alarms to break out at any moment. She darted up to the wall, pressed her back flat against it, started shuffling sideways. She'd seen characters do this in prison-break movies, but she wasn't entirely sure whether it would make any difference.

There didn't seem to be any guards. *How many of them have been hit by the plague?*

She reached a corner and, keeping her back to the wall, Abby cautiously peered around it. *If Pyrokine is the only one who's not an adult, then they could all be—Aw no!*

Abby stepped out. The side wall of the prison had been split open from the ground to the roof. The courtyard was almost hidden under tons of dust, bricks, and concrete debris. Nearby, protruding from the rubble, was a man's boot.

She stared at it for almost a minute, afraid to check whether there was a leg attached. If there was, then she was only two yards from a dead man.

She looked away. *Whoever he is, I can't help him now.*

Climbing cautiously over the rubble, Abby made her way inside the prison building, into a large open room lined on two sides with barred cells. The only sound was a faint drip of water from somewhere to her right. Overhead, neon lights blinked on and off in an irregular pattern, allowing Abby to half-see the carnage within.

The floor was strewn with bodies, most of them wearing dark orange jumpsuits.

The one nearest Abby—a gray-bearded man who looked to be in his fifties—twitched and moaned loudly. The noise set off a chorus of groans and weak cries from some of the others. The man's eyes flickered open, turned to Abby. "Sick . . . Help me . . ."

She moved a little closer—but kept herself out of his reach. His eyes, mouth, and nose were coated with drying mucus and saliva. Beneath a tear-streaked layer of brick dust his skin was a yellowish-gray, shot through with red and blue veins.

"Who did this?" Abby whispered.

The man groaned again, and his eyes closed. "Men . . . Woman in red. Strong . . . Help me, please."

"There's nothing I can do right now," Abby said. "But help *is* on the way," she lied. "It won't be long."

She stood up. *The woman in red. Slaughter.* She moved farther into the building, carefully stepping over and around the fallen prisoners and guards. A few of them made weak attempts to reach out to her.

In one of the cells Abby saw a man she knew for certain was dead. He was lying on the floor, a ragged hole in his throat big enough to fit a fist. His silver armor marked him as one of The Helotry's men. *They weren't tracking us*, Abby thought. *They'd already been here and were on the way back. So why did they come here? What was here that could be of any use to them?*

She ascended a metal staircase to the next level. Many of the cells' doors were open, but they all appeared to be empty. *They must have come for someone in particular. But the plague . . . No, they would have found a way to immunize him against it. Unless he was* already *immune.*

She stopped. *No . . .*

"Hey!" she shouted. "Can anyone hear me? Anyone not sick?"

There was no response.

Abby knew now who Slaughter had come to find. An unbelievably powerful superhuman. Someone who didn't need to be immunized against the plague because it wouldn't affect him.

And she'd already seen him back in the town. The burning man. Pyrokine.

A key turned in the lock, then the door creaked open.

Tied arm and leg to a chair, Lance heard heavy footsteps approach, then the canvas bag was removed from his head. He felt a rough hand grab his chin while another pulled the strip of duct tape from his mouth. He gasped, taking in deep lungfuls of warm, fetid air. "Who's there?"

A voice said, "He's not faking the blindness, then?"

There was a rustle of cloth, and a second voice said, "Didn't even flinch. He's not faking it."

"Look, what do you want from me?" Lance said. "I honestly don't know what's going on here or who you think I am!"

There was a slight sharp hiss from one of the men. "Not too convincing, kid. We already know you're not Jason Myers, so give it a rest."

"What have you done with Dylan?"

"The little girl? Gave her a cheese sandwich and a glass of milk. Brought her home."

"I wouldn't say no to a cheese sandwich and a glass of milk myself," Lance said. "I'm starving."

"Maybe if you tell us the truth. How about it, kid? Ready to spill the beans?"

"No beans for me, thanks—they give me gas. Look, who *are* you people?"

Someone slapped him hard across the face, and he almost toppled to the side.

"This is how it works," one of the voices said. "We ask. You answer. Comprende? Now. Tell us everything. From the car crash in Fairview onward. You found Marcus's briefcase. You opened it. You found the address of the warehouse. Marcus was dumb enough to write down the alarm code, so you went in, you took the jetpack. Am I missing anything?"

"Not so far," Lance said. "Carry on."

Another slap, much harder than the last. Lance tasted blood in his mouth.

"He doesn't know anything else, Mr. Remington," the first voice said. "Just finish him."

"I know all about the Fifth King," Lance said.

There was a pause, and Lance pictured the two men exchanging a look.

"That's right," Lance said. "One of your guys from the power plant talked. Told the FBI everything. Names, dates, places . . ." Then he forced a smile. "They know all about Windfield, and they know about the virus. They're already working on a vaccine."

"Well, good luck to them," one of the men said. "A vaccine is useful only for people who aren't already infected, and by now *everyone* is. The whole planet."

"Why?"

A third slap. Lance's face stung from the pain. He shook his head to try and clear it. "I forgot. I'm not supposed to ask questions."

"Who else knows about the Fifth King?"

Lance did his best to shrug. "Everyone, I think." His arms had been secured behind his back with cable ties. Ropes wouldn't have been much of a problem—Lance was sure he knew enough about knots to get out of any rope, but cable ties were made from plastic, almost unbreakable, and couldn't easily be opened once they were fastened—they had to be cut. It didn't help that he still couldn't see. For all he knew, there was someone standing silently behind him.

"The other kids with you . . . We know all about Roz Dalton. Who are the other two?"

Lance hesitated. "Before I tell you, I want permission to ask a question."

"Go ahead."

"Do you know anything about me?"

"Your full name is Lancelot Aaron McKendrick, fourteen years old. Father is Albert McKendrick, mother is Karina. You have an older brother called Cody." The man called Remington rattled off a list of facts and figures about Lance and his family.

"Right, but that's not the *real* me," Lance said. "In the past two years I've pulled dozens of scams and earned over five thousand bucks from people who still don't know they've been conned. I can get into and out of almost any building. I could list off a hundred standard alarm bypass codes if you were interested. I know how to disappear on an empty street. I can break into and hot-wire any make of car in under a minute. I know how to rip off cash ATMs so that the bank doesn't find out about it for weeks. So as for Roz and the others . . . I'm with them, but I'm not *with* them, if you know what I mean. I'm with them because I have nowhere else to go."

The man farthest away—Lance pictured him standing in front of the door—said, "This is the part where you pretend you're really on our side so that we'll cut you loose."

"What good would that do me? I'm blind."

"So it appears. But you weren't blind earlier. It's probably temporary."

Lance heard soft voices and shuffling feet from somewhere beyond the door, then an old woman's voice said, "Leave him, Mr. Remington. He is of little use to us now, except as bait to trap his friends."

That means they haven't been caught yet! "Who are you?" he asked. Taking a chance, he added, "Oh God. You're *her*, aren't you? The one your men were talking about."

The woman made a "Hmm?" noise.

"Yeah, they said . . . Well, I don't want to tell you what they said. I'm not allowed to use that sort of language. But you should probably be nicer to them. I mean, I know they're only the hired help but they have feelings too."

The woman laughed, a long, wheezing throaty noise that grated through Lance's nerves. "He has spirit," she said. "The Fifth King will find him amusing."

A thought struck Lance. "So you're bringing back the Fifth King. . . . How do you know he *wants* to be brought back?" There was no reply, so Lance continued. "He won't know anything about this world. Things like cars and airplanes and television will seem like witchcraft to him. He might have been a great warrior back in his time but he won't know one

213

end of a gun from the other. He won't be able to speak English either. Did you think of that? And even if he could, what are you going to say to him? 'Hi there, Fifth King. We brought you back. Look, we've killed more than half the people in the world just for you. Isn't that cool? Now you can rule over a desolate ruin of a planet.' Yeah, he's going to be really happy to get here."

One of the men started to speak, but Lance interrupted him. "And there's more. . . . What about the people he knew back then? How are you going to explain to him that they're all long dead and he'll never be able to see them again?"

The old woman finally spoke directly to Lance: "Young man, we have been planning this day for more than four thousand years. I think that by now we'll have thought of everything."

"Yeah, but suppose he doesn't *want* The Helotry following him around and worshiping him? You're totally screwed then. Or what if the process of bringing him back from the dead drives him insane? Then what'll you do?"

She shuffled closer. "He was the first superhuman. The father of us all. The greatest warrior this world has ever known."

"Can't have been *that* great if he got himself killed." Lance prepared himself for another slap but it didn't come.

Instead, the woman said, "You talk a lot, boy, but you say very little. And I suspect you *know* even less. I have met people like you before, many times. You think you can talk your way out of any situation, that you are smarter than everyone else. You are not. You are a blind fourteen-year-old boy with no friends and no hope of rescue."

214

"So what are you going to do next? Set your flying monkeys on me?"

One of the men laughed and hurriedly turned it into a cough.

"You think that if you enrage me I will order your death. Dead, you will not be able to betray your friends. A noble thought, perhaps, but it will not happen."

"Why not? You've already sentenced billions of people to death. You do realize that if there's a heaven you're not going to be allowed in, don't you? There'll be a sign on the gate: Mad evil old ladies who stink of poo need not apply."

She sighed. "A tiresome child, but perhaps he knows more than we realized. Feed him, Mr. Remington. Give him water. He will need his strength if he is to survive the interrogation long enough to give us the information we need. Then start with his fingers. For every answer that does not satisfy you, remove one knuckle at a time." She paused, then with a hint of amusement in her voice she added, "If *that* does not work, release the flying monkeys."

CHAPTER 24

Roz didn't know how long she had been fighting Slaughter. It felt like forever, but it might have been only a few minutes.

She was exhausted. Her head throbbed from the exertion of using her telekinesis so much. Her back and legs twinged with pain every time she moved, and inside her gloves she was sure that her hands were bloodied and a bruised.

Despite the situation, she was still unsettled by the dream she'd had when, half-unconscious from the ferocity of Slaughter's attack in Oak Grove, all she could think about was a tremendous sense of loss. Or rather the *memory* of a sense of loss.

But the feeling kept slipping away whenever she thought she was getting close to it. *I can't let myself think about that now. Whatever it is, it'll come back to me. Right now there are more important things to worry about.*

No matter what she did, Slaughter kept coming. She was

faster and much stronger than Roz, but Roz's telekinetic shield had so far been able to deflect most of the woman's kicks and punches. *She hasn't killed me yet. That's got to be driving her crazy.*

Roz knew that she wasn't facing Slaughter at her best: The woman's face was normally starkly beautiful—though cold and unsmiling—but now she looked even more exhausted than Roz felt. Her eyes were bloodshot, rimmed with dark patches, the lids heavy.

She looks like she's been going for days without a break, Roz thought. *Or maybe not even that long. . . . We all get wiped out if we use our powers too much, and it could be that Slaughter burns through her energy a lot quicker than the rest of us.*

That made sense. In top condition Slaughter was almost unstoppable. She blazed into action and any fight was usually over in seconds. Roz remembered one of her brother's many lessons: "No one has ever fought Slaughter for more than five minutes at most. She *has* been beaten, but it's always taken at least three of us. If you ever encounter her, run away. That's the only sensible course of action. She seems to act without thought, always operating on pure adrenaline and fury—so she can be distracted."

Throughout the battle with Roz, Slaughter had been using the same tactic again and again: strike hard, retreat, build up speed, strike again.

She's actually helping me, Roz thought. *Every time she goes away I get a few minutes to hide and recover.*

Now, Roz was in an old train station, hiding among the wooden rafters above the platforms. A few moments ago she'd spotted Slaughter soaring through the air, searching for her. *OK, enough rest. Have to get back out there.*

It was a simple plan, and one that Roz knew would freak out her brother if he ever found out about it: Roz could have remained hidden, but kept emerging to confront Slaughter.

When she was nine years old, when her parents were still alive and the family lived in a sprawling suburban neighborhood, one of the neighbors had a small nasty terrier that attacked the kids on the street every chance it could get. One day Roz decided she'd had enough: She went out on her bike and, as always, the dog chased after her, yapping and barking.

Usually Roz would just pedal faster until the dog grew tired and gave up, but on this occasion she kept her speed down, allowed the dog to get within biting distance of the bike's back tire, then sped up. Every time it looked as though he was about to quit, she'd slow down again. After twenty minutes of this the exhausted dog finally looked around and realized he had no idea where he was or how to get home.

The terrier didn't find his way home for three days, and after that his owners never let him out on his own again. For a while Roz was treated as a hero by the other kids.

Right now, she wasn't entirely confident of the same trick working on Slaughter, but it was all she could think of. She knew that if she stayed hidden, Slaughter would give up and go after the others.

She climbed down from the rafters and quietly made her way along the eastbound platform. At the end she dropped down onto the tracks and realized that the sky to the east was no longer a solid black—dawn was breaking. *That's not good. . . .*

A loud squawk and fluttering of wings from behind Roz: She turned to see a flock of pigeons take to the air, startled by Slaughter as she skimmed over the trees.

Roz crouched on the tracks, prepared herself for the assault. Slaughter would rush at her, Roz would form a telekinetic shield, Slaughter would collide with it, and the two of them would bounce apart.

But this time the growing light would make going into hiding again more difficult.

The solution hit Roz like a tidal wave: *She can only chase me if she can* see *me!*

She reached out with her telekinesis and forced Slaughter's eyelids shut. The woman panicked, lost control. She plowed into the tracks beside Roz, the impact tearing up the sleepers and showering the area with fragments of bedrock.

Lying on her back sprawled across the tracks and half-covered in debris, Slaughter screamed, "What have you done to me?"

"I've severed your optic nerves," Roz said. "Now give up or I'll do the same thing to your spinal cord."

Slaughter's gloved hands probed her face. "Liar.... You've closed my eyes!"

Roz had never imagined that superhuman strength would extend to the muscles in someone's eyelids, but now Slaughter was forcing them open and it was taking all of Roz's telekinetic strength to keep them closed.

But her telekinesis could control only one thing at a time. *There has to be a way I can* . . . Roz smiled. *I've got hands, don't I?*

She scooped up a pile of pebbles and dirt from the side of

the track, walked over to Slaughter, and allowed the pile to spill into the woman's open mouth. She darted back as Slaughter coughed and spat, rolled onto her hands and knees.

"I'll kill you for that!"

"Yeah, yeah. . . ." Roz lobbed a fist-sized stone that bounced off Slaughter's head. "Good shot!"

"You think a rock can hurt me? I've already taken a bullet to the head today!"

"I know. That was funny."

The woman rose into the air. "How far can your telekinesis extend? All the way into the upper atmosphere?" Her speed increased. "I'll kill you later."

Roz watched as Slaughter became a dot against the early morning sky.

She collapsed onto the ground and realized that she was trembling. *I won. For now.*

Abby de Luyando stood in the prison officer's staff room staring up at the TV set bolted to the wall. She had the remote control in her hand and flicked through channel after channel.

Most of the channels showed only static, but some displayed a message: "We are experiencing technical difficulties—please stand by."

How are we supposed to find out how far the plague has spread? Millions of people could have died already and we'd never know!

She wanted to go back out to the prisoners, but knew that it was pointless. The majority of them were unconscious and the rest were too delirious to communicate with her. At first she'd considered blocking up the shattered wall with some sort of barrier, but quickly realized that there was no point: The prisoners weren't in any condition to escape, and there were few people on the outside who were capable of breaking in.

Instead she'd spent an hour retrieving gray blankets and thin pillows from the cells and making the prisoners and guards a little more comfortable. She couldn't think of anything else to do—the phones were down and it was unlikely that any of the emergency services would answer.

Abby turned off the TV set, righted a fallen chair, and sat down. For the first time since she'd crept out of the apartment, she allowed herself to think about what might be happening at home.

She knew that her mother would be sick by now. Maybe her sister too. Vienna was just about old enough to be affected by the plague. Her brothers were too young to be able to cope on their own, and they certainly weren't capable of looking after their mom and older sister.

She thought of the sick woman in the car on the side of the road, of Lance and Thunder and Roz. *They could all be dead by now. And I don't even know Thunder's real name.*

They'd pinned everything on Lance's idea of recruiting Pyrokine. It had been a risk, but one that had seemed worth taking. *We were idiots—he was in prison! How could we not have expected him to side with the bad guys?*

Abby left the staff room and returned to the main part of the building. She leaned over the rail and looked down at the ground floor—none of the guards or prisoners had moved.

One of the prisoners had looked familiar as she was tending to him, and now she remembered who he was: the Scarlet Slayer, arrested a year earlier by Titan. On the TV news, the Slayer had looked menacing. He was tall, gaunt, almost skeleton-thin, with a shaved head and a long beard. He'd dressed like a cross between a pirate and a samurai warrior. His powers were basic; flight, enhanced strength, and speed, and he'd never seemed to be particularly smart.

Abby was about to move away when it occurred to her that a prisoner who could fly wouldn't be allowed out of his cell without some sort of restraint, but she hadn't seen anything like that on the Slayer.

She looked around. The cells appeared to be no different from those in any prison she'd seen on TV. Walls on three sides, barred door on the other. Nothing that would be strong enough to stop someone like Dioxin, whose acid-dripping skin could easily burn through steel bars.

So what do they do? Use a device or injection to inhibit their powers? No, I would have heard about something like that.

Unless the really dangerous ones are held someplace else. This place couldn't *keep Dioxin prisoner.* She made her way back to the staircase. *But Pyrokine was here. . . . At least, he was in this prison, but maybe not in this part of it.*

On the ground floor at the far side of the building she found a corridor sealed by a set of locked doors. The lock snapped with one blow from her sword, and as she was pushing the doors open she thought she heard a voice cry out.

"Hello?" Abby shouted. "Anyone there?"

A moment later a deep, rumbling voice called back, "Yes! Yes! In here! Thank God, I thought I was going to starve to death in this place!"

"Where are you?"

"Third room on the left. There's a steel door!"

Abby found the circular door and stopped. It was easily seven feet in diameter and looked like the door to a bank vault. A massive wheel was connected by heavy levers to eight bolts that sealed around the edges—the bolts were almost as thick as her arm—but there didn't appear to be a lock.

"Hello?" the voice called. "You still there?"

"Um . . . Listen. . . . Do you know what's going on?"

"A plague, right? Pretty much everyone who's over the age of twenty is infected. It was on the radio before it went off the air. Is that what's happened?"

"Yeah," Abby called back. "Look, it was done deliberately. There's an organization called The Helotry who've done this for, well, it's too complicated to get into it now. But I need to stop them, and I can't do it on my own. So I need two things from you before I let you out. First, I don't care what you're in here for, but if you're a superhuman then I need your help. The Helotry's plague is going to kill millions of people if we can't stop them. So you have to swear that you're going to help me."

"I swear!"

"OK. And the second thing . . . You're definitely a superhuman?"

"No doubt about that."

Abby turned the wheel counterclockwise, three full revolutions, and the heavy bolts drew back with a grating squeal.

She pulled the door open, and looked inside. Four mattresses were lying side by side on the floor, and getting up from them was the largest person Abby had ever seen. He was at least thirteen feet tall, heavily muscled, and completely hairless. His eyes were colorless—lacking even a pupil—and his skin was a deep blue.

She swallowed hard and stepped back into the corridor. "Remember the deal?"

The giant awkwardly squeezed himself through the round doorway. "I remember," he growled. "You know who I am?"

"Of course I do. You're Brawn."

"That's what they call me in the papers. Who are you?"

Abby started heading back up the corridor. "Um . . . Well, I don't have a superhero name yet. I haven't thought of one."

The ceiling was too low for Brawn to walk upright—he crawled on his hands and knees after her. "You should pick something from Roman or Greek mythology. I was going to call myself Hercules but . . ." He faltered. "Things didn't turn out the way I thought they would."

Abby couldn't help glancing back at him, half expecting him to grab hold of her and tear her apart. "Are you able to . . . change back?"

The giant shook his head. "Nah. Stuck like this forever, probably."

Abby pushed open the doors at the end of the corridor. "Better watch your step here."

Brawn squeezed through the opening, and was finally able

to stand upright. He looked around. "Oh man . . . I know some of these guys! Are they all dead?"

"No, but the plague hit them pretty bad." Abby stepped back and looked up at Brawn. He was naked except for a pair of crude orange trunks that looked like they'd been handmade from one of the prison jumpsuits. On TV he'd always looked ferocious, a barely human monster fired by rage and hatred, but now she could see compassion and concern on his face.

But there was still an air about him that set her nerves on edge. A small part of her mind told her that something so huge couldn't be human, that he was dangerous and she should run.

Brawn crouched down next to one of the guards and gently placed his massive hand on the man's chest. "Mr. Chapman . . ." To Abby, he said, "He's the only one who didn't treat me like an animal. God, I hope he pulls through. Mr. Chapman doesn't have a sense of smell, see. Some accident when he was a kid. So he's not afraid of me."

Abby didn't know how to respond to that.

Brawn sighed. "Apparently sometimes I give off a scent that triggers people's fear reflex. You can't detect it consciously, but it's there. I mean, *you've* been keeping your distance, right?" He stood up again, and shook his head. "The people who did this . . . Who are they?"

"A group called The Helotry. Slaughter is with them—"

"Aw, not *her*! I *hate* that woman!"

"And a guy we think is Pyrokine."

"Never heard of him. So who's this *we*?"

"Me, Max Dalton's sister Roz, a guy called Thunder who can control sound waves, and a guy called Lance. He's not a superhuman, though. And as far as we can tell, all the other superhumans are infected. Which reminds me . . . Why aren't *you* infected?"

Brawn looked down at her, spread his arms. "I'm tall for my age." He shrugged. "I'm only sixteen."

CHAPTER 25

Lance only realized he'd been left alone in the dark when the overhead lights came on, and he winced at the sudden brightness. He blinked rapidly, shook his head. His vision was definitely recovering. The shifting red and green afterimage was still there, but through it he could now see the room in which he was being held prisoner.

He'd imagined it was a dungeon of some kind, but instead it looked like a room in an ordinary apartment. In front of him was a closed wooden door and there were blind-covered windows to his left, but otherwise the room was bare.

The door opened, and one of the guards entered.

"Who's there?" Lance called. The longer they believed he was still blind, the greater his chance of escaping.

"Shut up," the man said. Lance recognized his voice as the one belonging to the man called Remington. The man moved to the left, but Lance kept his eyes focused straight ahead.

"Look, I'll tell you everything I know. But the old woman was right—I don't know much."

"Bring him in," the guard called out.

Lance heard footsteps and scuffling out in the hallway, and it took all his willpower not to react to what he saw: Thunder was dragged into the room, facedown, by two of the guards. They dropped him just inside the door.

Lance jumped at the sound. "What was that?" *Oh man, please don't let him be dead!*

Thunder's mask was gone, his costume—the black and green wet suit that had seemed so funny earlier—was ripped and covered in scorch marks. His hands were tied behind his back—his gloves had been removed, revealing blood-covered, bruised knuckles. His legs were tied at the ankles.

"What's going on?" Lance said. He sniffed the air. "Smells like something's burning."

One of the guards said, "This one *still* hasn't shut up?"

"He will soon enough." Remington approached Lance. "Kid, we've got your friend here. Thunder. Two down, two to go. What do you think about that?"

"No, *six* to go," Lance said, staring just to the left of Remington's face. "What, you thought there were only four of us? God, you people are such amateurs. There's eight of us. The other four are . . . Well, I'm not telling. But you guys really ought to get yourself some padded pants because pretty soon now the others are going to be kicking your butts all the way from here to San Jose."

On the edge of his vision Lance saw the blow coming and forced himself to keep staring straight ahead. Remington's fist slammed into his jaw, sent him sprawling—chair and all—onto the floor.

Lance groaned. He tasted blood again, and was sure that some of his teeth had been loosened. He coughed. "Proud of yourself, are you? Hitting a blind kid tied to a chair . . . What do you think your mother would say if she could see you now? When she phones you and asks how your day was at work, what are you going to tell her? Of course, that's assuming that your mom hasn't been infected by the plague that you morons created."

The man strode over to him, grabbed his arm, and hauled him upright. He took hold of Lance's chin and pressed his face close. "*Shut up, you snotty little punk!* I have had it up to *here* with your mouth! One more word and I swear to God I'll choke the life out of you!"

The other two guards grabbed his arms and pulled him back. "You're letting him get to you," one said. "That's exactly what he wants—to get us off guard." They ushered him toward the door and out into the hallway.

As they were pulling the door closed, Lance cheerfully shouted, "Bye! Tell your mom I said hello!"

Remington hesitated for a second, then slammed the door.

Then Thunder's weak voice said, "Lance, you *really* know how to get under someone's skin, don't you?"

"Aren't you dead yet?"

"Getting there." Thunder awkwardly rolled onto his side. "Man, that guy Pyrokine is an absolute maniac. The whole time he fought me he didn't say a word. Just kept coming. First he melted the ground ahead of the motorbike, then he zapped the tires. I nearly broke my neck coming off it. I hurt him, though. Hit him with a high-pitched squeal that sent him running for a few minutes. Then he came back and started pounding me. I got in a couple of good punches but they didn't slow him down." He stared up at Lance. "You were pretending to be blind?"

"Wasn't pretending. When they attacked the truck and melted off the doors the glare was . . ." Lance shook his head. "I was afraid it might be permanent. My eyesight's only just starting to come back."

"I guess that explains why you haven't escaped yet."

"Yeah. That, and the fact that I'm tied to a chair. Plus I'm not a superhuman, unlike some people. So . . . is this a rescue or what? 'Cos if it is, I can't quite see how it's going to work."

"Wish I could say it *was* a rescue. I thought you were still back in Oak Grove."

"What about Abby and Roz?"

Thunder did his best to shrug.

"Great. Why'd it have to be you? Why couldn't they have captured someone with *useful* powers?" He sat up straighter. "Hey, why don't you just blanket this whole building with your sound-damping trick? If they can't speak to each other they'll all freak out and stuff."

"And then they'll come in here and put a bullet in my brain. Now shut up a minute. I'm trying to listen in on them."

"Cool. Fire the sound my way so I can listen too."

Instantly it seemed to Lance that the room was filled with invisible people, their voices all chattering at once, the sounds overlapping, fading in and out.

He heard the old woman ask, "Mr. Remington . . . Everything is ready?"

A man's voice replied: "Almost, ma'am. The Pyrokine will reach the power plant within the hour."

"Good, good. . . . How much does he know?"

"Only that his powers are needed to trigger the temporal shift."

"Interesting," Lance said. "Wonder what *that's* about."

The woman's voice again. "Ensure that Slaughter is with them, understood?"

"Understood. She's currently resting from her battle with the telekinetic. The girl is proving to be a lot more resourceful than we'd anticipated."

"Indeed," the woman said. "An error on my part, I think. I should have taken more consideration of her pedigree. The girl with the sword?"

"Gone to ground," Remington said. "I doubt we'll be seeing her again."

"Then you are a fool, Mr. Remington." A long pause. "The children were not looking for our people in Oak Grove. They could not have known about our plans for the prison—Marcus was not privy to that information. It is possible—likely—that one of the children was smart enough to realize that the Pyrokine was too young to be affected by the plague. Yes . . . They were looking for him, to recruit him. An idea that was both clever and foolish at the same time—a trait that only the young truly possess. They encountered the Pyrokine in Oak Grove, but it is possible they did not know who he was. . . . I believe you will find the girl with the sword in the vicinity of the prison. Send a team, Mr. Remington. Immediately."

Remington began yelling, "Team Seven, this is Remington! Get to the prison right now! If you find the girl—if you find *anyone* still standing—terminate them on the spot!"

A radio voice replied, "Acknowledged. We're a couple of minutes away—will report back as soon as we have her."

Lance and Thunder stared at each other for a moment, then both began to struggle frantically against their bonds.

Then the old woman said, "No . . . No, that would not be wise. Send *four* teams, Mr. Remington. And have another four on standby."

Roz found out where she was from the freestanding maps on the train station's platform—she was in Greenwood, almost ninety miles away from Oak Grove.

She made her way down through the station, past the ticket counters, and stopped in front of the locked gates that spread across the entrance. *Oh great. Got to go all the way back up again and find another way out.*

She was about to turn away when she decided to test out an old idea. A few months earlier the superhero Impervia had visited the Daltons' home—Roz suspected that Impervia and Max had some sort of secret relationship going on, but had never been able to prove it—and the woman had chatted with Roz about her budding powers.

"Telekinesis?" Impervia had said as they sat in the sprawling lounge sipping iced tea while Max helped their younger brother Josh build monsters out of Lego bricks. "That could be useful, Rosalyn. Very useful."

"Yeah, but so far I can only lift things that I'd be able to lift with my arms."

"Then if there's a connection between your physical strength and your mental strength you'd better start hitting the gym. A few hours a day on the weights would do you a world of good. But of course telekinesis isn't just useful for moving *big* things. Small things could be just as important." She nodded over toward the piano. "You could play that from across the room."

"If I could play," Roz said. "And if I could move more than one thing at a time. And if I could actually *see* the keys. I can't move what I can't see."

"Why not?"

"Because . . . Well, I just can't."

"If you know where something is, but can't actually see it, can you move it?"

Roz shrugged. "I haven't tried."

Impervia took the TV's remote control out of the hands of the boy sitting next to Roz, and placed it on the coffee table. "Try it now. Close your eyes, picture the remote in your head, and move it."

Roz gave it a go, but it didn't work. The remote control remained where it was.

But now, facing the gates, Roz thought she knew what to do. When she grabbed or touched something with her telekinesis she could feel a sort of feedback, resistance from the object due to its mass or inertia.

She probed the gate's lock. She could sense the tumblers and pins inside, and was sure she felt one of them move—but it wasn't much use. Without knowing exactly what the inside of the lock looked like, she didn't know what to do next. After a minute of trying, Roz gave up and simply used her telekinesis to remove the pins from the gate's hinges instead.

Back out on the street, it was now close to full daylight. The small town was still, silent. It looked as though it was deserted, but she knew that there were sick—dying—people behind almost every window. Scraps of litter blew lazily along the gutters and twenty yards away, a shaggy black-and-white mongrel was sniffing around an overflowing garbage can.

The dog raised its head, saw Roz, and trotted over, its tongue lolling and tail wagging. It sat down in front of her and slightly lifted its paw. She scratched its head between the ears. "Good boy. Go home. Home, boy!"

It tilted its head to the side as it stared at her with a look of expectancy in its brown eyes.

"I don't have any food for you, boy. Now go on. Go home!" She pointed back down the street.

The dog looked at her finger for a moment, then back to her face.

"Listen, dog. Go away, OK? Go off into the fields and find some rabbits to eat. Um . . . Not baby ones, though. Or cute ones. Only eat the *evil* bunnies."

It wagged its tail and raised its paw again.

"Not getting the message, are you?" Roz crouched down next to it and stroked its back. "There's going to be a lot more hungry doggies like you in the next few days if they can't find a cure for this plague."

For the first time, the enormity of the situation struck her. *If The Helotry's plague is fatal then . . . That's pretty much the end of the world as we know it. There's no way back from that. Max will die. God, he could be dead already!*

She stood up and looked around. "All right. *That's* what we need." At the far end of the street was the familiar white and blue of a police car. With the dog trotting after her, Roz ran toward it. *Should be able to drive this most of the way to the power plant, as long as the roads aren't blocked.*

She slowed as she reached the car. Sitting in the driver's seat, slumped over the wheel, was a uniformed officer.

Roz opened the door, put her hand on the man's shoulder and pulled him back. He was alive, but only barely. He was breathing through his mouth, a ragged and weak uneven gasp. A thick plug of mucus had formed and solidified around his nose. *God, he's going to suffocate!*

Even though the officer wasn't aware of her and there was no one else around to see, Roz tried not to make a face as she reached out with her telekinesis and pried the crust of mucus away from his nose. Almost instantly, his breathing eased and he groaned softly. His eyes began to flicker, trying to open—but they were gummed shut.

"Take it easy," Roz said. "Just stay calm. . . ." She placed her gloved palms on either side of his face and used her thumbs to gently wipe away the sticky substance that was gumming his eyes shut.

The officer's eyes darted around wildly for a moment, before settling on Roz. "Who . . . ?"

"My name is Roz Dalton. Max Dalton's sister. . . . Look, I need to borrow your car."

He shook his head. "No gas."

"All right," Roz said. "Your radio, then." She reached in past him and grabbed hold of the radio handset, its coiled cable stretching out past the officer.

There was a brief click from the speaker, then Roz pressed the button on the handset. "Can anyone hear me? Is anyone listening?"

The radio hissed static. *Come on, come on.* . . . *The police bands are always monitored.* She tried again. "Hello? If there's anyone listening please respond!"

Still nothing. She switched the frequency dial from channel 1 to channel 2. "Hello? Is anyone listening?"

For a moment there was only static, then a woman's voice said, "I hear you! Who are you? *Where* are you?"

"My name is Roz Dalton. I'm trying to get in touch with someone in the Centers for Disease Control in Atlanta. Who am I speaking to?"

"Oh thank God, thank God! Listen, this is Doctor Janine Gertler at CDC. We're in a sealed environment here and we've been working all night on decoding the virus. We're pretty much one hundred percent sure that it's Orthomyxoviridae Class H_3N_2 modified by an artificially induced antigenic shift!"

"Uh, right," Roz said. "You sound excited to have discovered that, but I've no idea what it means."

"What? Jeez, where the heck did *you* study microbiology?"

"Nowhere, yet. I'm fifteen."

"*What?*"

Roz raised her eyes and shook her head. "Doctor, can't you just treat the infection with antibiotics?"

"Listen, kid . . . The difference between a bacteria and a virus is like the difference between . . . a comatose elephant and a hyperactive rat. It's much harder to stop a rat from getting into your apartment. It's also a lot easier to *find* an elephant. Understand?"

"Can I speak to someone who doesn't have an attitude problem?"

There was a sigh. "OK. Listen carefully. A bacterium is pretty much self-sufficient, but a virus needs a living host in order to survive and multiply. *Now* do you get it? A virus is really just a bunch of genetic instructions—it changes whatever it infects. To get rid of a bacterial infection it's often simply a matter of flushing the bacteria out of the system—that's where antibiotics come in. But to beat a virus you need to develop a set of counter-instructions for the host's body to adopt."

"All right, I get it. So what are you telling me? What's the prognosis?"

"The prognosis is that it takes a lot longer to develop a cure for a virus. And since viruses change the host, they also change themselves in the process: Viruses can and often do mutate from one form into another. Which means that by the time we develop a cure for The Helotry's virus, it could already have changed into something that's *immune* to the cure. Most viruses mutate at random—but we've been analyzing this one's RNA and, well . . . a whole section of the genetic structure is designed to only modify itself. It's continually changing, and at a steady rate. Near as we can tell, it's a counter."

"I don't like the sound of that."

"Nor should you. Whoever constructed this thing is an absolute genius. Every sample we've examined has the counter and they're within seconds of each other. It's constantly increasing. We can't tell what number it's aiming for, or what'll happen when it reaches it, but they didn't build it in for no reason. *Something* is going to happen. But it's likely that people will start to die before then. The virus primarily infects the host's respiratory system, causes the body's immunities to go into overdrive. Their lungs clog up with fluid and mucus. That makes breathing difficult, which puts a huge strain on the heart and brain. When the level of oxygen in the blood drops below—"

"I don't need to know all that. How much time do we have?"

"Some of the infected people are already close to death. The strongest might last a couple of days. That's the other odd thing. . . . The plague broke out all over the world at pretty much the same time. This suggests it wasn't just passed from one human host to another—that would take weeks or months. So The Helotry must have had some other method to disseminate it. You and your friends need to find out what that method is. We might be able to use the same trick to spread the cure."

"OK. But . . . We got separated. I don't even know where the others are."

"Where are you? I'll send a copter. We have a couple of pilots here who haven't been infected."

"Don't. Slaughter is probably still looking for me. If she sees a helicopter approaching she'll destroy it. I'll get a car."

"Do you know where The Helotry are?"

"No, but I think I know where they're *going* to be."

CHAPTER 26

"Stand back," Abby said to Brawn as they approached the high wire fence. "I'll cut a hole big enough for you."

He looked at her. "Why?" Before she could stop him, the giant grabbed hold of the fence, ripped out a four-yard-wide section, and tossed it over his shoulder.

"Oh great!" Abby said. "My way, the prison would at least have *looked* secure."

"You mean, aside from that great big hole in the wall back there?"

He stepped through the remains of the fence, and Abby followed him. "Ah, free at last!" He grinned at her. "Well, nice meeting you. I'm outta here."

"We had a deal!"

"So we did. Duh! Supervillain, remember? Good luck saving the world."

He took off, moving with surprising speed for someone so

huge. He bounded over the fields and in seconds had disappeared into the woods. Abby was tempted to chase after him, but she knew that there was no way she could force him to work with her. *Now what do I do?*

Keeping to the trees that lined the road, she started back toward the town. *Maybe Thunder or Roz is still around.* On a whim, she said, "Thunder? Can you hear me? Hello? Abby calling Thunder? Are you there?"

There was no response, and she felt like even more of an idiot. *Great. Not only did I break a dangerous supervillain out of prison, now I'm talking to myself. Some hero I turned out to be.*

She stopped, ducked down behind a tree. From somewhere ahead came the rumble of approaching engines. Seconds later a small convoy of armored vehicles roared past—Boxers, the same make as the one that had chased her out of the town.

OK, they haven't seen me. I can—

The last Boxer skidded to a stop. Its steel doors rolled open and five of the silver-armored men jumped out. One of them shouted, "Those trees!"

Farther along the road, the other Boxers were already turning back.

Abby turned and ran, still keeping to the trees. She ducked under a low branch, leaped over a fallen trunk, and was debating whether it would be faster to move out into the field when she heard gunfire behind her.

I can lose them in the town. I did it last night and—

Ahead, four silver-clad men were approaching on foot.

Abby darted to the right, across the road, and into the field on the opposite side.

More men.

Then a low roar came from overhead, and she looked up to see a sleek black helicopter bearing down on her.

Back into the trees—but they didn't provide much cover. The one advantage she had over the soldiers was her speed, but the helicopter took care of that.

There's no way I can hide from them. What do I do?

She knew there were only two options: surrender or fight.

Then a bullet clipped the left shoulder of her jacket, and Abby knew that surrender was no longer on the menu. She pulled the sword from its scabbard and darted in a straight line toward the nearest trio of men. *They won't risk shooting me in case they hit their own—*

There was another *bang* from somewhere behind her—one of the soldiers clutched his neck and fell backward.

They don't even care about their own men! Abby zigged and zagged through the trees as she rushed at the remaining two. They opened fire.

Abby dropped to the ground, rolled, came up running. She leaped onto a large granite boulder and somersaulted over the soldiers' heads, landed in a crouch behind them and swung the sword.

It sliced into their armored legs and they collapsed screaming to the ground.

She felt like she was going to throw up, but she forced herself to keep going. She'd never hurt anyone before. Now those two men may have lost the use of their legs. *God forgive me, what have I done?*

Then gunfire erupted again and she reminded herself that

they'd been trying to kill her—she was only acting in self-defense.

Ahead, the line of trees was coming to an end—beyond that, the open road leading into the town. The copter was almost directly overhead now, its rotors' down-blast whipping the treetops, and Abby knew that as soon as she left the cover of the trees it was all over.

She remembered the last words she'd exchanged with Thunder: "If we don't make it, then we're going to take down as many of these guys as we can."

Too right, she said to herself. She slowed, looked up at the copter. Pulled her arm back.

And threw the sword.

The heavy weapon streaked into the air, struck the copter close to its rear rotor, embedded itself deep into the fuselage. The copter shuddered, began to spin out of control. It dipped and wavered, lost height for a moment, and almost recovered before it suddenly tilted to the side and plummeted.

Abby threw herself to the ground and covered her head with her arms. The ground shook as the copter crashed down. Its main rotors sliced into the dirt field before shattering and filling the air with razor-sharp fragments.

The men inside were still screaming as Abby scrambled to her feet and ran toward the copter. One of them opened fire, but his aim was off and the bullets plowed harmlessly into the ground to her right.

She pulled her sword out of the copter's fuselage and immediately threw herself backward onto the ground—the copter was raked with large-caliber bullets and the men inside were silenced. Abby rolled underneath the copter, got up, and ran. *They killed their own men just to get to me!*

Behind her: the roaring engines of the Boxers, shouting and screaming from the soldiers, gunfire.

Ahead: the open road. Nowhere to hide.

She kept her head down and ran. *Any second now,* she thought. *A bullet in my back or my head. I wonder if I'll feel it.*

Then something else roared, and it wasn't an engine. There was a crash, terrified screaming, more gunfire.

Abby reached an abandoned car and ducked down behind it, peered around it to see what was going on.

Two soldiers raced down the road toward her, but they were clearly unarmed and one was even tearing off his armor as he ran. They darted past Abby's spot and kept going, though she was sure they must have seen her.

A Boxer rocketed at full speed in her direction, weaving from one side of the road to the other as its occupants leaped clear. One of the soldiers clung desperately to its swinging door and let go seconds before another vehicle—enveloped in a ball of flame—soared through the air and crashed down on it. The tangled mass of steel and rubber scraped along the road for fifty yards and came to a stop in front of Abby.

Then past the smoke and flames she saw something massive and blue approaching.

Brawn stepped around the burning Boxers, almost casually dragging a struggling man behind him. His huge blue fist was locked around the man's head.

The giant circled slowly around the ruins. "Now, *that* was a good shot! Did you see that? Pow! Hit it dead-on!"

He turned to Abby. "I saw you take down the copter—nice work."

Abby swallowed. "God, those men . . . They shot their own people!"

"Yeah, well, don't shed any tears over them. They were trying to kill you. Plus, y'know, there's that whole thing about the plague and trying to take over the world and stuff." He lifted up his right arm, and the soldier's arms and legs twitched and flailed. "I kept this one in case we need to interrogate him or something." He opened his fist and the man collapsed to the ground. Abby didn't know what to say.

"So, anyway," Brawn rumbled. "I came back. You were right. We had a deal. So . . . Let's break bits off this guy until he tells us what we need to know."

Abby started to protest, but Brawn reached down to the soldier's head and covered the man's ears with a thumb and forefinger. Quietly, he said, "We're not *really* going to torture him. I may be a villain but I'm not a monster. But we want him to *think* we'll do it so he'll talk."

Abby nodded dumbly.

"Cool!" Brawn said. He released the man's head and straightened up again. "Um . . . What exactly *do* we need to know?"

"You need to create some sort of sonic vibration thingy to loosen the knots," Lance told Thunder.

"Thanks. I'd never have thought of that on my own."

"I'm just *saying*," Lance said.

"Already tried it," Thunder said.

Lance sighed. "They haven't come to interrogate us yet."

"What, are you disappointed?"

Lance ignored that. "Here's an idea. . . . You have complete control over all forms of sound, right? Does that mean you can mimic voices?"

Thunder nodded. "Yeah. Anything I hear, I can replicate." His voice changed. "Like this. No one would be able to tell the difference."

"Who's that supposed to be?"

"You, you idiot."

"Get lost! I don't sound anything like that! That was all . . ."

"Nasal and whiny? Trust me, that's what you sound like."

"Whatever. So here's what you do: There's a guard outside the door, right? You pretend to be the old woman talking to him on his walkie-talkie, order him to let us go."

"That's nuts! It'll never work."

"You won't know until you try. Go on, give it a shot. And let me listen in."

Lance watched Thunder as the older boy frowned in concentration, then there was a quiet static-filled beep.

The guard's voice said, "Talbot."

"Have you checked on the boys, Mr. Talbot?" Thunder said. To Lance he sounded exactly like the old woman.

"Not scheduled for another fifteen, ma'am."

"Did I *ask* when it was scheduled? They're no longer of any use to us, nor are they any danger. Release them."

"Ma'am?"

"You heard me."

"Yes, ma'am."

Seconds later, the door opened and the guard entered. "All right, kids. We're letting you go." He pulled a small knife from his belt, crouched down next to Thunder, and cut his ropes. "Come on. Get up."

Thunder sat up and began to massage his calves. "Give me a minute to get some feeling back."

The guard walked around to the back of Lance's chair. There was a series of snips, and Lance's arms and legs were free. He jumped up and stretched. "About time!"

Lance glanced at Thunder, tilted his head slightly toward the guard. A tiny voice next to Lance's ear whispered, "What now? How do we get out?"

Lance thought for a moment, then froze. "What was *that*? Sounded like gunfire downstairs!"

The guard began, "I didn't hear—"

The building was suddenly rocked by gunfire and explosions. The guard's radio squawked into life. "This is Remington—we're under attack! Every man to his post—now!"

The guard ran from the room and pounded down the hallway.

"Nice one," Lance said. He reached down and helped Thunder to his feet. "Was that just for him or the whole building?"

"Just for him, but I can extend it."

"Not yet. Pretend to be Remington again. Tell him that it was just a weapons malfunction and that he has to . . . go on patrol on the roof. Oh, and he has to maintain radio silence. We can't have him mentioning to the real Remington that he's cut us loose."

Thunder nodded. After a moment, he said, "Done. Now we sneak out?"

"Yeah. But I still can't see too well—you'll have to watch out for me."

"Now I'm your guide dog too?" Thunder moved toward the door. "This is turning into a very one-sided partnership. What exactly are *you* bringing to the party?"

"My brains," Lance said. "And certain other skills." He raised his hand. Protruding from the sleeve of his jacket was the guard's knife.

CHAPTER 27

Roz tried not to think of the brand-new camper van she was driving as stolen. She had only borrowed it. Besides, if anything happened to it she'd get Max to buy the owners a better one.

On the drive back to Oak Grove she didn't encounter any other traffic—with her foot on the gas the whole way the journey took under fifty minutes.

A few miles outside the town she passed the prison. *No point stopping there now. Pyrokine is long gone.* A minute later she slowed the camper down. Something large and coal-black was blocking the road ahead. "What on earth . . . ?" The air was heavy with the pungent odor of burning rubber and scorched metal.

As the camper slowly maneuvered around the burned object, Roz saw that it was the front half of an armored vehicle, a GTK Boxer. She couldn't see the other half anywhere.

Then she saw the cause: Next to another burning Boxer a

thirteen-foot-tall blue man was crouched over something on the ground.

Brawn! Lance said that he was in the prison—he must be immune to the plague! Either that or his body is so big it's taking longer for the infection to take hold.

I can't face him now—there's no time. Got to just hit the gas and go around him. If I'm lucky he won't take any notice of me.

Brawn looked up as she approached, and put out his arm with a thumb raised as though he was hitchhiking. It was such an ordinary action from someone so extraordinary-looking that Roz couldn't help slowing down.

And then Abby stepped out from behind Brawn. "Roz!"

"Abby?" Roz couldn't stop staring at Brawn. "What . . . um . . . what's going on?"

"Pyrokine was already gone when I got to the prison. The Helotry have him. But I found another ally. Brawn, this is—"

"We've met," Brawn rumbled.

Roz pursed her lips. "I know where The Helotry are going, and I know what they're going to try to do. Exactly *how* they're going to do it, I have no idea. But we've got to try to stop them. What about Thunder and Lance?"

Abby shook her head. "We were just heading into the town to see if we could find them." She stepped aside so that Roz could see the armored Helotry soldier sitting slumped over on the edge of the road. "We were trying to question this guy but he passed out."

"All right. Get in." Then Roz looked at Brawn, and considered the size of the camper van. "Get *on*. Hope this thing can take your weight."

The camper swayed and its roof buckled as Brawn climbed up. "Just don't go under any low bridges!" he shouted.

Abby ran around to the passenger side and climbed in. "Let's go."

Roz floored the accelerator. "You sure we can trust him? Guy gives me the creeps."

"We need him. Besides, he saved my life. You should have *seen* him. He beat up one of the armored cars with another armored car. That's the kind of power we can use."

"Abby, he's a villain!"

"So's Pyrokine, and we didn't let that stop us from trying to recruit *him*."

Roz considered this. "All right, you've got a point there."

They passed through the center of the town. It looked smaller and much less threatening in daylight. The black shell of the burned-out car and several shattered windows were the only clear signs of the previous night's battle. Even their army truck was gone.

"Helotry must have cleaned up their stuff," Abby said as the truck slowed to a stop. "Me and Thunder left a good number of them lying around before we had to split up."

"What about Lance? When did you last see him?"

"Just before Slaughter grabbed you something burned through the doors—but there wasn't any heat, only light. Must have been Pyrokine. I kicked out the windshield and threw Lance out onto the street. We saw him staggering into one of the stores . . ." She opened the door and jumped out. "Lance!"

Her voice echoed around the square. After a moment she called again, "Lance!"

Brawn jumped down from the camper van's roof. "This the guy you were talking about? The human?" She nodded.

The blue giant straightened up, filled his massive lungs, and bellowed, *"LANCE!"*

Abby jumped. The echo seemed to go on forever. Hundreds of startled birds took to the air, dogs for miles around began barking and howling.

Brawn gave Abby a yellow-toothed grin. "That oughta do the trick."

Hiding behind wooden packing crates at the dark end of the narrow corridor, Lance felt Thunder grab his arm. "What?"

So far they had discovered that the entire apartment building belonged to The Helotry. They had managed to sneak down four floors without being seen, but they still had three more floors to go, and the ground floor was packed with soldiers. Getting out without being seen would be almost impossible.

"I just heard someone calling your name," Thunder said. "It was pretty far away too. Several miles."

"Abby or Roz?" Lance was using the guard's knife to prize open the lid of one of the crates.

"Neither. It was a guy."

"Oh. Well, maybe he's looking for a different Lance." He inserted the small knife into the gap under the lid and jabbed at the hilt with the heel of his palm.

"Right. Because it's such a common name."

"There's nothing wrong with the name Lance!"

Thunder grinned. "What's it short for? Lancelot?"

"No, it's just Lance. My folks just liked the sound of it."

"You're lying, Lancelot," Thunder said. "I can tell by your heartbeat. Lancelot, like the Knight of the Round Table. Well, that'd make me King Arthur."

"No way! If anyone's King Arthur, it's me. You're . . . I dunno. One of the ones no one ever remembers."

"So who's Guinevere, then? Roz or Abby? It's Abby, isn't it? Your heart went into overdrive the first time you saw her."

Lance felt his face flush. "Give it a rest!" He popped the crate's lid and peered inside. "Looks like another one of the jetpacks they copied from Paragon."

"Think we could use it to get out of here?"

"No. Paragon said the other one was a death trap. I don't know how to control it anyway. But *this* might come in handy." He reached into the crate and pulled out a metal cylinder about the length and thickness of his arm, and passed it to Thunder.

Thunder read the letters stenciled on the side. "Whoa, it's heavy. N_2O_4 slash H_2O_2 . . . That's dinitrogen tetroxide and hydrogen peroxide. This is the fuel the jetpack uses?"

"Yep. We're taking it. If they don't have fuel they can't fly after us."

"They might have another supply."

"Good point." Lance used the knife to slice through the jetpack's straps. "*Now* I'd like to see them fly it."

"Get ready," Thunder said. "OK, next floor down's clear."

Lance slipped the knife back into the back of his jeans, then hauled the cylinder onto his shoulder.

With Thunder leading the way, they darted out from behind the packing crates, along the corridor and down a flight of stairs. They didn't need to worry about moving quietly—Thunder had them cocooned in a bubble of silence.

They stopped before they reached the next floor. Thunder listened for a moment, nodded, and they continued down.

Thunder stopped on the metal stairway halfway between the second floor and the first. "Just had a thought. . . . How long has it been since we got out of the room?"

Lance slapped his palm against his forehead. "You're right. The guard said he wasn't due to check us for another fifteen minutes. It's got to be that long already." He sniffed. "Smell that? Fresh air! We're close to a door. . . . Want to make a run for it?"

Thunder hesitated. "Even if we do get away, how are we going to find Roz and Abby? Can you drive?"

"Officially? No."

"Unofficially?"

"Uh, that'd also be no. But how hard can it be? You steer the steering wheel the way you want the car to go, and you press the pedals or something."

Thunder rolled his eyes. "Then it's a good thing *I* can drive. Well, kind of. A bit."

"All right then. . . . Can you use your power to tell us where the door is?"

"Yeah, it's . . . Oh no."

A voice from the floor above said, "That's far enough. Stay exactly where you are or we *will* open fire."

Lance slowly turned to look back up the stairs. Two of The Helotry's guards were looking down at them, both with their weapons aimed.

There was a scuffle of footsteps and four more guards appeared on the floor below. "Hands on your heads! *Now!*"

Lance carefully lowered the fuel cylinder onto the step at

his feet, then raised his arms. "OK, you caught us. But do we get points for trying?"

"Shut up, McKendrick!" Lance saw that it was Remington, the guard who'd threatened to choke him. "Any more of your mouth and I swear . . ."

"All right, all right!" Lance said. "But just so you know, this thing at my feet is one of the fuel cells from the jetpack you guys made. It's a mixture of . . . Well, I can't remember what it's called."

"Dinitrogen tetroxide and hydrogen peroxide," Thunder said.

"Yeah, what he said. Anyway, it's extremely unstable. You'll notice that it's resting against my foot. And that we're standing on a metal staircase. If any of you shoot, all I have to do is give this thing a nudge. It hits a few steps down and it's sayonara. You get what I'm saying? There'd be nothing left of this building but a crater with red bits in it."

Some of the guards stepped back.

"Drop your guns," Lance said. "I'm serious. I'm more than willing to blow the lot of us to kingdom come."

The old woman's voice could be heard from farther down the corridor. "Do what the boy says. You will allow them to leave unharmed."

The guards reluctantly lowered their weapons.

Thunder said, "In case you're thinking of changing your minds, just remember that even from miles away I can rupture that cylinder with a sonic burst."

Lance and Thunder exchanged a glance, nodded at the same time, and they resumed their descent.

The guards watched them with stone faces and sullen eyes

as they made their way along the final corridor and pushed open the outer door. Another dozen weapons were suddenly pointing at them.

Remington followed them out. "Stand down! Let them pass!"

The building was part of a complex of identical apartment blocks, with a small road winding away through a landscaped green area. The large parking lot at the front of the building was lined with two dozen jeeps.

Lance tried to walk as though he was a lot more confident than he felt. "Step aside there, ladies. The good guys are comin' through!"

Thunder whispered, "Jeez, Lance! Don't push it!"

"Think you can handle that?" Lance asked, pointing to the nearest vehicle.

Thunder walked around to the driver's side, and climbed in. "Yeah, it's an automatic."

"Cool." Lance turned to Remington. "Keys?"

The man scowled, then tossed a set of keys to Lance, who snatched them out of the air.

"Thanks. Have a good one, guys. It's been fun. Next time we'll hold the party at my place, OK?"

Through gritted teeth, Thunder muttered, "Will you just stop showing off and get in?"

After a couple of minutes and several undignified false starts, Thunder got the jeep moving. It surged away from the apartment complex.

Lance let out a deep breath he hadn't realized he'd been holding. "Oh man, that was intense! OK, Thunder. . . . Find us somewhere to hide. We don't know how to get to the power plant but they do—we'll wait until they pass and follow them."

"Good thinking."

"I don't do any other kind." He grinned. "They're going to be so mad when they figure it out!"

"Yeah," Thunder said. After a moment, he added, "Wait, figure *what* out?"

"That you were faking the old woman's voice again."

"Oh. No, that wasn't me."

"What? *Seriously?* Man, I was wrong—it was *double-intense!*"

Thunder suddenly laughed. "You realize we just talked our way out of the enemy's HQ?"

Lance couldn't help grinning. "Yeah. More than once I thought we were dead for sure." He laughed.

"Hey, if they find us, we're definitely toast."

For some reason that made Lance laugh even harder. With tears in his eyes, he said, "They're trying to bring about the end of the world and *we stole their jeep!*"

Thunder snickered. "There'll be a bunch of them left behind going, 'It's not fair! We're going to miss it!' and they'll all be squeezed into the other jeeps and some of them will have guys sitting on their laps!"

Lance was doubled over clutching his stomach. "Right! Or they'll be going, 'Now we have to get the bus! Oh, wait, there *aren't* any buses because we infected everyone with a plague and they're all going to die!'"

They both instantly stopped laughing.

Lance put his hand over his mouth. "Oh man."

CHAPTER 28

Slaughter strode toward the main entrance doors of the Windfield nuclear power plant. In the parking lot behind her, six large trucks—now empty—were preparing to leave.

A guard saluted as he approached, and unrolled a large blueprint. "We're just about finished with the alterations. You were right—the layout is a perfect match for the plant in Midway."

She held the blueprint up to the light. "Excellent work." She gave the man a cold smile. "Once this is done, we'll break the Midway team out of prison."

The man saluted again, glanced at the teenaged boy beside Slaughter, and resumed his post outside the door.

The boy was wearing an old pair of jeans and a T-shirt. He was barefoot, had close-cropped blond hair and dark brown eyes. As he followed her into the building, he said, "We've still got some time to go. So what's the plan exactly?"

"We need to hook you up to the output from the reactor."

"And it's safe, right?"

"Of course it is. You're the most valuable member of the team. You're the last one we'd put at risk."

He considered that. "All right, then. What about those kids back in Oak Grove? They're not going to come along and mess things up, are they?" He paused for a moment, frowned. "There was something about that girl that . . ."

Slaughter placed a hand on his shoulder. "They've been taken care of. Trust me."

He looked around the expansive lobby. Guards and engineers were filing out of the side rooms in groups of two and three. "So the Fifth King really *was* real, then?"

"Absolutely. He was the first of us. The first superhuman."

"But I don't get how he died. I mean, you kept saying he was immortal."

Slaughter led him deeper into the building. Unlike the power plant in Midway, this one was fully furnished, equipped with the latest nuclear technology. "Immortal just means that he wasn't ever going to die of old age. But he wasn't completely invulnerable. Something got to him."

"What, though?"

"We don't know that. But he might be able to tell us. It could have been another superhuman. He was the first superhuman born, but he was close to six hundred years old when he died—that's plenty of time for another one to show up." She stopped in front of a pair of sealed metal doors and looked at the boy. "What's your real name? I can't keep calling you Pyrokine."

"Fabian," the boy said. "I don't know where the name Pyrokine came from."

"It's from the word *pyrokinesis*—the ability to start fires with the power of the mind."

"But that's not really what I do. I turn matter into energy."

"I know that. That's what makes you so powerful." Slaughter keyed a code into the pad next to the doors, which slid open with a faint hiss. They stepped through into the heart of the power plant where dozens of men and women were checking readings and working at computer stations.

Slaughter pointed up to the eight-yard-diameter metal sphere. "And it's what makes *this* so powerful. Controlled atomic decay releases energy in the form of heat, which . . ." She saw the glazed look in his eyes. "You don't care about that, do you?"

"Not really. Where do I come into all this? I mean . . ." He sighed. "Look, don't take this the wrong way, but . . . Well, everyone thinks that you're one of the bad guys."

"Good and bad are just points of view," Slaughter said. "Look at any conflict and you'll see that everyone on every side thinks *they're* the good guy. There's no doubt that what we're doing here looks like evil to some people, but that's a small price to pay for saving the world. You don't see *yourself* as a villain, do you?"

He shook his head. "No. I never did anything wrong. Not deliberately."

"Then why were you in prison?"

"They said I was too dangerous to be allowed to go free."

"Yes, but *who* said that?"

"You know. The superheroes. Titan, Quantum, Max Dalton. . . . Those guys. I can see why they thought that. If I lost control I could destroy the world. Last year I met this girl and . . . We never really got that close—can't even remember her name now—but that was just as well because I was putting her in danger just by being near her."

"Those days are gone, Fabian. You are powerful, and that's why we need you. But you don't have complete control over your abilities, and that's why *you* need *us*. That's what this is about. You can transform matter into energy. Have you ever wondered what would happen if you applied that same process to energy itself?"

Abby and Roz drove in silence for the last five miles—from the moment they saw the domes of the power plant each was wrapped up in her own thoughts.

Even when they passed the six large trucks going in the opposite direction they exchanged only a glance.

Finally, Abby said, "Listen . . . If something happens to me . . ."

Roz glanced at her. "Don't talk like that. That doesn't do anyone any good."

"My name is Abigail de Luyando. I live in Apartment 4C in 655 West Franklin, Midway. You'll tell my mom everything, right? *Everything*."

"OK. But it won't come to that."

"And . . ." Inside, Abby cringed. This was harder to talk about than anything else. "I have an older sister and four younger brothers. My sister has a job but she doesn't earn a lot. . . . Mom can't work much. She's in a wheelchair and my sister and me have to take care of her. So, uh . . ."

Roz reached out and patted Abby's arm. "It's all right. You don't have to say any more."

But Abby knew she had to say the words. "They'll need money. But only if I don't come back from this, OK? It's not charity, it's . . . Well, maybe it *is* charity, but . . ."

Roz nodded. "I understand." After a moment, she added, "I have to say something to you too. Ever since our parents died, Max has been looking after me and Josh. He's made a lot of money, more than we could ever spend. But I'm not trying to put on the 'poor little rich girl' act. . . . The moment Max found out about my powers he started training me. I was eleven. He took me out of school and I haven't seen any of my friends since." She gave Abby a thin-lipped smile. "Sometimes I worry that he might be using his mind control on me, making me *want* to train all the time."

"God, that's horrible!"

"I know. But there's no way I can prove it. Or at least I don't *think* I can prove it. For all I know, I've already found proof a dozen times and he's just made me forget."

"But . . . Max is a super*hero*. He's not one of the bad guys!"

"Yeah. Anyway. . . . The point is that because of the way things have been going for me the past few years, you and Thunder and Lance are pretty much the only friends I have."

"But you've only known us since yesterday!"

Roz laughed. "Crazy, isn't it?" She glanced upward—one of Brawn's huge blue feet was sticking out over the edge of the roof. "And who knows? Before this is over *he* might be on the list too."

"So . . . No boyfriend then?"

"Who has time?" Roz asked. "There was a guy I met a while back and he was, y'know, kinda . . ." She shrugged. "I can barely remember him now. You ever get that? Where you meet some guy and you're absolutely crazy about him for, like, a couple of weeks, and then one day you realize that you haven't even thought about him for ages?"

"Yeah, that's happened to me a couple of times," Abby said. "My sister says it's the brain's way of weeding out the dweebs."

Minutes later they reached a narrow side road. A sign at the entrance read WINDFIELD NUCLEAR POWER PLANT. UNAUTHORIZED ENTRY PROHIBITED.

"Oh no—they have a *sign*!" Abby said. "Well, better turn back, I suppose."

Roz grinned, steered the van onto the dirt road, and floored the accelerator.

Then they heard Brawn's voice bellow, "Incoming!"

Roz slammed on the brakes—the camper swerved and screeched to a halt. Brawn tumbled from the roof and landed on his feet.

"Take cover!" he yelled. "Now!"

Abby and Roz darted out of the camper—as she ran, Abby heard the sound of approaching helicopters. "Which way?"

Brawn pointed back the way they had come. "There! Man, I hate being such a big target! Look, I'll hold them off for as long as I can—you two try to get past the guards."

"I'm not sure we'll even get past the *gate* without your help."

"Just go for it," Brawn rumbled. "I'll take care of the gate before you get there. And don't get killed."

Abby raced ahead with her sword drawn. She could hear Roz behind her, but the older girl couldn't match her speed.

How many of these guys are we going to face . . . ?

A siren blared and Abby had her answer: The open wasteland in front of the gate was suddenly swarming with men in silver armor.

There were at least a hundred of them. Abby fought the urge to turn and run.

Slaughter reacted to the alarm by simply saying, "Well, they're here."

Pyrokine looked concerned. "We should get out there. We can stop them."

"We certainly can. But that's what the grunts are for. Let the heroes tire themselves out on the help, then we can go out and mop up later."

"But—"

"There's a right time for everything, and this is not the right time for putting *you* in the line of fire. Now . . . Everything in the universe is either matter or energy or a combination of both. Unless you're getting down to subatomic particles, matter and energy cannot be created or destroyed, but they *can* be changed . . ." She noted his expression and let out a sigh. "You want me to dumb it down for you? OK. We're going to feed you a very large—and very precise—burst of energy from the reactor. You'll use your power to change that energy into . . . something else."

"How?"

Slaughter nodded toward a dozen people sitting at a cluster of workstations. "These guys here have figured it out to a thousand decimal places. You won't have to do anything but work your magic on the energy, and the machines will do the rest. . . . Your power is going to punch a wormhole—a tunnel—through time and space. One end of the tunnel will be here, and the other end will open four thousand, four hundred and fifty-six years ago in the city of Alexandria on the Mediterranean coast of Egypt, exactly one second before the Fifth King died."

"Why not do it earlier? If we're late by a couple of seconds then we'll just be bringing back a corpse."

"There wasn't a corpse—he was completely destroyed in a pillar of fire. If we took him, say, the week before he died, then all the decisions he made during that week would never have happened. Someone he ordered put to death would have lived. That person might have had children, grandchildren, great-grandchildren, and so on. Everything in the present is built on the foundations of everything that has gone before."

He nodded. "Got it. So we take him at the last possible second and there won't be any changes."

"That's the theory."

"How can you be so sure about the time? People back then didn't have clocks!"

"No, but they did have the sun. He died at dawn, the instant the light of the sun hit him. We know exactly where he was standing, we know the sunrise time to the microsecond, and we know the heights of the other buildings in the city."

"And you're certain that it's safe? The reactor isn't going to go into meltdown or anything like that?"

"If there was even the slightest chance of that happening, we wouldn't do it. The Helotry have been working on a way to get him back for four and a half thousand years. They haven't gone to all this trouble just to risk everything at the end."

The boy looked around the cavernous room. "OK then. I'm ready. Where does this all happen?"

Slaughter led him to a small side room lined with thick steel panels. In the center of the room was what looked like a metal dentist's chair. Thick cables and tubes snaked from the chair and disappeared through holes cut into the walls.

"It's like being inside a giant microwave oven," Fabian said. He walked once around the chair, then sat down. "It's not very comfortable."

The radio on Slaughter's belt beeped. She put it to her ear. "Yes?"

"Slaughter, we need you out here! It's the girls—and they've got Brawn with them!"

"And?"

"He's completely bulletproof, and he's already taken down two of the choppers! You're the only one strong enough to take him on."

"Do I have to think of everything for you? Sort out the girls first—shoot to kill—then go after Brawn." She clicked off the radio. "Humans, eh?" she said to the boy. "Always worried that they're going to be killed."

It's working, Abby said to herself. *Maybe we're going to make it!*

There was still the gate to breach, but right now she wasn't allowing herself to think about that. The armored men were rushing her in twos and threes.

Roz was somewhere behind her, using her telekinesis to trip the men up, knock their weapons out of their hands, pelt them with rocks.

Abby leapfrogged over one man, slashed at another with her sword—it sliced off the top of his helmet and gave him an instant crew cut.

She swiveled on one foot, jabbed the other into a third man's midriff, slammed the hilt of her sword down on his head as he pitched forward. Abby felt a vague sense of shame to be using some of the same moves she'd seen Slaughter use.

Then the man started to get up again. Abby swung at him with her left fist: Just before the blow connected, his helmet was suddenly pulled up and off his head by an invisible force. Her fist slammed into his jaw and sent him staggering backward.

And then they were *all* losing their helmets, one by one. Abby took a moment to look back at Roz and give her a thumbs-up.

Without any protection on their heads, the guards were much less inclined to fight, especially since Roz was showering them with fast-moving rocks that followed them whichever way they dodged.

Farther down the dirt road, Brawn was still where they had left him. He was using an eight-foot-long wooden fence post as though it was a baseball bat. The Helotry's men were being batted in every direction. The giant seemed to be thoroughly enjoying himself. As Abby watched, he knocked one straight into another twenty yards away, and shouted, "Yes! Home run!"

Abby shouted down to him. "Brawn! The gate!"

He nodded, dropped the fence post, grabbed hold of the camper van, and lifted it over his head. "Heads up!" he roared.

The three-ton vehicle soared through the air and demolished the heavy gate.

"Swish!" Brawn yelled.

The rest of the armored men scattered and ran.

Roz darted up to Abby. "How are we doing?"

"We've just got to . . ." She looked around. "I think that's all of them." On the ground at her feet, one of the fallen men stirred and moaned.

Abby put her foot on his chest, and lightly rested the edge of the sword against his throat. "You. Talk."

"Wh-what do you want to know?"

"Slaughter. Where is she?"

"Inside. With the Pyrokine," he stammered.

Roz asked, "How much time do we have before they try to bring back the Fifth King?"

"A—an hour, maybe a little more. The leaders of The Helotry will be coming to greet him."

Roz dragged Abby aside so that the man couldn't overhear. "So we have time to stop all this," Roz said. "But . . . we need The Helotry to tell us how to cure the plague before the virus's timer hits its target. So what do we do?"

"Slaughter's got to be pretty high up the chain of command. We get to her, force her to tell us."

"This close to the end, she's not going to be playing nice.

267

She's going to live up to her name. Last time I got away through luck more than anything else."

"But now we have something that we didn't have before," Abby said. "Brawn."

Slaughter clicked off her radio again. "They're doing well—I thought the men would hold them off for longer. But there's nothing they can do now anyway. So, Fabian . . . Ready?"

He jumped. "What? You mean we're doing this right *now*?" His eyes were wide with fear. "No way!" He started to get out of the chair, but Slaughter put her hand on his chest and pushed him back.

"What do you want?" she asked. "A fanfare? A digital counter that will activate when it reaches zero? We're all set up and ready to go. As soon as the power surge hits, close your eyes and let the machinery guide you."

"But you said we have to wait until the old woman gets here!"

Slaughter smiled. "Kid, you've got a lot to learn about people. That disease-ridden old bat has been running The Helotry for a very long time. She worships the Fifth King. She thinks he's going to bring about a new golden age on Earth. Well, he is, but she's not going to be a part of it. Her day has passed. I'm in charge now."

"She'll have you killed when she finds out!"

"No she won't." Slaughter lightly ran her fingers over a large red button on the arm of the chair. "See, The Helotry want to be his *slaves*, that's the saddest part of it all. For forty-five centuries they've been worshiping a man who wouldn't think twice about killing them all if he was in a bad mood.

Now, we're going to bring back the Fifth King and he's going to need someone to guide him through this world. I don't want that someone to be a crazy old woman. I want that someone to be *me*. So . . ." She raised her hand over the button.

"Well, give me a count to three at least!"

"All right. On three. . . . Three." Slaughter slammed her fist down on the red button.

The machinery hummed into life. Pyrokine screamed, his body erupted into cold blue fire, twitched and shuddered. Luminescent sparks rippled across his body, blinding arcs of light leaped from his fingers and toes into the metal framework of the chair.

And just as suddenly it was over. The fire enveloping his body melted away and Pyrokine slumped down in the chair. He took a long, deep, ragged breath, shuddered once more, and opened his eyes. "That *hurt!*" His voice was weak, almost inaudible. "You said . . . it was safe!"

"You're still alive, aren't you?"

"So . . . Now what? The next part better not hurt that much!" Pyrokine rolled his shoulders back and flexed his arms. "How long do we have to . . . ?" He froze, staring past Slaughter's shoulder.

She turned around.

There was a man standing in the room, naked from the waist up. He was bearded, heavily muscled, bronzed from the sun.

Slaughter dropped to her knees. "Hail the Fifth King."

CHAPTER 29

Now . . .

Krodin stared at the pale-skinned woman kneeling before him.

Moments earlier he had been on his balcony in Alexandria, glaring at the woman after whom he had named his city.

There had been a flash of black, excruciating agony, and now he was in a metal room with a strangely dressed woman and a pale young man sitting on an elaborate silver throne.

The woman was speaking in an incomprehensible language, but she knew the protocols: She was staring at the ground, unwilling to look him in the eye.

The boy, however, clearly did *not* know how to behave in the presence of a king. He was staring openmouthed at Krodin.

The warrior-king ignored the woman's babbling and slowly turned around.

In his long life he had seen many things, heard many strange tales, yet he had rarely encountered anything that gave credence to what the humans would call magic. But this . . . He shook his head.

Through a transparent portion of the wall he could see many people in a much larger room. They were all on their knees, facing his direction.

What is this place? So many metal . . . contraptions. Not even the people of the Indus have the skill to create such devices.

Behind him, the woman continued to talk, and Krodin realized that she was trying to use one of the Sumerian dialects. He turned back and addressed her in the same tongue. "Who are you?"

"I am your servant, Lord Krodin." Her accent was unlike any he had heard before.

"Where have you taken me, servant?"

She hesitated for a moment. "You are safe, Lord."

Krodin recognized the woman's evasiveness. *She thinks I will not understand.* "Where am I?"

"A land called America, Lord Krodin. On the other side of the world."

"You lie. It is not possible to travel such a distance in so short a time."

"Lord Krodin, it has not been a short time. Please allow me to explain."

He nodded. "Proceed."

"This is not the time in which you lived. That was more than four thousand years in the past. Our records show that you died on that morning in Alexandria. We have used our science and our powers to take you from your time

271

before your death could happen. It was the only way to save you."

"If you are lying I will kill you and every other human in this America of yours."

"I do not lie, Lord Krodin. And I am not human. I am like you: *more* than human. Superhuman."

"The boy does not show the proper respect."

"Forgiveness, Lord Krodin. He is not familiar with the customs." The woman turned to the boy and hissed at him in her strange language. After a moment, he climbed down from the silver throne and got to his knees beside the woman.

"What is your name, woman?"

"I am called . . ." She frowned as she sought the correct word in the Sumerian tongue. "Slaughter."

"Slaughter. You are a warrior."

"The greatest warrior of this time, Lord Krodin. Until now, of course."

Then the building trembled. From far away came the sound of crumbling stone and the clash of metal on metal.

"What is happening?" Krodin asked.

"Our enemies, Lord Krodin. They have come to destroy you."

"Destroy *me*?" A smile crept across his face.

"They too are superhuman. A girl who can move objects without touching them, another girl who is as fast as a cheetah and stronger than ten men. And a giant."

"Then let us greet them, Lady Slaughter. And when they are dead you will show me this America. I expect that it will be a little different from the Egypt of my time."

• • •

Roz used her telekinetic shield to protect herself and Abby from the flying debris and concrete dust as Brawn tore his way into the side of the building.

Most of the remaining guards inside the complex had scattered and run when they saw Brawn, but a few had stayed to fight. They'd shot at him, driven a truck at high speed into his leg—Brawn had angrily kicked it over—and two of them had even leaped onto his back and tried to strangle him. They'd been there for almost a minute before he'd noticed them and flicked them away.

And now a handful of civilians were trying to sneak past the blue giant.

Roz decided that she wasn't about to let them escape. They might not be soldiers, but they were part of The Helotry and therefore bore a responsibility for everything that had happened.

"Abby? On your left."

"I see them!" Abby called. She grabbed the nearest one—a woman covered in dust and scratches—and threw her to the ground. "Who's in charge?"

The woman's eyes were wide with fear—she couldn't stop staring at Brawn.

"Answer me or I'll turn him loose on you!" Abby yelled at her. "What do you know about the virus?"

"N-nothing! That's a separate division."

The woman's colleagues abandoned her, running in every direction. *All right,* Roz thought. *The older ones are usually in charge, and they're the ones who can't run too fast.*

She picked a white-haired man and telekinetically tripped him up, then dragged him facedown toward her, his hands desperately scrabbling at the rubble. *Either this guy's very light or I'm getting stronger.*

She crouched down next to the man. "Same question. The virus."

"I swear, we don't know anything about it! Our task was just to get the reactor online and hooked up to the Pyrokine!"

"You must know *something.* How come you're immune?"

"They injected me with a vaccine last month."

"Where?"

He looked confused, almost embarrassed. "In my left buttock."

"I mean where did it *happen*? Where can we find stocks of the vaccine?"

"A place about sixty miles north of Dallas. A ranch. We were brought there, injected, brought back. That's all I know!"

"No, you knew that this was going to happen!" Roz balled her fist and slammed it down into the man's face. "Billions of people are going to die because of you!"

"Please! It's not like that!"

Roz hit him again. There was a walkie-talkie clipped to the man's belt—Roz pulled it free, hit the talk button. "This is Roz Dalton trying to get in touch with anyone in the CDC."

There was only static in reply. Roz repeated her message. After a moment, a voice said, "Roz? Doctor Gertler. Where are you?"

"At the Windfield power plant. Some of The Helotry are already here. They're going to try to bring back the Fifth King as soon as the leaders arrive. That's only a few minutes away. We . . ." Roz realized that both Abby and Brawn had stopped fighting and were backing toward her. The walkie-talkie slipped out of her hand and clattered to the ground.

Two figures were coming out of the dust-filled building.

On the left was Slaughter. She grinned at Roz, nodded, then drew her index finger across her throat.

The figure on the right was Pyrokine, floating a few feet above the ground. Blue-white fire wreathed and swirled around his body.

Roz felt her heard skip a beat. "Oh my God. . . . Pyrokine."

"Watch him," Abby said quietly. "He's not as crazy as Slaughter but he's much more powerful. He can—"

"I know what he can do," Roz said. "I don't know *how* I know, but I do." The half-remembered dream was closer now, so close she felt as though she could almost touch it.

And then a third figure emerged from the dust. A tall, bronze-skinned, bare-chested bearded man. He was looking at them with curiosity, as though wondering in which order he would kill them.

"Three against three," Slaughter said. "I'd advise you to stand down, but there's no point. We're going to tear you apart anyway."

Beside Roz, Brawn went into a crouch. A growl rumbled in his throat. His muscles tensed.

He launched himself at the Fifth King.

"How much longer now?" Lance asked. The jeep raced along the deserted freeway—Thunder was keeping them a mile behind The Helotry's forces—and the wind whipped at his hair, stung his eyes. He found it hard to believe that less than a day had passed since he'd been rocketing along a similar freeway on his bike.

"Not sure," Thunder said. "They're not talking much."

Lance grabbed Thunder's arm and pointed to the left. "There! Those towers—that's the place!"

"You're sure?"

"Well, it's not Disney World. Point your super-hearing over that way and see what you can pick up."

After a second, Thunder nodded. "You're right. That's the place. . . . Sounds like there's a lot of fighting going on." He suddenly grinned and pumped the air with his fist. "Yes! Abby and Roz are there—they're OK! Well, they're in the middle of a battle but . . . Whoa . . . *Brawn* is with them!"

"What? Aw, no!" Lance put his head in his hands. "But that guy's a total *animal*!"

"No, I mean, he's with Abby and Roz—he's on our side!"

"I always liked him," Lance said. "Floor it!"

"We'll catch up with The Helotry—they're already slowing down."

"Catch up? We have to *overtake* them! Can you do anything with your powers to slow them down even more?"

"I can make them all deaf—that should disorient them."

"Go for it, Thunder!" Lance grinned. After a moment, he said, "Hey, I still don't know your real name."

"This is true."

"Well?"

"Well, I'm not going to tell you. What's the point in having a secret identity if you tell people who you really are?"

"Hello? Your mask is long gone, remember? Everyone can see your face."

"No, I made a vow never to reveal my identity."

"Right. Well, instead of that couldn't you have made a vow to not have such a dumb superhero name? I mean, *Thunder*? It sounds like a dinosaur farting in a cave. What made you choose that one?"

"There's already at least two guys called Shockwave. And Thunder's a *good* name. A lot of people are scared of thunder."

"Huh. If it was fear you were after, you should have called yourself The Monster Who Lives Under the Bed."

Thunder sighed. "You never, *ever* stop talking, do you?"

"It's a gift."

"Well, I hope you kept the receipt—Whoa! Crash! One of The Helotry's jeeps just hit the median and another one plowed into the back of it! I've blocked all sounds from reaching their ears, but I can still hear them. . . . It sounds like they're trying to coordinate everything through hand signals."

"Nice work. Off-ramp's coming up on the right."

Thunder slowed the jeep down to twenty miles per hour: The road ahead was almost blocked with The Helotry's soldiers and jeeps. Many of the men were staggering about, tapping at their ears and shaking their heads.

Thunder grinned. "Hey, I've just thought of something. . . . Balance is controlled by the fluids in the inner ear." He pointed to one of the few men who was standing still. "Let's see what happens to *that* guy."

The soldier suddenly swayed back and forth, then toppled over.

Lance laughed. "Oh, that is priceless! Do them all!"

"I would if we had time." He steered the jeep around some of the lurching, disoriented soldiers, then onto the off-ramp. "Almost there. Lance, you stay out of sight when we get there, OK?"

Less than a minute later they reached a turnoff leading to the power plant. The road and the fields on each side of it were covered in small craters, fragments of metal debris, and the unmoving bodies of The Helotry's men.

"I don't know if that's a good sign or a bad sign," Lance said.

Thunder steered around the wreckage of a Sikorsky S-70 helicopter. "Abby, Roz . . . Can you hear me?"

Abby's voice appeared next to them. "Thunder? You're alive!"

"So far. We're almost with you now. How are you guys doing?"

Roz said, "The Fifth King is real. He's here. I've never imagined—Thunder, is Lance with you?"

"Yeah, we're both—"

"Go! Turn around and leave this place! Just keep going and don't look back! Oh God, he's out of control. . . ."

There was a deafening *crack*, and something blue streaked into the air from the grounds of the power plant.

It reached its apogee within seconds, and came plummeting down toward the road.

Thunder stamped on the brake pedal. The jeep went into a skid, hit a fence post side-on, snapped through it, and slid halfway into a ditch.

The blue object plowed into the road with a trembling crash, and lay still.

Shaking, Lance and Thunder climbed out of the jeep. In front of them, the road had a new crater, and at its center was the giant, unmoving figure of Brawn.

CHAPTER 30

Krodin flexed his fists. That had hurt. The blue giant was the strongest opponent he had ever faced. *And yet I bested him,* he told himself. *Even in this future world with its flying metal carriages, I am the greatest warrior.*

He watched the battle for a moment. The woman called Slaughter was a ferocious fighter, but that very ferocity was her weakness. She lacked control.

At the moment she was grappling with the dark-skinned girl, who was also clearly untrained. But what the dark girl lacked in training and experience she more than surpassed in natural skill. Of the two, she was by far the better fighter.

The girl swung her strange-looking sword with enough force to remove a man's head. Slaughter caught it by the blade, twisted it out of the girl's grip, and cast it aside.

Slaughter struck a vicious jab at the girl's throat, but it

wasn't quite fast enough: The girl ducked aside and in the same motion she dropped onto her hands and swung her feet into Slaughter's midriff.

Krodin also found the fight between the pale-skinned girl and the burning boy fascinating to watch. This girl was extremely well-trained, but she appeared to have only the strength and speed of a human. She would not be a match for the burning boy if not for her arcane power.

As she launched punches and kicks at the boy, he was also reacting as though struck from behind by an unseen force.

A fist-sized stone raised itself from the ground and streaked toward the boy's head—but he waved a hand at the stone and it immediately turned to flame and disappeared.

But Krodin could see that the fight was restrained, that neither of them wanted to engage fully in battle.

Krodin shook his head. *I will have to train them myself. Why does the fire-boy not simply use his magic to turn the girl into flame? Why does Slaughter not change tactics? She has the power of flight—she could lift the sword-girl into the air and throw her against the side of the building. Or she could pick up the sword and use it against her.*

Then a low growl reached his ears, and he smiled. *Ah, the blue giant awakens and returns for another beating!*

The giant ran toward Krodin, leaped into the air, and crashed down in front of him, teeth bared and hands in grasping claws.

He struck with his right hand, and Krodin stepped to the side. The giant whirled about, lashed out with his left. Krodin grabbed the smallest finger on the giant's hand and wrenched it back. The giant roared in pain, scuttled away clutching his hand.

Are these beings truly the greatest champions this America has to offer?

He spotted the dark girl's sword protruding from the ground, and walked over to it, pulled it free. Its balance was odd, clearly made for someone with great strength.

He swung the sword lightly and briskly, as though slashing at weeds. *A good weapon.*

In the Sumerian language, he called to Slaughter. "Enough play. End this battle now." He tossed the sword to her.

Somehow, the sword passed far out of the woman's reach. Puzzled, Krodin looked around. He had missed his target. *Trickery of some kind. I do not miss. I can shoot an arrow on the darkest night and always hit my quarry.*

He saw the burning boy launch a ball of blue fire at the pale girl. *Of course. Her ability to move objects—she diverted the sword's path.*

The blue giant attacked again, this time from behind. Krodin ducked down and rolled backward, passed between the giant's legs and landed on his back. He kicked out at the backs of the giant's knees.

The blue man pitched forward, screaming even louder this time. Krodin walked over to the giant and kicked down hard on a certain part of the small of his back: at a point that Krodin knew would temporarily paralyze a human.

He had already decided not to kill the giant. He would make an excellent trophy to take back to Alexandria.

The thought of his city reminded him of his wife. She would

be long dead now, her bones turned to dust and scattered by the winds. His sons and daughters, their children, their grandchildren . . . All gone.

But I am not forgotten. More than four thousand years and my followers are still loyal. Surely no other leader could make such a claim.

There was movement at the edge of his vision, and Krodin turned to see two more children approaching. Two boys. One dark-skinned, the other pale.

The battlefield instantly fell silent, though Slaughter and the burning boy were still fighting the two girls.

Strange, Krodin thought. *Another piece of trickery? Or more magic from these superhumans? No matter. I can fight as easily without sound as with.*

He stepped toward the two boys, and the ground seemed to sway and shift. He heard a large fly—perhaps a hornet— buzzing about his head and he absently swatted at it. The buzzing grew louder.

He looked, but there was no insect. Still the noise increased in volume, and with it came a high-pitched shriek, like the scrape of metal on stone.

The noise vibrated through his skull, so loud now that he could feel his teeth chattering.

From the concentration on the dark boy's face, Krodin knew that he was the cause.

The sound ripped at him like the strongest wind, shuddered his bones, was now so ferocious that even his eyeballs were trembling.

A useful ability, Krodin thought. *Surely this would kill an ordinary man.* But he was not an ordinary man, and he knew that the boy could not continue this assault indefinitely. Krodin sat down, and waited.

Abby heard Lance shouting, "Oh for crying out loud! He's just *sitting* there taking it!"

Everyone—even Slaughter and Pyrokine—paused in what they were doing long enough to stare at Lance.

Slaughter had Abby's left arm up behind her back, had her own arm around Abby's throat. "What is *wrong* with that kid?" Slaughter said.

Abby jabbed with her right elbow, felt it scrape uselessly against Slaughter's rock-hard ribs. She stepped back, hooked her foot around Slaughter's ankle, and pulled it forward.

Slaughter shifted her stance to compensate, and Abby jumped up, spun about to free her arm, and at the same time swung a kick at Slaughter's chest. Slaughter blocked the kick with a down-sweep of her forearm, carried the movement through into a lunge, and locked her hands around Abby's throat.

Abby threw herself backward, knowing that she couldn't break Slaughter's grip—she wasn't trying to. She tucked her legs up, slammed them against the woman's hips and pushed. Unbalanced, Slaughter began to topple forward.

Abby landed on her back, with Slaughter's hands still on her neck—and her feet pressed into the woman's hips. She kicked up and back, pushing Slaughter over her head.

Finally, the woman's hands came free.

But Slaughter didn't land on the ground—she had turned her fall into flight. She hovered out of Abby's reach. "Got to hand it to you, little girl. You're good. But you don't have what it takes. You don't have that killer instinct."

Abby took advantage of the lull to catch her breath. She peered at Slaughter, tilted her head slightly to the side. "Is that a gray hair?"

"You little—!" Slaughter launched herself at Abby once more.

Abby spun out of the way, rolled across the ground, and passed over her fallen sword. She came to a stop faceup just as Slaughter threw herself onto her.

Slaughter stopped, her face inches away from Abby's.

She shuddered, the color drained from her skin. She swallowed, twitched. A thin line of red trickled from her mouth.

No . . . Abby looked down to see that her sword was buried almost to the hilt in Slaughter's stomach. The woman's eyes flickered, and she slumped forward on top of Abby.

And then Abby heard someone rush over to her. Abby shook her head. "I didn't mean to . . ."

"It wasn't your fault," Lance said. He pushed Slaughter aside, grabbed Abby's arm, and pulled her to her feet. "She was trying to kill you. *She* did this, not you."

"But . . ."

Lance put his hands on her shoulders. "Come on, Abby—get with it, OK? Slaughter's not dead—you think this is the first time she's been stabbed? She was shot in the head last night, remember? The woman has healing powers! Abby, Roz needs your help."

Abby took a deep breath, and her trembling subsided. "OK, OK. My sword . . ."

"Leave it!" Lance said. "It'll be no use to you against Pyrokine and the longer it's inside Slaughter the longer it'll take for her to heal. Now go!" He pushed her in the direction of Roz and Pyrokine.

A hundred yards away she found Roz crouched into a ball as Pyrokine bombarded her with fireballs. Most of them seemed to dissipate before they reached Roz, but it was clear that the girl was weakening: Her clothing was scorched, her hands and face covered in red blisters.

Abby launched herself at Pyrokine, slammed him into the ground.

He twisted away from her, jabbed his elbow into her face. Abby flinched, cracked her own elbow into the pit of his stomach.

Pyrokine shuddered, turned onto his side, and coughed uncontrollably.

Roz climbed unsteadily to her feet. She limped over to Abby: Much of the skin on Roz's left hand had been burned away.

Pyrokine was getting up. Abby began to move toward him, but Roz grabbed her arm, held her back. "No . . . I owe him."

The boy rose into the air as though an invisible cable was tied around his waist. Roz lashed out with her foot, a spinning kick that slammed into Pyrokine's face and sent him tumbling on the spot.

He hung limply, facedown, and Abby reached out and lifted up his head. "He's out."

Roz released her control, and Pyrokine dropped. The glowing, crackling shield of energy around his body faded as he passed out.

Roz stared down at Pyrokine's face, as though seeing it for the first time. "I think I *know* him . . ."

She snapped out of it when Abby grabbed her arm. They looked at each other for a moment, then turned toward the Fifth King, still sitting on the ground and unconcernedly weathering Thunder's sonic assault.

"Last one's gonna be tough," Abby said. "You ready for this?"

"No. But let's do it anyway."

They charged.

CHAPTER 31

Something slammed into Lance's back, pushing him face-first onto the ground. Strong hands grabbed his arms, pulled them together behind his back, and before he could react he felt the familiar ratchet of a tightening cable tie around his wrists.

As he was hauled once more to his feet, a coarse voice nearby said, "Your friends' courage is impressive, but futile."

He whirled around. Remington was holding his arm, and to the right an old woman was standing between three other guards.

The woman was wearing a long white hooded robe bearing the symbol of a blue eye surrounded by a golden sun. The same symbol was on the upper arms of the men's uniforms.

The woman was watching the battle, but the men had their weapons aimed at Lance's head. Behind them was a helicopter that Lance hadn't even heard approaching, its rotors slowing to a stop.

Lance couldn't take his eyes off the woman—he'd never seen anyone so old. Or so ugly. The woman looked furious: Her eyes and lips had narrowed and she reminded Lance of when he was six years old and his grandmother had caught him digging up her prized flower beds because he was looking for treasure. "I'm guessing that you're the Fifth King's welcoming committee. Bit late, aren't you?"

Speaking slowly, the woman said, "It was not meant to happen like this. Slaughter should not have taken matters into her own hands." Her teeth gritted, she added, "For four thousand years we have prepared for this day. Four thousand years. There was a ceremony prepared. . . ." The woman sighed. "She will *die* for this."

So she's the one behind it all, Lance thought. *If I can . . .* He felt Remington's grip tighten on his arm, and knew he could do nothing: The man was looking for an excuse to kill him.

Instead, Lance said, "Your Fifth King isn't doing much. But you should have been here earlier to see him and Brawn going at it. That was great."

The woman said, "You are a fascinating young man, Mr. McKendrick. You possess no superhuman abilities and yet you are even more courageous than your friends." She turned to him. "You won't win, of course. Nothing can defeat the Fifth King."

He shrugged as well as he could. "Well, I don't know about that. Something defeated him once, didn't it?" He paused. "No, wait a second. . . . If you've taken him from the past before he was killed, then . . . He never got killed, so, yes, you're right. Nothing has defeated him. Not yet, anyway." Doing his best to keep his voice cheerful, he asked, "So, who *are* you, then?"

She returned her attention to the battle: Abby and Roz were kicking and punching at the Fifth King, but still he sat there and didn't react. "I am but a pawn on the chessboard of the Fifth King's glorious reign."

"Nice to finally put a face to the voice, Mrs. Pawn. And by 'nice' I mean 'extremely scary.'" Lance cautiously raised his hands a little. The small knife was still tucked into the back of his jeans—either Remington hadn't noticed it, or he didn't care.

"Your forced optimism does not fool me, boy."

"Why are you doing this? I mean, the plague . . . Billions of people infected. Why? And for that matter, how?"

The woman raised a liver-spotted, wrinkled hand and showed her palm to Lance. It was covered in small red blisters and open sores. "I too am what you would call a superhuman, Mr. McKendrick. I was a little younger than you are now when I contracted typhus—but it did not kill me. My ability allows me to neutralize or change any bacterial or viral infection, and I soon learned that I can modify even a simple strain of acute viral nasopharyngitis—the virus that causes the common cold—into whatever form I wish."

Lance said, "You're a snot-monster? Ew! As powers go, that's not one I'd choose. So instead of using your ability to do good—like cure the sick—you created a virus that's going to wipe out most of the human race. But how did you get it to infect everyone at the same time?" He knew that he had to keep the old woman talking. He pushed his thumbs against the knife's hilt, forced it up an inch, two inches. . . . Then he shifted his arms down a little, tried to press the thick plastic cable tie against the blade.

"It was a simple matter of constructing the virus so that it became active only after a certain amount of time had elapsed," the old woman said. "In the last two months our people have acted as carriers, taking the virus to every major city in the world."

"And all this just because you wanted to bring back the Fifth King?"

"When we learned of the Pyrokine's ability to manipulate matter and energy, we realized that given sufficient energy it would be possible for him to create a . . ." She looked toward Remington.

"A tachyon well," Remington said. "Tachyons are subatomic particles that travel faster than light—with the right guidance they can breach time."

Lance nodded. "Clever. But I don't understand your obsession with the Fifth King. Why him and not, say, Attila the Hun or Alexander the Great?" Finally, he felt the cable tie snag against the small knife's blade. He began to slowly work his hands up and down.

The old woman looked insulted that he would even ask. "The Fifth King is a *god*."

"No he's not. He's a superhuman. Powerful, I admit, but still only a superhuman. I mean, he—" Lance paused. "Hold on. . . . Give me a second here. Something one of us said." Then he remembered, and grinned. "Got it."

She turned to him once more. "Yes?"

"Oh, you people are in *so* much trouble! Your Fifth King is going to kill you. Doesn't matter how much you worship him, that psycho is going to absolutely *murder* you. And that's if you're lucky."

The woman dismissed him with a wave of her hand.

"I'm serious, granny. Look at what you've done to him: You took him away from his own time, when he was the most powerful—and most feared—man in the world. How long do you think it's going to take for him to adjust to this century? He'll hate it here. You ripped him away from everything he knows."

Remington took a swing at Lance, who ducked out of the way. "He'll understand that we saved his life!"

Lance paled—when he dodged Remington's punch his right hand scraped against the knife's blade. The pain flared along his arm and he had to bite the inside of his cheek to stifle the scream. "Uh . . . No . . . you didn't. How was it he died? Consumed in a pillar of fire, right?" Lance forced a laugh. "You idiots! That wasn't a pillar of fire. He wouldn't have died that day. All those people who saw his supposed death . . . What they really saw was an energy flare. The same one that happens when your little pal Pyrokine destroys something."

The woman stared. "No . . ."

"Yes," Lance said. He was sweating heavily now, and his hands were slick with his own blood. But still he kept working the cable tie against the blade. "They didn't witness the Fifth King's death—they witnessed him being pulled through time."

She screamed, *"No!"*

"Look at what you've done. You've spewed out a virus that's going to kill billions of people, and all because you wanted everyone out of the way so you could pull the Fifth King out of danger that he was never in."

The old woman staggered, swayed a little. One of the soldiers lowered his weapon to grab her arm.

"You know it's true," Lance said. "And as soon as he figures it out, you're dead."

At that moment, a guttural cry erupted from the battlefield. The Fifth King jumped to his feet, swatted Roz and Abby aside with a single blow. He roared something in a language that Lance couldn't understand, but he knew what it meant: "Enough!"

All of the men were watching the battle now—Lance clenched his fists and tried to force his arms apart. Beads of sweat ran into his eyes and he had to shake his head to clear his vision.

Struggling against Thunder's sonic attack, the Fifth King planted one foot in front of the other. His body trembled and his skin rippled as though he was fighting through a hurricane—but he was making progress.

Thunder began to back away.

Abby threw herself at the Fifth King, slammed shoulder-first into the small of his back. Roz telekinetically lifted a foot-thick lump of masonry and launched it at him—it struck the side of his face, set him staggering.

Come on, Abby! Lance said to himself. *Don't let up—flatten him!* He took a deep breath, held it as he once again tensed his muscles and pulled. The cable tie snapped suddenly and Lance almost cried out with relief, but he forced himself to keep his arms behind his back.

Abby leaped onto the Fifth King's back, locked her arms around his throat. He reached over his head and grabbed her by the shoulders, threw her straight at Thunder.

But they didn't collide—Abby slowed, floated gently to the ground.

The king whirled about almost faster than they could see. He lunged at Roz, his fists swinging. Then he lurched to the side, hit by another sonic blast from Thunder.

The old woman barked an order to the men: "Target the boy!"

The guards swiveled their weapons in Thunder's direction.

Lance shouted, "Thunder! Get down!" and at the same time pulled the knife from his belt and threw it at Remington— its point struck the man's armored chest dead-center and bounced away.

The man looked down at the knife and grinned. "That was a good throw. Absolutely futile, though."

"That depends on whether I was trying to kill you or distract you."

Remington swiveled back to the battlefield; Thunder had darted to the side and was now keeping the Fifth King between them.

Lance threw himself against the guard who was closest to the old woman—she shrieked as he then locked his arm around her throat.

"Drop your weapons or I'll break her neck!" Lance screamed.

Remington glanced at him. "You wouldn't. Murder is not your style."

"Oh, I *would*. I told you before: I'm not one of the good guys. They've just been a convenient cover. And this wouldn't be murder—it would be an execution."

To one of his men, Remington said, "The chopper." The man darted away.

"What do you think?" Lance asked. "Which way do you want to play this, Remington? If Thunder dies, so does the old woman. . . . And I think you need her alive to ensure that the Fifth King doesn't get out of control." He risked a glance at the King, then smiled. "You thought you had it all planned out, didn't you?"

"We had. And we do." Remington nodded past Lance. "See?"

Lance didn't turn around. "See what?" He heard footsteps approaching, and the sound of something being dragged. An unconscious man was thrown to the ground. Lance thought he recognized him from somewhere.

"This is Maxwell Dalton," Remington said. "Your friend's big brother. He's infected—and he's got it *bad*. So . . ." Remington lowered his weapon so that the barrel was resting on Max's forehead. "Let her go."

Lance relaxed his grip and stepped away from the woman.

"Are you all right, ma'am?" Remington asked.

She nodded. "This is not the first time my life has been threatened." To Lance, she said, "You would not have done it. You claim to not be 'one of the good guys'—but I have been around a long time, Mr. McKendrick. I know about people. Mr. Remington? Kill the boy."

Lance backed away. "Wait! Wait! You shoot me and you'll lose the chance to *really* save the Fifth King's life!"

"What do you mean, boy?" the woman asked.

"He's bluffing—again!" Remington snarled.

"No! Speak. What do you mean?"

Lance pointed to the battle. "Look. He's weakening. Three teenagers are defeating your mighty immortal warrior. But if he's half as good as you people seem to believe, he should be able to overpower them with ease. So why is the fight still going on? It's because you geniuses haven't figured out what you've done to him. You pulled him through time and dumped him here. What was it like, four and a half thousand years ago? A lot different, I'm guessing. The people were different, the cultures were different . . . and so was the environment. Your homemade plague is still around. You think *he's* got any resistance to it?"

The old woman froze. "The boy is right. The Fifth King is infected. Remington—your hand!"

Remington reluctantly stretched out his right hand toward the woman. Her lined face frowned in concentration for a moment, then she pressed her hand into his. "A counter-virus—it will instantly nullify the effects of the first. Run to the Fifth King, touch his skin!"

Remington swallowed. "He . . . He won't know that I'm on his side."

Lance stepped up to Remington. "You have to do it! If you don't, he'll die!"

The soldier was trembling. He looked toward the battle—Brawn had recovered and was locked in a strangling embrace with the Fifth King.

"Look, she was right about me. I don't want *anyone* to die," Lance said. "Especially not me. I know we're not going to win this. I just want you to cure him and make him promise not to hurt the others."

"Go, Mr. Remington!" the old woman snapped.

He swallowed again, and nodded, but still didn't move.

Lance said, "Approach him from the front, OK? Let him see you coming, openhanded so that he knows you're not a threat. You can do this." He grabbed Remington's hand and shook it. "Good luck."

The man's eyes were wide with fear as he passed his gun to one of the other soldiers, then turned and walked slowly toward the battle.

To the old woman, Lance said, "You're sure this will work?"

"It will work. The moment Mr. Remington's bare skin touches the Fifth King's, the counter-virus will be passed to him. It will race through his system and override the first virus. He will recover his strength in seconds."

Lance nodded. "Good." He carefully lowered himself into a sitting position. "I don't know about you people, but this has been a tough couple of days. I could do with a rest."

He watched the woman and the soldiers, and—sure that their attention was on Remington—he reached out and placed his right hand on Max Dalton's neck.

Max groaned. His eyes flickered open. Lance whispered, "Read my mind."

A voice inside his head asked, "Who are you?"

Never mind me, Lance replied, *these people are trying to kill your sister.*

The three soldiers instantly screamed, dropped their weapons, clutched at their heads, and dropped to the ground twitching and convulsing. Seconds later the old woman toppled over on top of them.

"That guy too!" Lance said, pointing toward Remington. He toppled over on the battlefield and lay still.

Lance helped Max to his feet. "Over there—the guy fighting Brawn. Stop him!"

Max briskly shook his head. "No, I can't. I've never been able to control Brawn. It just doesn't work on some people."

"Not Brawn," Lance said. "The *other* guy!"

Max suddenly flinched, as though hit by something invisible. "Whoa. . . . Who is he? I've never met anyone with a mind like that. . . . It's . . . My God, so much *power*! It's not going to be easy to get in." He looked around at the battlefield, then turned back to Lance. "What is going on here?"

"Too long to explain," Lance said. "Just try to knock him out. Or at least slow him down."

We need help, Lance said to himself. *If Dalton can't stop the Fifth King then who can? All the other superheroes are out of action because of the plague. Right*—that's *what we need to do!* To Max, he said, "Listen, that mad old woman created a plague. That's what made you and your guys sick back in Midway. Everyone in the whole world is infected. But you've got the counter-virus in your system now. The old woman gave it to Remington, I got it when I shook his hand, and now I've passed it to you—you need to get to other people, spread the counter-virus. Get to Quantum and Titan and all the others. All you have to do is touch their bare skin and they'll recover. Then you can all gang up on the Fifth King."

Max was staring at the Fifth King. "That's *not* the best use of our resources. I've got a better idea."

CHAPTER 32

Lance hated to leave the others behind, but Max Dalton's idea made sense.

Far behind him the battle still raged: the Fifth King against Roz, Abby, Thunder, and Brawn, while Max tried to find a way into his mind. The King had been weakened by the infection, but he was still almost impervious to their onslaught.

"Faster!" Lance said to the copter's pilot.

"Already at top speed, sir," the pilot said.

Lance was astonished at how simple Max had made it look: The superhero had simply ordered The Helotry's pilot to do whatever Lance asked, and the man seemed more than eager to obey. Now the copter rocketed over the Nebraskan landscape, aiming for a specific destination.

"We're close, sir," the pilot said. "Two minutes." He tapped at one of the screens with his forefinger. "That's got to be it there."

The screen showed an aerial view of a large, ramshackle farmhouse. "Set us down as close as you can!"

The copter descended at a dizzying, stomach-churning speed, but Lance wouldn't allow himself to throw up.

Lance jumped the last two yards, raced up to the farmhouse's front porch. There was a wooden barn star next to the door: Lance ripped it off to reveal the hidden keypad. He entered the ten-digit code Max had given him, and the door swung open.

The inside of the farmhouse was completely at odds with its weathered and faded wooden exterior; it was bright, sleek, modern, and very much the style Lance always associated with ultrarich people like Max Dalton.

Lance took the stairs three at a time. One of the bedroom doors was open, and lying on the bed was a man in his early twenties, barefoot, dressed in only a sweat-soaked T-shirt and jeans. His entire body was trembling, and he was moaning softly. Lance put his hand on the man's bare arm.

Instantly, the man was off the bed and staring at Lance. "What the—? Where did *you* come from?"

"Are you Quantum?"

"What? Who, me? No, I—"

"We don't have time for all that," Lance said. "You're Quantum and you're the fastest human being who ever lived. So listen. Everyone—pretty much the whole planet—has been infected with an artificial virus. That's why you got sick. But you're carrying the cure now. You have to spread it to everyone. Just touch their bare skin."

The young man looked at him. "Everyone?"

"The whole world. You're going to have to become Santa

Claus. Every home in the world in one day. There's going to be a lot of locked doors, so I don't know—"

There was a blur, and the man was now dressed in Quantum's all-white costume. "Locked doors are not a problem for me."

"Then get moving. And try to find people like Titan and Energy—they'll be able to fly you anywhere you need to go. Oh, and you need to get to the CDC in Atlanta—give them a sample of your blood so they can replicate the cure."

"This is for real?"

"Yes. Just go."

The man nodded, and vanished.

Five minutes later, as the copter began its journey back to Windfield, they passed low over a small town. Lance looked out to see that some of the people were already beginning to emerge blinking and confused into the sunlight.

Why do they not submit? Krodin wondered. *They must know they are beaten.*

The children shouted orders to each other in their strange language, but it was clear to Krodin that their desperation was growing by the minute.

The white-skinned girl used her power to raise a thick cloud of dust, caused it to fly at the Fifth King, to swirl and condense around his head.

Krodin closed his eyes, stretched out with his senses. He allowed his consciousness to rise up, out of his body, to float over the battlefield and see everything at once.

The sound-controlling boy was keeping his distance from Krodin, but then he did not need to be close to use his power.

The boy still blasted at Krodin's body with tremulous shock waves, but their effect was considerably less now.

The sword girl continued to attack though her weapon was now lodged in Slaughter's midriff. She had found a long metal bar and was striking over and over—Krodin snatched the bar from the girl's hands, spun around, and struck back at her.

She raised her forearm at the last moment—the metal bar slammed into her arm with enough force to split a normal man in two, but had no such effect on the girl. Instead, the bar twisted around her body as though it was a rope and she was a stone pillar.

She pulled the bar back from Krodin's grip—that in itself impressed the Fifth King, for no one had ever been able to break his grip—and tossed it aside. She launched herself at his legs, seeking to topple him.

In his mind's eye Krodin saw the blue giant approaching him from behind. *Ah. She tries to distract me.*

He grabbed the girl's arm before she reached him, threw her back over his shoulder and into the blue giant's face.

Krodin allowed his mind to stretch further. On the edge of the battlefield a man stood still, staring at him. *Another of these superhumans? What strange abilities does this one have?*

No matter. I will adapt. I always adapt.

And then he felt something rip into his skull, a pinpoint of agony that ruptured, filled his head with incomprehensibly alien words and images.

Roz groaned, and sat up. Her body was a mass of bruises and she knew that even if they survived this day she'd never be whole again: Pyrokine's fireball had almost completely burned the skin from her left hand. The pain was almost unbearable; the stench of burned flesh was worse.

Nearby, Brawn and Abby were still pounding the Fifth King without much sign of damage.

Inside her head, Max's voice said, "I'm in, Roz. . . . His mind is very strange. Not like any other I've ever seen."

A few minutes earlier, Max had taken over the minds of The Helotry's soldiers, woken them, and ordered them to open fire on the bronze-skinned warrior. Somehow he had successfully dodged every bullet. Roz had once seen Quantum in action—or rather she *hadn't* seen him, because the man moved so fast he was invisible—but this was different. The Fifth King seemed to be able to anticipate where the bullets were going to strike. And he did it with his eyes closed.

Roz limped over to her brother.

"It's working," Max said. "He thinks he's invulnerable, but he's not. At least, not in the way we think of the word. His power enables him to adjust to any situation. If we were able to shoot him, the bullets would do some damage, but he'd heal quickly and then next time they wouldn't affect him at all. That's why he doesn't age and doesn't get sick. He caught the plague that old woman created, and it slowed him down for a few minutes, but now he's adapted. He's immune. My God—he's going to outlive the entire human race! And he's alone, so alone . . ."

Is he kidding? Roz thought. "Max, if you can't stop him he's going to *kill* us!"

"He's hundreds of years old. Everyone he's ever known is dead." Max turned to Roz. "You can't imagine what that feels like—to know that you're going to be here long after everyone else is dead."

Roz grabbed her brother's arm. "You're letting his feelings infect you. You have to put that aside. Just force him to stop fighting!"

Max nodded, looked back to the Fifth King. "You're right. . . . I'm pushing through. I can see his memories. . . . He's killed hundreds of people with his bare hands, thousands more using swords and spears. And he doesn't care. He's never regretted anything. But he's not evil, Roz. Not the same way that old woman is. He's better than us—our morals don't apply to him. Krodin knows that he was born to rule. He's above good and evil."

"No, he's not. Just stop him!"

"I'm not sure I can. I . . . I'm not sure I *should*."

"What!?"

"Roz, the whole world's in a mess. Always has been. People just don't *want* to live in peace. Krodin thinks—he *knows*—that his function is to unite the entire human race. He could be right. Think about it, Roz. . . . What if there were no nations, no discrimination, no war?"

"You can't save the world by beating it into submission, Max! There must be something in his memory that you can use against him. That's how you normally do this, isn't it? You take something that scares them and magnify it."

"But . . . his memory is huge, Roz. He's never forgotten anything. His mind is like . . . a desert filled with blood and bones, scattered with rusting shields and swords. Wait, I can see his parents. They died young. Food was scarce—they starved themselves so that Krodin and his brother would live. That's got to be painful for him. . . ."

This has to work, Roz thought. *I don't think even Titan could defeat him.*

On the battlefield Krodin swung a punch at Abby and missed. Then he staggered, bellowed in pain, swayed, shuddered, and toppled over.

Exhausted, Max slumped to the ground. "It's done. I'm telling Abby and Brawn to tie him up with the strongest stuff they can find. If we're lucky, we'll be able to keep him down long enough for Titan to get here."

From the far side of the battlefield Thunder approached, keeping his distance from the Fifth King's unconscious body. Roz walked out to meet him. "You OK?"

The boy shook his head. "Not really." He looked even more drained than Roz felt. He ran his hands across his face. "I hope he's down for good because I don't think I can go through this again. Look at us, Roz. With Max there's five of us. Five superhumans. And we barely made a dent in this guy!"

There was a scuffling behind them. Roz turned. Pyrokine was climbing to his feet. Roz and Thunder turned to face him, fists clenched.

Pyrokine held up his hands. "Don't. I'm not going to fight you—you've won. I . . . Sorry about your hand."

They stood facing each other for a moment. Roz was torn between the urge to attack him and a powerful, inexplicable desire to run toward him and wrap her arms around him. And she could see in his eyes that he was caught in a similar confusion.

"I *know* you," she said. "But that's impossible. We've never met before."

"I . . . I get the same sort of feeling."

Thunder looked from one to the other. "What's going on here?"

Pyrokine stepped closer to Roz, and reached out his hand toward her face.

The moment his fingers brushed her cheek, she remembered. She remembered everything.

They had met over a year ago. A chance encounter as they both rushed to save people from the same disaster, a collapsed suspension bridge in Arkansas.

"Fabian. . . . You saved me," Roz said. "I was trapped under a metal beam. It was crushing me, and you turned it into light."

Pyrokine clasped his hand to his mouth. "Oh my God. We went out. . . . We were together for *months*! How could I have forgotten that? I was falling in love with you!"

Roz nodded. "And then . . . something happened. You left. I . . . We couldn't be together. It was too dangerous."

"They locked me away," the boy said. "There was an accident and I caused it. I *know* I did, but I don't remember what it was. And then I forgot about you. How is that possible? You're the only one I've ever loved and I forgot about you!"

"You used to take me flying," Roz said. "You'd hold my hand and we'd just take off. . . ." She smiled. "Remember how mad my brother got when he found out? He kept saying that we were too young to be in love and we didn't know anything about the world and that . . ." She found that her mouth had gone dry. "It was him. It was Max. He said it would be for the best. He made us forget. He wiped our memories. He set you up!"

With Pyrokine and Thunder following, she strode back to Max. He wouldn't look at them. "Roz, I know what you're thinking, but this isn't the right time. It's all I can do to keep Krodin unconscious."

Roz swore at him. "You messed with our minds! How many times, Max? Who *else* have you done this to? Josh? Is that why our brother is so different from other kids his age? He's ten years old and he has no friends, no hobbies. He hardly does *anything* kids his age do. All he does is study! Have you been using your power on him too?"

Pyrokine stepped in front of Roz, pushed his face close to Max's. "When this is over you are going to pay. You set me up, got me sent to prison. You ruined my *life!*"

Still staring at the Fifth King, Max said, "This is not the time."

Thunder took hold of Pyrokine's arm, tried to pull him away. "Hate to agree, but he's right. Save it for later."

Pyrokine shrugged free of Thunder's grip. "No! How dare you, Dalton! Do you know what your lies did to me, to my family? You destroyed them! My folks lost their jobs, they had to move to a new town!"

"Get him away from me, Roz," Max said, his teeth gritted. "Right now."

"What you did to her is even worse!" Pyrokine screamed. "You twisted her *mind*, you sick son of a—"

Max lashed out, struck Pyrokine across the face with his

307

fist, sent him sprawling to the ground. Pyrokine reacted instantly—he launched a fireball at Max.

Roz instinctively leaped at her brother, knocked him out of the fireball's path.

Max's head smacked off the ground.

And the Fifth King awoke.

CHAPTER 33

Two hours after it left, the helicopter carrying Lance returned to the power plant. The military had evacuated a twenty-mile radius around the battle zone: The fight was still raging.

As they reached the perimeter the pilot said, "Sorry, sir. This is as close as we're allowed to get."

"Says who?"

"Says Colonel Morgan—it's been declared a no-fly area. If we attempt to breach it, we'll be shot down."

"Get him on the radio, will you?"

A few seconds later, the pilot passed Lance a headset. "Go for it."

Lance put the headset on. It was too big for him and he had to adjust the microphone. "Colonel Morgan? This is Lance McKendrick."

The colonel's voice came back crackling with static. "Who? No, not the kid Paragon brought in?"

"That's me."

"What do you want, McKendrick? We're kinda in the middle of something here!"

"We need permission to get to the battle."

"No chance, kid. You're a civilian, and you're not superhuman. I'm not putting anyone else at risk. That monster has taken everything we can throw at him and he's still going strong. You cross the perimeter and we will use whatever force is necessary to bring you down."

"Wait. . . . In order to protect us from getting killed by the Fifth King, *you're* willing to kill us? Wow, that's smart."

"Stop wasting my time, McKendrick."

"So you've recovered from the infection, then? Oh, of course you have. Because it was *me* who got the cure to Quantum and got him to pass it on to everyone else. You're welcome, by the way."

Lance thought he heard a muttered curse, then the colonel said, "All right. Get the pilot to drop you no closer than five miles from the site. Then he's to fly back here—a copter is just another source of ammunition for the Fifth King. You're on your own out there, Lance. I don't know what good you're going to be able to do."

"Me either, but I'm sure I'll think of something." He removed the headset. "Better take it in low and slow."

The pilot nodded. "Yes, sir."

Lance smiled to himself. He decided he liked being called sir.

The copter crossed the twenty-mile perimeter and a minute later, over the constant roar of the rotors, Lance heard a knocking on the copter's hatch. He unclipped his seat harness and started to rise, then paused. "OK, I don't know much about helicopters but I'm guessing *that's* not normal."

Then a silver shape darted around to the side of the canopy—and Paragon saluted to Lance. The armored hero pointed back to the hatch, and beckoned to Lance.

"Is it safe to open the hatch at this height?" Lance asked the pilot.

"Safe enough," the man replied, "long as you hold on to something."

"OK. Steady as she goes. Or whatever the proper expression is. No loop-the-loops or sudden dives."

Lance got out of the copilot's seat and opened the hatch. The wind rushed through the copter and he had to brace himself against the bulkhead to avoid being pulled out.

Paragon had dropped back a little, and was now flying level with the hatch. He reached out his hand to Lance, and nodded.

Why not? Lance asked himself. *What's one more crazy stunt after everything I've done in the past couple of days?* He took hold of Paragon's arm and jumped.

We're beaten, Roz thought. *There's no way we can stop him now.*

Max was once again trying to get inside Krodin's mind, but it wasn't working. The Fifth King had already adapted to his attacks. Even with Pyrokine's aid, they were still only barely holding the warrior at bay.

Exhausted, and in almost constant pain, Roz wanted nothing more than to lie down. She knew she couldn't do that. She had to keep going.

If Max is right about Krodin being able to adapt to any attack, then we need to find something he hasn't encountered yet.

Roz knew then what she had to do, and the thought of it sickened her.

She walked over to Slaughter, who was still lying on the ground, feebly trying to remove Abby's sword from her stomach. "You can't remove it until your strength returns, and that won't happen until you're healed, right? And you can't heal with the sword inside you."

The woman swore at her.

"Slaughter, you know what's going on here. We can't control the Fifth King. He's going to defeat us and he's going to remake the world in his own image. Do you honestly believe that he'll let you live?"

"Go to hell, Dalton!"

"We need you. With your strength and speed we might be able to turn this around. All of us working together. You, me, Abby, Max, Thunder, and Pyrokine. That's a lot of firepower right there. The deal is this: You help us defeat him and everything is forgiven."

"You know you can't trust me—why should I trust you?"

"Because if he wins he's going to destroy you anyway. Max told him, spoke into his mind," she lied. "At that level they don't need language—only images. The Fifth King knows that it's The Helotry's fault that he was taken from his time. He'll never see his wife and children again. So your only chance is to work with us. What do you say?"

For a long moment, Slaughter was silent. Then, "I'll do it. Get this thing out of me."

Roz reached down and grabbed the sword's hilt with both hands, pulled the blade out of Slaughter's stomach.

The woman winced in pain. "Give . . . Give me a few minutes to recover."

Roz nodded. The sword floated from her grip and sailed over to Abby, who snatched it out of the air.

And when Roz looked back, Slaughter was gone.

CHAPTER 34

Abby ducked under the Fifth King's reach and slashed at his thigh with her sword—though she knew it wouldn't do any damage. She'd already struck him dozens of times, blows that would slice a normal man in two, and each time the wounds healed within seconds

He made a grab for her and she threw herself backward, rolled head over heels, and landed on her feet.

Before he could get any closer, Pyrokine swooped at him, his body wrapped in a sheath of blue-white fire. The Fifth King swept out his arm and knocked Pyrokine to the dirt.

Abby darted in again before the king's powerful foot could stamp down on Pyrokine. Her sword flashed twice, and for a moment twin streaks of red appeared on the warrior's bare back.

From a hundred yards away, Max Dalton shouted, "Abby, pull back! Roz, take over!"

Abby threw the sword into the air as she retreated—Roz caught it telekinetically and resumed her attack.

"You holding up OK?" Brawn asked as Abby collapsed next to him.

She nodded. "Think so. Exhausted, though. How long have we been fighting?"

"About four hours," Max told her. "Brawn? You're up next."

The giant pushed himself to his feet. "Yeah. I know. Don't see *you* taking a turn, Dalton."

"That's because I'm not much stronger than an ordinary human. I wouldn't last a second against him. Get ready." Max resumed barking orders at Roz and Pyrokine. He'd been doing that almost since the moment he was cured.

Abby found Thunder lying on his back, still trying to catch his breath. A few minutes earlier, the Fifth King had struck Thunder a glancing blow across the chest—they had all heard his ribs crack.

"Anything I can do?" Abby asked.

He shook his head. "No. . . . Look, don't worry about me. I can't fight him physically, but I can still use my power."

"He's not even tired yet."

"Abby . . . I don't think he *gets* tired. I think he's actually enjoying himself."

A familiar low whining noise came from the west. Abby raised her head and saw Paragon preparing to land—he was holding on to Lance with one arm.

With every muscle burning and every joint feeling like it was made of sandpaper, Abby slowly walked over to them.

"I got to Quantum," Lance said. "Passed the cure on to

him. He's spreading it everywhere else." He grinned. "It's working, Abby. The geniuses at the CDC created an airborne strain from Quantum's blood and right now Titan, Heimdall, Energy, and—uh, the guy with the thing . . ." Lance tried to describe it with his hands, and gave up. "Can't remember his name. Anyway, they're seeding the atmosphere with it."

Paragon said, "Abby, I got the police to check on your family. Your mom and sister are worried about you, but they've recovered. They're fine. And so are the boys." He looked toward the battle: Brawn had the Fifth King in another headlock. "Nothing's working, is it?"

"He's unstoppable." Admitting that out loud made Abby's heart pound faster. "I can cut him, but he heals almost immediately. I'm hoping that eventually he'll pass out from loss of blood."

Max Dalton approached, shook Paragon's hand. "If we can stop him long enough . . . I have an island off the coast of Newfoundland. Nothing but sea and rocks for fifty miles in every direction. I'm thinking that we can strand him there. I doubt he can breathe underwater."

Lance said, "Yeah, but maybe he can swim."

Max briefly looked at him, then back to Paragon. "The other option is to wait for Titan."

"The Fifth King is stronger than Brawn," Abby said. "And Brawn is stronger than Titan."

"I know that," Max said. "But Titan is still strong enough to lift him. Strong enough to carry him out of the atmosphere and throw him into the sun."

Abby's mouth dropped open. "What? You're serious?"

"Do you have a better solution? Abby, if we don't stop him he'll kill us all and keep on killing."

Lance said, "No. We don't kill. We have to stop him long enough that we can talk to him, let him know what's—"

Max jabbed a finger at Lance. "*You* don't have a say in this. You're not a superhuman. You shouldn't even *be* here."

Lance muttered, "Saved your life, you ungrateful jerk."

Then a roar echoed over the battlefield.

Abby saw the Fifth King slam his fist into Brawn's throat, grab his arm, and throw him into the air. The giant collided with the floating Pyrokine.

"Enough!" the Fifth King roared. "I have had enough!" He began to stride toward them. "You—mind-speaking man!" He pointed at Max. "You lead these people?"

Max nodded. "I do."

The Fifth King stopped ten yards away. "I grow . . . weary of this . . . confrontation. You cannot best me—you know this to be true. You will stop. Now."

Lance said, "OK, exactly *when* did he learn to speak English?"

"I am Krodin, the undefeated!" the warrior bellowed. "Ruler of Assyria, Sumeria, Egypt, and all the lands of the world. In my time no man could stand against me. My word was law. I have beaten your . . . champions again and again. If this does not stop, I will kill them. Do you understand? I am invincible. I am immortal." He glared at Max. "You lead these people, so you are the most powerful warrior of this land, this . . . America. Yet you have not faced me in battle. Do so now. Prove your worth and I might allow your people to live."

Max swallowed. "I . . . I am not the most powerful warrior."

"You are a coward, then. You are not fit to lead." Krodin turned to Paragon. "You, man-of-metal. Strike him down."

"I will not," Paragon said. He took a step forward, putting himself between Max and the warrior. "You have no dominion here. You have great strength, but we do not follow strength. In this time, we follow wisdom, and justice."

The Fifth King seemed to consider this. "Your ways are no more." He raised his hand, clenched his fist. "*This* is justice: Power. And I am your king. You will kneel in my presence or you will die." He watched them for a moment. "You fear me, yet you do not obey. I have seen such courage before, sometimes even from the weakest of men, but bravery is a poor weapon against an enemy who cannot be defeated. You *will* die. I will hunt down your families and kill them slowly. By the end they will be cursing your names."

Max roared, "Everyone at once! *Now!*"

Abby charged at Krodin with her sword raised. Paragon aimed and fired his armor's grappling gun. Brawn launched himself into the air and came down on the Fifth King's back. Pyrokine streaked in low over the ground, slammed into the king's legs. At the same time, Thunder hit him with a sonic shock wave and Roz attacked the loose ground under Krodin's feet.

The Fifth King grabbed the grappling gun's hook out of the air, backhanded Abby and sent her soaring, threw Brawn over his shoulder, and jabbed down at Pyrokine with his elbow.

Then he wrapped the grappling gun's thin cable around Pyrokine's neck, pulled it tight. There was a loud *snap*, and Pyrokine slumped to the ground.

"No!" Roz screamed. She reached out with her telekinesis, lifted Pyrokine up, and pulled him back to the others.

The Fifth King said, "He is but the first."

Brawn's massive hands locked around Krodin's head from behind, lifted him off his feet. The giant roared, raised his arms above his head, slammed Krodin downward with every ounce of his strength.

Even as he was plummeting, Krodin tucked his legs up, kicked back at Brawn's face, sent the giant stumbling backward. Then he closed his eyes, spun on one foot, and whipped the other out at Brawn's stomach. Krodin doubled his fists and his arms were a blur as he hit the giant again and again.

Abby dug her hands into the dirt, hauled herself toward Roz and Pyrokine. Lance rushed up to her, took her arms, and helped her to stand.

Thunder too was standing now, one arm clutched tightly around his ribs. He shuffled awkwardly over to Lance. "You were a fool to come back, Lance."

"Well, I haven't finished picking on you yet."

"Shut up!" Roz yelled at them. She was crouched close to Pyrokine's head. "Oh God. . . . His neck is broken."

Twenty yards away Brawn staggered under the Fifth King's onslaught, collapsed to the ground, and lay still, moaning weakly.

Krodin stopped, turned to the others. "The flame-boy still

lives? He is stronger than I thought. Step aside, girl. I will finish him. He was a powerful opponent and deserves a quick death."

Roz got to her feet, stood over Pyrokine. "No."

Abby shouted, "Roz! Get back!"

The Fifth King suddenly reeled as though hit by an invisible force. He staggered once, twice. "*Still* you resist me? You are a fool, girl. You will die next."

Abby and Lance grabbed Roz's hands. "Come on!" Abby said. "You can't help him now!"

Before any of the others could react, the Fifth King struck: He knocked Abby and Lance aside, locked his hand over Roz's face, and lifted her into the air. "Little witch. . . . You. Are. Next!"

From the ground at his feet, Pyrokine screamed, "No!"

He rose into the air, his limp, broken body crackling with blue, white, and green fire. "Let her go!"

Burning brighter than ever before, he launched himself at the Fifth King, crashed into his arm, forcing him to drop Roz.

Abby darted forward, dragged Roz away.

Krodin tried to shake him off, but Pyrokine continued to press himself against his arm. The blue flames seared Krodin's skin, and for the first time in his long life he screamed in pain. "No! Enough!"

With the last of his breath, Pyrokine said, "No. You don't get to decide when you've had enough. *We* have had enough!"

The flame was so bright now that Abby could barely look at Pyrokine. It continued to spread, burning through Krodin's flesh faster than he could heal.

"Shield your eyes!" Paragon yelled. "Everyone get back!"

His warning was almost too late: Pyrokine's body flared.

Krodin screamed, now completely consumed by the fire. He thrashed and roared, collapsed to the ground.

There was a final, searing flash so hot that it scorched the earth. And there was nothing left of them but cinders.

CHAPTER 35

"What do we tell the rest of the world?" Lance asked Abby and Roz.

Thunder limped over to them. "That flash . . . I've never seen anything like it. How did he . . . ? I thought he just turned everything into light, but there was heat too."

Slowly, they moved closer to the blackened circle on the ground. Lance saw Roz's knees start to buckle—he grabbed for her, held her upright.

"He's gone . . . ," Roz said. "We only just found each other again and now he's gone." She pushed herself away from Lance, whirled around to stare at her brother. "I will never forgive you for this!"

Max Dalton looked at his sister for a moment, then turned away. "Roz, it was the only way. I was trying to protect you. To protect all of us."

"You wiped our memories! You framed him, sent him to prison! Why? *Why*?"

There was no answer.

In the failing light Lance saw Paragon approaching.

"Radio's down," the armored hero said. "Could be a side effect of the flash. But the last I heard was that everyone is recovering. There are reports coming in from all over the world. It's going to be a long time before everything is back to normal, but we'll get there. You kids should be proud of yourselves."

Quietly, Abby said to him, "But Pyrokine died."

Paragon put his hand on her shoulder. "I know, Abby. But . . . I'm sure you don't want to hear this now, but sometimes that's the price we pay." He paused for a moment, then said, "Max? You and I need to have a talk. Back this way. *Now*. And Thunder? This is not for your ears, or anyone else's. Understood?"

The tall boy nodded, and the four of them watched as Paragon led Max back toward the power plant.

They were silent for a few moments, until there was a long, low moan followed by scuffling sounds as Brawn regained consciousness and climbed to his feet. "Did we win?" the giant rumbled.

"Sort of," Lance said. "Pyrokine beat him. Killed himself in the process."

Brawn looked down at the scorched patch of ground. "Oh man. . . ." He looked over to where Max was returning, and said to Roz, "Has he admitted what he did yet?"

"What do you mean?" Roz asked.

"Pyrokine," Brawn said. Seeing her frown, he added, "The way Max made you forget you were ever with him."

She laughed. "Are you nuts? What are you talking about? I never met Pyrokine before today!"

Abby said, "My God, he's done it again! Roz, you were . . ." She frowned. "You were . . . What was I talking about?"

"Well, if *you* don't know, how are we supposed to?" Lance asked. "We're not mind-readers, you know. Anyway, this guy Pyrokine. I guess we should find out who he was."

Roz nodded. "I'll get Max on to it." She looked down at her bandage-wrapped hand. "I guess he wasn't a bad guy, in the end."

Thunder said, "Good and bad . . . it's all a matter of perspective." To Brawn, he said, "You get what I'm saying?"

"What are you looking at me for? I helped you, didn't I?"

"I guess." Thunder turned to Lance. "And I really hope *your* thieving days are over."

"What? After all the great new tricks I've learned?"

Max Dalton said, "All right, kids. Time to clear out. We still can't get a signal on the radio so we're just going to have to walk back to the perimeter."

Abby moved to give Roz a hug, but Roz held up her bandaged hand and backed away. "Better not."

Thunder said, "Me either. I can barely stand."

She looked at Brawn, but the expression on his face told her he wasn't the sort of person who was into hugs.

Then she turned to Lance, who was grinning at her and had his arms already outstretched.

"Oh dream on!" Abby said.

There was a crunch of heavy boots on the rubble as

Paragon returned. He was holding a thick jacket in one hand. "All right, kids. Max will get the rest of you home. Stick with him. Brawn, you're probably going to have to go back to Oak Grove, but I promise we'll put in a good word for you." He tossed the jacket to Lance. "Put this on. I'll fly you home."

"Yes!" Lance pulled on the jacket and zipped it up. To the others, he said, "OK, guys. It's been fun. I don't suppose we'll ever meet again, but I shall always treasure this short time we've spent together."

"Yeah, yeah," Thunder said. "Go. You've already outstayed your welcome."

Abby smiled at him.

Then Lance felt Paragon take hold of his arms. The jetpack whined into life, and suddenly they were soaring into the air.